'A [...] [...]ed
conseq[...] [...]ving'

'[...]rises and twists are engineered with literary dexterity. A dark, compelling book, which exposes the reader to a raw brutality of both crime and poverty'

ARBUTURIAN

'The master of razor-sharp one liners, David Jackson's *The Rule* is an absolute belter'

MANDASUE HELLER

'Brilliant. Spiralling tension, wit and heart, this is British crime writing at its best'

MARK EDWARDS

'I really enjoyed [it]. Jackson doesn't do cosy thrillers. There is dark, ultra dark and then there is *The Rule*. You've been warned'

PAUL FINCH

'An intense and compelling read that will evoke complicated emotions in every reader. Highly recommended'

LISA HALL

'Excellent as always. Grimy and heartbreaking in equal measure, peppered with Jackson's trademark wit and humour. May be his best yet'

WILL CARVER

'A stomach-lurching descent into parental desperation, full of surprises from start to finish. A gasp-out-loud read after which I dare you to break *The Rule*'
JANICE HALLETT

'Jackson is one of the finest British thriller writers. A thrilling, propulsive and ultimately heartbreaking tale of the lengths a father will go to in order to protect his family'
MARTYN WAITES

'A pacy, smart and darkly funny heartbreaker of a crime novel'
SUSI HOLLIDAY

'David Jackson has done it again. *The Rule* is incredible. Creepy, emotive, dark, tense and disturbing'
NOELLE HOLTEN

'A stupendous piece of literary engineering. When high-rise tenants meet the local vicious lowlife, who knows what the outcome will be'
JENNY O'BRIEN

'A dark, poignant and perfectly observed page-turner that asks: How far would you go to protect the people you love? A triumph'
VICTORIA SELMAN

Also by David Jackson and available from Viper

The Resident

THE RULE

DAVID JACKSON

 VIPER

This paperback edition first published in 2022
First published in Great Britain in 2021 by
VIPER, part of Serpent's Tail,
an imprint of Profile Books Ltd
29 Cloth Fair
London
ECIA 7JQ
www.serpentstail.com

Text design by Crow Books

1 3 5 7 9 10 8 6 4 2

Printed and bound in Great Britain by
CPI Group (UK) Ltd, Croydon, CR0 4YY

The moral right of the author has been asserted.

A CIP catalogue record for this book is available from the British Library.

ISBN 978 1 78816 4382
eISBN 978 1 78283 6520

THE RULE

DAVID JACKSON

This paperback edition first published in 2022
First published in Great Britain in 2021 by
VIPER, part of Serpent's Tail,
an imprint of Profile Books Ltd
29 Cloth Fair
London
ECIA 7JQ
www.serpentstail.com

Copyright © David Jackson, 2021

Text design by Crow Books

1 3 5 7 9 10 8 6 4 2

Printed and bound in Great Britain by
CPI Group (UK) Ltd, Croydon, CRO 4YY

A CIP catalogue record for this book is available from the British Library.

ISBN 978 1 78816 4382
eISBN 978 1 78283 6520

For Irene

PROLOGUE

'Bloody hell. Not you lot again.'

The furious manner in which Suzy Carling was drying her hands on a faded tea towel threatened to peel off her skin. She turned away from her front door and marched back into the gloomy interior of her terraced house.

Detective Inspector Hannah Washington looked at her colleague standing next to her.

'I think that's her way of inviting us in.'

Detective Constable Marcel Lang nodded. 'She's obviously in a rush to get the kettle on. I do like a friendly welcome.'

They entered the hallway. Marcel closed the front door and said, 'I hope she's got some Hobnobs in. Or KitKats. I'm not fussy.'

'Didn't I just see you wolfing down a pasty and chips in the canteen?'

Marcel rubbed his belly, which belied what he shovelled into it on a regular basis. He was one of those people who was always charged to capacity with nervous energy. He could cram in a four-course meal, then burn it off within the hour. He was neither tall nor stocky, but in a fight he was tenacious and ferocious. A darting, snapping terrier rather than a lumbering Rottweiler.

'Yeah,' he said. 'I'm sure Vera was a bit stingy with the chips today.'

The hall was papered in busy patterns that made Hannah's eyes wobble. It was like one of those optical illusions where you had to look at it a certain way to make it pop out in 3D. She was glad to get past it and into the living room, where Suzy had plonked herself down on an armchair and was lighting up a cigarette. The room already reeked of stale smoke.

'Mind if we sit?' Hannah asked.

'I don't care if you do handstands if it helps get this over with. Ask your questions and get out.'

Hannah lowered herself onto the sofa. It was upholstered in a floral fabric that didn't match the chairs. A stack of interior design magazines was balanced on one of its arms, although it was clear that the advice within their pages had not been taken on board. To Hannah's right, a gas fire was fixed to the wall on an obvious slant, as though it might fall off at any second. Behind Suzy, a large window with failed double-glazed units offered a fogged view of a garden crowded with weeds and junk.

Marcel didn't sit down. He hardly ever relaxed in other people's houses. Hannah didn't mind on this occasion. His steady pacing, coupled with the occasional surprise launch of a question, would unsettle Suzy.

Hannah studied the woman for a few seconds. She was thirty-nine. Coffee-coloured hair that she'd endeavoured to make more interesting with some blonde streaks. Trim figure and a push-up bra straining against a vest top. Cartoonish doodles of eyebrows. Inflated lips that made it look as though she'd stick fast if she walked into a plate-glass window.

'This doesn't have to be difficult,' Hannah said.

Suzy snorted out two streams of smoke, like an angry bull.

'Try saying that when a gang of hairy-arsed coppers breaks down your front door at four o'clock in the morning and then rips your house apart.'

Hannah sighed. She could do without the attitude. It was wearying, draining. She didn't have the patience for this shit anymore.

'We didn't rip it apart. We searched it. And we were acting on information received that Tommy was here.'

'Well, he wasn't, was he? Which just goes to show how crap your information is. He wasn't here then and he isn't here now, so why don't you just sling your hook?'

'Have you seen him recently?' Marcel asked.

'Not since the last time you asked me, no.'

'Has he phoned you?'

'Nope.'

'What, not a single call? I thought you two were inseparable. Suzy and Tommy sitting in a tree.'

She showed him her middle finger. 'Don't take the piss, all right? You're the ones who are keeping him away. Don't know if I'll ever see him again now.'

Hannah shook her head. 'My heart bleeds for you. Not as much as his fiancée's, mind.'

Suzy stabbed her cigarette into the overflowing ashtray on the table next to her and jumped to her feet.

'That's it!' she yelled. 'Get out of my house.'

Hannah stayed put. 'You need to talk to us, Suzy. You're not helping him or yourself.'

'I said get out!'

The command was followed by a thunder of footsteps rolling down the staircase. Hannah saw Marcel's eyes widen. He dived for the doorway to intercept whatever was heading their way. Hannah had faith in him. He would handle it. And if he didn't . . .

Well, did it matter? Did anything really matter? Sometimes she thought someone beating the crap out of her might do her some good.

She remained on the sofa, staring philosophically at Suzy, wondering if she had a similar attitude to life. Despite the heavy foundation, the bruise on her cheek still shone through. Why would she put herself through that? Why would any sane woman stay loyal to a violent nutcase like Tommy Glover?

'What are you doing to my mother?'

Shane Carling. Eighteen years old and straining to fill the shoes of the man of the house. Still baby-faced but attempting to counter the apparent innocence with a scalp of stubble and a tattoo of three swords on his neck. Now getting gobby like he always did. He stood in the doorway, jabbing his finger at the detectives while the unintimidated Marcel blocked his path and itched for an excuse to get him in an armlock and call for a van.

'We're having a quiet chat,' Hannah told him. 'Nothing to get your knickers in a twist about.'

'Quiet chat, my arse,' Suzy said. 'They're accusing me again. I want them out!'

'You heard her,' Shane said. He tried to take a step forward, but Marcel didn't budge. Shane's glower became increasingly aggressive, but it was no match for Marcel's unwavering stare.

Hannah kept her voice flat, calm. 'We're not accusing you of anything. Can we have a proper adult conversation now, please?'

Suzy mulled it over. Gradually, the tension drained from her and she lowered herself onto her chair. Shane and Marcel continued their staring match, like championship boxers at a weigh-in.

Realising she had just stubbed out her cigarette, Suzy picked up a carton from the table, but discovered it was empty.

'For fuck's sake.' She looked across at her son. 'Fetch me some cigarettes, lad.'

Shane seemed relieved at the excuse to break eye contact. 'Ma . . .'

She waved him away. 'It's all right. Let them say their piece and go. I've got nothing to hide.'

'Where are your cigs?'

She snapped again. 'I don't bloody know. Try my bedroom. One of my bags. Use your head.'

Shane took one last glance at Marcel before disappearing upstairs. Hannah gained the impression he was more scared of his own mother than he was of the police officer.

She turned back to Suzy. 'We're not trying to make life difficult for you, but you don't seem to appreciate how dangerous Tommy is.'

'He's not dangerous. Not to me. He loves me.'

Ah, Hannah thought. So there it is. Love. Everything can look brighter through the prism of love.

'You've heard what he did to Marie, haven't you? That was his *fiancée*. The woman he once *loved*. We don't know if she's ever going to come out of hospital. And even if she does, she'll never be the same.'

Suzy turned away as if she didn't want to hear any more, but Hannah pressed on.

'Did you know he insisted on getting the engagement ring back? And when she refused, he attacked her. And when she still refused, he cut off her finger to get it. That's the kind of man your Tommy is. That's what he does to the women he claims to love.'

Suzy's head was still turned to the side, but there was a discernible tremble in her lower lip.

'Where the hell is he with those ciggies?' she said. 'I'm gasping here.'

Hannah watched her for a few seconds, allowing her words to percolate further into Suzy's brain. If the woman could see sense, if she could just allow herself to step back and see the danger she was in . . .

And then there was a movement in the corner of Hannah's eye. At another doorway, leading to the kitchen.

She was standing there, as pretty as a field of flowers. Only eight years old. A sunshine smile that seemed to fill the room with birdsong. She was wearing her school uniform: bottle-green sweater, black skirt, shiny black shoes, and white socks pulled up tight and precisely aligned below her kneecaps. As always, a lock of her hair had escaped to coil between her eyes.

And then she was gone, retreating into the depths of the kitchen.

Hannah stood, moved towards the kitchen. She couldn't help herself.

'Hey!' Suzy said. 'Where do you think you're going?'

Hannah heard the voice but couldn't stop. From behind her came further protestations from Suzy, then words from Marcel as he tried to hold the woman back. It was all just background noise to Hannah now.

The kitchen was empty. The back door was open, admitting a broad wedge of warm September sunshine, but there was no sign of anyone in the garden.

Hannah surveyed the room. Finger-stained cupboards, one absent its door. The washing machine thrumming its motor and sloshing its contents. A basin full of soapy water. A precarious mountain of dishes on the draining board . . .

The voices grew louder. Shane pounded downstairs again and joined the commotion. Marcel had his hands full back there.

She took a step closer to the sink . . .

Something winked at her. A brief glint of brilliance. Like a lightbulb moment. Hannah could almost hear the *ding* in her head.

Yes. There. Evidently, Suzy had been washing the dishes when they'd arrived. Hannah remembered her drying her hands on that grubby towel. And in preparation for the task, she had removed her ring.

It rested on a window ledge above the sink. Rose gold, with a bulbous central blue stone surrounded by smaller white gems. Exactly as she had seen it in the crime reports.

This ring had belonged to Tommy Glover's fiancée, before he hacked it from her hand.

Tommy had been here.

A rush of movement behind her.

She whirled to see Suzy racing out of the back door and across the garden. Hannah threw the ring down and took up the chase.

'Marcel!' she yelled.

She dashed outside but could see that Suzy had already reached the fence and was pulling a couple of the panels aside to duck through. Hannah sprinted through the tall weeds, hurdled over a broken lawnmower. When she reached the dilapidated fence, she looked back to see that Marcel had been tackled to the ground by Shane, and was now wrestling with him. She debated whether to go back and help, decided against it. She had confidence that Marcel could handle himself.

She pushed through the hole in the fence, then barged through dense shrubbery that seemed intent on clawing her back. She was unprepared for the steep slope that met her on the other side. She lost her footing, rolled down the bank, slammed hard onto a pathway and felt sharp-edged stones cutting into her knees and shins.

'Shit!'

She clambered to her feet. Saw the blood oozing from the puncture wounds on her legs. She fought through the pain and started running again. Ahead, Suzy was widening the gap, but there didn't seem to be anywhere she could go. To her left were the steep, slippery, grassy banks bordering the rear of a long row of houses, and to her right was a tall wire fence closing off access to a railway line. Another section of fencing ran perpendicular to it in the distance, terminating the path.

Jesus, Hannah thought. For a chain-smoker in her late thirties, that woman can move!

As she picked up the pace, her mind began to make sense of the situation. She realised that Tommy had been visiting Suzy via this route to her rear fence, and that was why he had never been picked up by surveillance officers stationed on the road at the front. Perhaps Suzy was heading towards him now, to warn him off. Or perhaps she knew that she was in deep shit herself. Was it Tommy's idea to bring his fiancée's ring to Suzy, or had she insisted that he do it to prove his devotion?

And then Hannah realised something else. A short distance in front of Suzy was an opening in the fence – a pedestrian level crossing to the other side of the tracks. Hannah could see the bright warning lights flashing.

And she could hear the train.

It was coming up behind her. She glanced over her shoulder. Still at some distance, but it was probably going at a hell of a speed. She looked again at Suzy and the crossing, performed some crude mental calculations. Decided that it wasn't worth the risk.

Don't do it, Suzy. You won't make it.

She found some acceleration. Her heart was pounding, her lungs were ready to burst, her legs were burning, but still she ran.

Suzy looked back. Saw Hannah and the train. Carried out her own instant risk assessment.

No, Suzy. Please. It's too dangerous.

Hannah heard the train roaring up behind her, the sudden ear-splitting two-tone blare of its horn, and she kept her eyes focused on Suzy, kept willing her not to attempt it because *No Suzy, you won't make in time, you're too late*, and then there was a rush of wind and thunderous noise and the sight of Suzy jinking to her right, onto the level crossing, and all that Hannah could do was collapse against the fence, her fingers clutching the wire as she stared at the blur of darkness rocketing past her, praying with all her might that Suzy had made it across that track, that she would soon be seen running in the distance and flipping two fingers up to her pursuer, because that would be so much better than the alternative.

But then the train was gone.

And so was Suzy. What remained of her was now scattered far and wide.

Hannah slid down the fence. She threw her head back and let out a howl of anguish. When she dropped her chin again and blinked away the mist of tears, she yearned to be proved wrong, to be shown that Suzy had evaded both capture and death.

Suzy wasn't there.

Somebody else was, though.

Standing to attention atop a small hillock, stiff and proud in her new school uniform.

1

The hiss of the bus doors made Daniel Timpson look up from his comic. He peered through the grimy window to check where he was. The journey home took in a total of ten bus stops. This was number eight. He had to be careful about his count, because sometimes drivers skipped a stop if nobody wanted to get on or off.

'I thought you'd gone to sleep.'

Daniel turned to the woman sitting next to him. He thought she looked very old. Maybe more than a hundred. She'd probably die soon. He hoped she didn't die on the bus.

'I don't sleep on the bus,' he told her. 'I might miss my stop if I do that.'

She smiled. She had a nice smile, but it made him wonder if her teeth were real.

'Very wise,' she said. 'I only mention it because you haven't moved an inch for the past few minutes. You seem very engrossed in your comic.'

This puzzled Daniel. He didn't know what *engrossed* meant, but he knew that a thing was horrible if it was gross, so why would he be reading something horrible?

'It's about Adam-9,' he told her.

'Adam-9? Is he a superhero?'

'Not really. He's a secret agent. That's him.' He pointed to a figure in his comic.

'What's so secret about him?'

'Well, nobody knows what he looks like.'

'Oh. Now I'm confused.' She touched a withered finger to his comic, and he hoped that she didn't put old-person germs on it. 'Doesn't he look like that?'

Daniel wasn't surprised she was confused. Old people could get very muddled.

'No. He puts on rubber masks that make him look like other people. He can look like anyone. Maybe even you if he had a really wrinkly mask.'

She laughed, and he didn't know why.

He continued: 'So nobody knows what he really looks like, and Adam-9 is just his call sign, so nobody knows his real name either.'

'Gosh, he *is* secretive, isn't he? But he doesn't have any special powers?'

'No. But he does have a special briefcase with lots of special gadgets in it.'

The woman moved her skeletal digit to Daniel's own briefcase on his lap. 'A bit like this one, I imagine.'

He stared at her. How did she know? Was she an enemy spy?

No, he decided. She was just old, and old people are very wise. Like owls.

'A bit,' he said. He went on to explain that Adam-9 carried his briefcase everywhere, and that it was the most amazing briefcase that had ever been made. He told her that it didn't just hold his disguises and other useful stuff, but that it could also do really clever things, because the top of the handle could flip up and show buttons and dials, and one of the buttons made it fire knockout darts, while another made panels slide out from the briefcase to turn it into a bulletproof shield. And in last week's story on TV (because Adam-9 isn't only in comics), Adam-9 was thrown out of a plane, and it looked like he was going to die, but he didn't die because by pressing the right button on his briefcase he made it release a parachute.

What Daniel didn't admit to the old lady was that his own briefcase didn't do any of that stuff. It didn't even have buttons on the handle. But he could pretend it did. His mum had wanted him to have a backpack or a sports bag like everyone else, but he'd insisted. It was the briefcase or nothing. So they had gone shopping and looked at every single case in town before deciding on the one that most looked like Adam-9's. This was it, and that was why it was special.

The bus doors hissed again.

'Oh,' Daniel said. 'I have to get up now and wait for the next stop.'

'Well,' said the woman, 'it's been a pleasure talking to you, young man, but I wouldn't want you to miss your stop.'

'Thank you. Don't miss your stop either. Old people can forget things. My nan used to forget everything. She used to fart a lot, too.'

The woman laughed again, but Daniel didn't know why.

When it came time for him to alight, he made sure to thank the bus driver. He always made a point of doing so.

'Politeness costs nothing,' his mother always told him. That, and 'Manners maketh the man.' He never understood why she said *maketh* instead of *make*, but he knew she was right. More often than not, his courteous behaviour provoked a smile, and that made him happy.

At the bus stop he looked around to make sure his mother wasn't there. He had informed her many, many times that he was perfectly capable of getting home by himself now, but she often turned up nonetheless. Sometimes she would lurk in the shadows of a shop doorway and then follow him at a discreet distance, like a spy. Like Adam-9.

He turned off the busy main street and onto Marlborough Road. Home was only a short walk from here. A few minutes, although he didn't know exactly how many. He wasn't very good at telling the time. He was good at drawing pictures, though. Today he had drawn a picture of Adam-9 destroying a missile, and Mrs Collins had said it was AMAZING and put a gold star on it, *that's* how good he was at drawing. And when she did that, he felt he should say something nice back to her, so he told her that the spot on her nose looked a lot better and that she was wearing a pretty bra today, and Mrs Collins smiled and went red, probably because they were such nice compliments, and she hurried away with one hand on her nose and the other pulling together the top of her shirt.

He was looking forward to getting home and telling his mother all about his wonderful day, and what Mrs Collins had said. He was also looking forward to his tea, which tonight would be chicken nuggets and chips and two slices of bread and butter, and he'd have a diet cola with it because *diet* meant it didn't make you fat. Then he'd have ice cream with strawberries, and he'd have five strawberries because he was supposed to have Five A Day. That was his Friday night meal. Not the Friday after next, though, because that Friday would be his birthday, and on that day his diet would go out of the window and he'd have his favourite chippy meal of all time, which was steak pie with chips and gravy, and then his mum would bring out a Colin the Caterpillar cake, because that was his favourite cake of all time.

Halfway down Marlborough Road he crossed over. That was because he could see the Dirty Man sitting on his front step. Daniel called him that because he didn't know his real name and because his hands and clothes were always dirty, like he'd been working in a coal mine or down a sewer. It wasn't the dirt that made Daniel cross the road, but the fact that the Dirty Man owned a dog that ran out at anyone who got too near the house, and it would yap and try to bite their ankles. Daniel didn't like angry dogs like that, so he crossed the road and then crossed back again a few yards farther along.

At the end of Marlborough Road, he turned right onto Pickford Avenue. Mrs Romford was in front of her house, polishing the letter box on her front door. Usually when she was out like this, it was to wash her car, but today it was to polish the letter box.

'Hello, Mrs Romford,' he said, being polite.

She looked up and smiled and said, 'Oh, hello, Daniel. How are you today?'

'Fine, thank you. I'm having chicken nuggets and chips

tonight. Not chippy chips. Frozen chips. I'll have chippy chips when it's my birthday, which is very soon.'

'That's nice. How's your father?'

Mrs Romford was always asking about his dad. He didn't know why, because she saw him often enough. She was always taking her car into his dad's garage. The last time it was because one of the seats was making a funny squeak, and the time before that it was because one of the wipers wasn't cleaning the windscreen properly. When his dad said Mrs Romford was his best customer, Daniel's mum said it wasn't only her car she was looking to get serviced. Daniel didn't know what that meant.

'My dad's fine, thank you. He said to tell you something.'

Mrs Romford suddenly perked up. She got to her feet, still clutching her cloth and can of Brasso.

'Oh,' she said. 'What's that?'

Daniel put a finger to his chin as he tried to recall the exact words. 'He said, "Tell Mrs Romford that if she ever needs anything lubricating or pumping up, I'm her man."'

Mrs Romford suddenly emitted a deep-throated chuckle, which startled Daniel. The remark had seemed so ordinary at the time, although he had wondered why his mum had jabbed her elbow into his dad's ribcage.

When she had finished laughing, Mrs Romford pointed with her oily rag and said, 'You look very smart with that briefcase.'

Daniel raised the briefcase in the air, offering her a better view. 'I use it every day. It's special.'

'It certainly is,' she replied, clearly spellbound.

He hoped she wouldn't ask him why it was so special,

because then he would have to answer, and he had already gone through all that with the old lady on the bus.

'I'm going home now,' he told her. 'My mum will be waiting. She gets worried if I'm late.'

'You do that, Daniel. Tell your dad I'll see him soon.'

Daniel nodded. Then, feeling the need to pass a compliment, he said, 'I'll bet the postman will enjoy putting his package into your lovely letter box.'

Mrs Romford exploded into laughter again. Through her tears she barely managed to get out the words, 'Like father, like son.'

Daniel didn't know why she was saying that, or what she found so hilarious, so he waved goodbye and moved on.

The flats loomed into view. Twelve storeys high. Daniel lived on the top floor. There was a lift, but unless he was with someone else he always took the stairs because it was healthier. And because the lift usually stank of wee. He didn't understand why anyone would want to wee in a lift unless they were trapped in there for a long, long time.

A gang of boys came around a corner, heading towards Daniel. They were on the opposite side of the road at first, but then they saw him and crossed over. He told himself not to worry.

The boys were dressed in school uniform. They carried backpacks and sports bags rather than briefcases. One of them was bouncing a football on the pavement. The steady banging echoed off the buildings and made Daniel feel a little uneasy. He felt even more unsettled when the boys spread out to block his route.

'Where you going?' said the lad with the ball.

Daniel pointed. 'Home. I live there. 1204 Erskine Court.'

The boy grinned, and his mates sniggered.

'Why've you got a briefcase? Are you a bank manager or something?'

The laughter grew more intense. Another boy said, 'Maybe he's the prime minister.'

'Is that right?' said the first. 'Are you our leader? Are you going to save the country?'

'No. I—'

'What's your name?'

'D-D-Daniel.'

'Duh-Duh Daniel? That's a funny name. Well, Duh-Duh, what's in the briefcase?'

'Yeah, Dodo,' said a voice behind him. 'What's in the case?'

Daniel turned to face the new interrogator, and the ball hit him on the back of the head. He whirled back to face the group's leader.

'Sorry about that, Doo-Doo. My hands slipped. Anyway, you were about to tell us what's in the briefcase.'

'My lunchbox,' Daniel said. 'It's empty now. I ate all my sandwiches and my fruit and my biscuits at lunchtime. Oh, and my picture is in there too. I drew a picture, and Mrs Collins gave me a gold star. I'm going to show it to my mum.'

There was another splutter from behind, and again when Daniel turned, the ball was bounced off his head.

'You shouldn't do that,' Daniel said. 'It's not nice.'

'It was an accident,' said the lad. 'Come on, then, Dumbo. Show us your picture.'

Daniel contemplated the request. He wasn't very good at

working out whether people were being sincere or not. He liked to be honest at all times, but experience had taught him that the words of others didn't always match their thoughts.

'It's for my mum,' he said.

'Yeah, well, if it's good enough for your mum, it's good enough for us. Don't you agree, lads?'

There was a chorus of assent. Another voice said, 'Get on with it, Dildo. We haven't got all day,' and when they all laughed and Daniel turned, the ball once again smacked the back of his skull.

'Nice header,' said the leader as he caught the ball. 'Keep that up and you'll be playing in the World Cup soon.'

'I don't want to play in the World Cup. I want to go home. My mum's waiting for me.'

'Well, we don't want to stop you going home now, do we? All you've got to do is show us your picture, and then you can go home to Mummy.'

It sounded a fair enough deal to Daniel. Not such a great hardship to let them see his drawing if it meant he could go. And besides, it was a drawing to be proud of, to be appreciated by an audience.

He unclasped his briefcase, pulled out the piece of paper.

The lad whipped it out of his hand. He wasn't being the least bit careful with it, and Daniel worried that it might get creased.

'What's this, then?'

'It's . . . it's Adam-9. He's blowing up a rocket.'

'Adam-9, eh? Off the telly? Wow. What do you think, boys?'

The other lads nodded, whistled, uttered words of

appreciation. Daniel began to think he had finally made a good impression, and that this might convince the gang to be a bit more friendly towards him.

'Yeah,' said the leader. 'This is really . . . shit.'

And then he ripped it up. Tore it in half and then into quarters and then let the pieces be snatched away by the wind.

'Oops,' he said. 'Butterfingers again.'

Daniel felt a sudden stab of pain behind his eyes and in his heart, and without knowing what he planned to do next he took a step towards the boy, and yet again the ball was fired in his direction, but this time from the front, and it hit him with full force in the face, and he felt the hurt, the sting, and he halted in shock and looked into the eyes of the boy and saw that they no longer carried amusement but instead a fierce aggression.

The lad sneered. 'What are you going to do about it, Danny boy?'

What Daniel wanted to do was cry, but crying was for babies and he wasn't a baby. He wanted to run, but running away was for cowards. He wanted to fight, but if there was one thing his parents had told him time and time again, it was that violence was never a solution, that it always made things worse rather than better. And yet his fists were bunching, the leather-bound handle of his briefcase squeaking in complaint against the tightness of his grasp.

Yes, the briefcase . . .

'Well, Duh-Duh? What's your answer?'

It was an Adam-9 briefcase, wasn't it? What would Adam do in a situation like this?

And then his thumb was flipping open the secret compartment on the handle, manipulating the controls only he understood, selecting the gas jet, which was now spurting forth a dense white plume from the end of the case. Daniel closed his eyes and held out the briefcase and began to twirl on the spot, spinning and spinning while the gas created an impenetrable cloud all around him. He could hear the insults and the laughter, but he kept on revolving, keeping the attackers at bay while his special briefcase did its job of enveloping him in its protective smokescreen.

And then the voices were gone, and Daniel stopped spinning. He felt a little sick and dizzy, and so he opened his eyes.

The boys had disappeared.

Daniel looked down at his trusty briefcase. It had rescued him, but he was still saddened by what had happened.

He started for home again, trying to ignore the blood trickling from his nose and across his swollen lip, trying to avoid thinking about the drawing that had been destroyed.

Think about nice things, he told himself. Happy things.

And so he thought about his upcoming birthday. His chippy meal. His Colin the Caterpillar cake. His mother would put candles on it.

She would need a lot of candles.

In a couple of weeks, Daniel would be twenty-three years old.

2

Scott Timpson was glad to get home. For the most part, he loved his job at the garage, but sometimes it could be a pain in the arse. It wasn't the cars; it was their owners. Most were friendly enough, but some were never satisfied. One guy today was convinced that he'd been charged for an oil change that had never actually taken place. It was nonsense, of course, but to keep him happy Scott had had to do it all over again for free while the man watched. Then there was the idiot who claimed that someone had been on a joyride in his car while it had been in for a service, putting hundreds of extra miles on the clock. Other than deny it, there was nothing that Scott could do about that one.

So he was glad to be home, even though home wasn't exactly a mansion, and this neighbourhood of Stockford wasn't exactly well-to-do. He hoped one day to save enough money to put a deposit on a nice little house somewhere, but his job didn't pay a lot, and their finances always seemed tight. Bills had an annoying habit of cropping up at the most inconvenient times. For now, Erskine Court would have to do.

The structure itself was a depressing sight. A drab grey

column with no redeeming architectural features. It was the residential equivalent of the coffee cream at the bottom of the chocolate box. It had two entrances: one on the street at the front of the building, and the other here facing onto the car park. Scott felt the familiar stab of irritation as soon as he reached the door.

It was *supposed* to be secure. It was *supposed* to be protected by a lock that required a magnetic key card. It was *supposed* to keep out intruders.

The problem was that there was a certain local element that didn't believe in doing what they were *supposed* to do. Instead, they would wait for a resident to open the door and sneak in behind, which they could usually get away with because there were so many people in this building that nobody knew who lived here and who didn't. Another trick was to keep buzzing individual flats in turn until someone surrendered and unlocked the door remotely. It only took one undesirable to gain entry; they would then act as gatekeeper for their mates.

Or they would simply do what Scott was looking at now.

He bent forwards and picked up the half-brick that was jamming the door open, then went inside.

They were here, in the cavernous foyer. About half a dozen of them this time. The numbers varied. They were in their late teens, early twenties. All wearing hoodies, the uniform of their generation. Supping from cheap cans of lager and smoking roll-ups. Usually, Scott would ignore them and head straight for the lift, knowing that to challenge them would be to take his life in his hands, especially now that everyone and his dog seemed to carry a knife.

Today, he was feeling either particularly brave or particularly foolhardy.

He wandered over to the gang. He had never spoken to any of them before, but he had noticed the way they always paid deference to one particular member. He had heard them call him 'Biggo', even though he was the shortest there. Or perhaps because of it. Slightly older than the others, his shaven red hair and round pale face made Scott think of a matchstick.

The youths turned as one to face Scott. They were young and fit and confident in their superiority.

'What you going to do with that?' Biggo asked with a smile.

Scott looked down at the brick still in his hand. Yes, he thought, what am I going to do with it?

'You're not supposed to prop open the door,' he answered.

'Wouldn't dream of it, mate.'

Scott knew he had to be careful. He couldn't just come right out and call Biggo a liar. That would be suicide.

'The door is supposed to remain shut. Somebody used this to keep it open.'

'Well, it wouldn't be us, would it? In case you haven't noticed, we're already inside. We wouldn't want any riff-raff coming in here and giving us grief, would we?'

'You don't live here.'

'Doesn't matter. We were invited in.'

'Who by?'

Biggo took a drag on his cigarette and blew smoke in Scott's direction.

'What's it got to do with you?'

'You're not supposed to smoke or drink here. There are signs up.'

Biggo looked around. His eyes alighted on a notice taped to the wall near the front door. He nodded to one of his friends, who then strolled across to the notice, tore it down, and stuffed it into the pocket of his hoodie.

Biggo turned to Scott again. 'What signs?'

Scott felt his anger mounting, but it was directed more at himself than these scum in front of him. He felt utterly powerless and insignificant. His legs were actually beginning to shake.

'Just ... just stop coming here,' was the best he could do, and then he walked away, wishing that he had ignored them as he did every other day, because to act otherwise was to invite in this overwhelming sense of humiliation.

'Have you adopted that brick?' Biggo called after him. 'You should get a pram for it. What's its name?'

The raucous laughter crushed him even further. In the lift, he jabbed the button frantically, desperate to get away.

As the lift moved, he took deep breaths in an effort to calm himself. The acrid odour of urine made him cough. It invariably smelled of piss in here, and the lift seemed determined to keep its occupants confined for as long as possible, freeing them only when they were at the point of vomiting. Scott guessed that it was probably the yobs downstairs who emptied their bladders here for amusement.

I'll raise that issue with them tomorrow, he thought sarcastically. See if that goes down as well as tonight's little chat.

What an idiot.

He felt more in control when the metal doors eventually whined open. This was the twelfth storey. His domain. He told himself that if he ever came across any of those fuckwits on this floor, he'd really show them what he could do. It would be a long time before they found anything funny again.

That's what he told himself. It helped for now.

He turned left and through the fire door, then along the corridor to his flat. He pulled out his keys, opened the front door and entered. The hallway stretched ahead of him. To his left were doors to the two bedrooms and the bathroom. A door to his right took him into an open-plan area comprising the living room, dining area and kitchenette. Scott hung up his jacket and went in search of his family, to put his shit day behind him.

Gemma's face warned him to think again.

She was directly in front of him as he came through the door. Usually a fizzing bundle of energy, this evening she was wearing an expression that said, *You're not going to like this, but . . .*

'What's up?' he asked.

She opened her mouth, but then her eyes flicked downwards. 'Why are you carrying a brick?'

Scott looked around for a surface that wouldn't be scratched or soiled. Eventually, he lowered the brick to the carpet.

'Long story,' he said. 'What's wrong?'

'It's Daniel. He's . . . he's been in a fight.'

Something rolled over in Scott's stomach. He looked back to the hallway, at Daniel's closed bedroom door.

'Oh, shit,' he said. 'Not again.'

'It's okay,' Gemma said, coming towards him. 'It's not what you're thinking.'

'He didn't—?'

'No. He was good. A gang of schoolkids came up to him on his way home. He's got a bloody nose to show for it, but he didn't fight back. He's really upset, though.'

Scott looked imploringly at the ceiling. 'Fucking hell. I hate this place. Isn't life difficult enough for him already?'

Gemma came closer and folded her arms around him. She had a knack for calming him down when things became too much.

'Daniel was as good as gold,' she said. 'You need to go and tell him. It'll make him feel better.'

Scott nodded, then kissed his wife and headed towards Daniel's bedroom. He knocked, opened the door.

Daniel was sitting on his bed, staring at a book. Scott often wished that Daniel's books didn't all have pictures in them, that at least one of them could be a textbook on maths or physics, or even just a novel for grown-ups.

He should be a university graduate by now, Scott thought. Maybe training to be a lawyer or a doctor or a dentist. Maybe engaged or married. Just having a girlfriend would be a start. Or—

No.

Stop it. You're not being fair. You're letting one crap day ruin everything.

'Hi, Daniel,' he said cheerily.

'Hi, Dad,' Daniel said. But he didn't look up from his book.

Scott sat down on the bed next to Daniel. It could still

27

surprise him that he was dwarfed by his own son. Scott was tall and broad. Gemma was also tall. Their ancestors were no Lilliputians. But as for Daniel . . .

He had been born by Caesarean section. No other option for a baby that size. And when he was hauled into the world, it was as if he was determined to continue expanding into his more spacious environment, the way goldfish grow in proportion to their bowls. With his increasing size came mounting strength, which, alas, was not matched by his intellect. In that regard, Daniel was, and always would be, a young child.

'What are you reading?' Scott asked.

'*The Gruffalo*. I like the story, but . . .'

'But what?'

'Somebody once said I looked like the Gruffalo.'

Scott sighed. It was just the latest in a string of insults. Some called him Lennie, or Desperate Dan, or Tank, or the Hulk, or Shrek, or Bigfoot, or . . . the list went on.

He put his arm around Daniel's shoulders. He could sense the raw power beneath. 'People sometimes say and do cruel things. I think you got a taste of that tonight, didn't you?'

Daniel nodded dolefully. 'I wasn't doing anything. I was just walking home. Some boys started saying things. One of them hit me in the face with a football.'

He started crying. Scott rubbed his back. 'Don't cry. They're not worth it.' He hesitated. He didn't want to ask this, especially as Gemma had already tried to reassure him, but he felt he had to. 'You didn't . . . you didn't hit any of them, did you?'

Daniel looked him straight in the eye. 'No, Dad. I promised, didn't I? I said I would never do that.'

'Yes, son, you did. I just need you to be careful, that's all. You remember what happened to Perry, don't you? And to Ewan?'

'Yes, Dad. I remember.'

Daniel lowered his head again, and Scott hated himself for dredging up the past. But it was the only way to keep the need to remain in control lodged in his son's consciousness.

'Tell you what,' he said. 'How about helping me out at the garage tomorrow?'

Daniel brightened. 'Can I?'

'Absolutely. And after that we'll have lunch, and then we'll do something in the afternoon.'

'Ooh, ooh, what about ten-pin bowling?'

Scott recalled the havoc that Daniel had wreaked the last time he got his hands on a bowling ball. They'd had to close down two of the lanes.

'Er, I was thinking the cinema. That new Disney film starts today – the one about the professor who uses science to pretend he's a wizard.'

'*Kupp and Sorcery*? Yes! Can we go? Can we?'

Scott briefly considered how much it would cost – the tickets, the petrol, the popcorn, the hot dogs, the drinks – but then he looked again at his son's face and his mind was made up.

'Course we can. It'll do us both good.' He stood up, buoyed by the sight of Daniel's beaming smile. 'Dinner will be ready soon. I'll give you a call.'

'Thanks, Dad,' Daniel said. And then: 'I love you.'

Something splintered in Scott's chest. 'I love you too.' He started to turn away, then halted. He opened his arms for an embrace. 'Come here, son.'

Daniel looked back at him with uncertainty. 'Dad ... The Rule.'

Scott beckoned. 'It's okay. Come on. Just be careful.'

The Rule was that Daniel should avoid physical contact with others as much as possible. It was a tough decree to enforce, but it was the safest option. The problem lay not so much in Daniel's sheer strength, but in his inability to control how much of it he was applying, especially when his emotions were running high. Right now, though, Scott felt compelled to take a risk.

The hug was brief, and Daniel's touch mercifully light.

'Good lad,' Scott said.

As he left the room, he decided not to tell Gemma about breaking The Rule. The last time Daniel had hugged his mother, he had fractured one of her ribs.

When he was alone, Daniel opened a drawer and took out a fistful of socks. He carried them across to the bed and lined them up.

For as long as he could remember, he had employed his socks as puppets. He would hold each one vertically, the toe end jutting upwards between his fingers and forming the head of a character. He would make them walk or run by bobbing them along the bed or carpet at the appropriate speed. Usually, he would have one in each hand and they would converse, Daniel speaking all their lines out loud. Sometimes he would make them fight, the bottom end of one sock being whipped into the 'face' of the other.

His parents had bought him all kinds of alternative puppets and action figures, but he always returned to his socks. Their stories gave him the comfort he struggled to find elsewhere, and acted as a vehicle for him to explore the confusing worlds of his imagination.

Right now, most of his puppets were naughty young lads. The sock in Daniel's right hand – bigger and thicker than the others – was Adam-9, and he was standing for no nonsense from the cheap cotton scallywags confronting him. Within seconds he had laid several of them out flat and made the rest run away like the chickens they were.

To Daniel's mind, this was not breaking The Rule. This was Adam-9, and Adam-9 was allowed to fight back. Daniel had never actually seen him kill anyone in the programmes or comics, but he was quite sure that people must have died. When Adam made that missile reverse back into the rogue space station, the people on board must have been blown to bits. How could they have escaped alive?

Yes, it was okay for Adam-9. The Rule wasn't meant for him.

3

Hannah didn't even bother to take her coat off. She went straight to the kitchen, where she dropped her bag in the middle of the floor. She took a glass from the shelf and a bottle of red wine at random from the rack next to it. She poured until the glass was full, then gulped most of it down. She didn't savour it; she just wanted the hit of alcohol.

She heard a noise behind her, and turned to see Ben wandering into the room. As always, he looked so chilled, so at one with his universe, his universe being largely confined to this address. They'd built a studio in the garden, where he spent most of each day creating sculptures and listening to weird electronic music. He even took his breaks out there, drinking herbal tea or contorting his body into impossible shapes on his yoga mat. He was the total opposite of the men with whom Hannah shared her working day. She believed that was why their relationship worked so well. She couldn't have stood being married to a bloody copper.

He smiled with his whole face and issued the brightest 'Hey', but his eyes were on the wine glass and it annoyed her, because why shouldn't she have a drink after work like lots of other people?

Ben stooped to pick up her bag, then tossed his head to clear the hair from his eyes as he placed the bag gingerly on the breakfast bar. Hannah had always liked the way he kept his hair long, but even that was starting to irritate her. Everything irritated her.

'Tough day?' he asked, and she took it as a slight because the implication was clearly that she was resorting to alcohol as a solution to her problems, which may have been true but that wasn't the point.

'Par for the course,' she said. She began to recharge her glass, and was convinced that Ben's eyes widened at the rising wine level.

'Need a hug?' he asked.

'What I need is work.'

He smiled again. 'Oh, I don't know. Some Botox, perhaps. And okay, maybe a slight boob job.'

She kicked out at him half-heartedly and he bounced out of range.

'They don't trust me,' she said.

'Who doesn't?'

'The top brass. My own boss. They think I've lost it. They don't trust me to do a proper job.'

'Maybe they're just protecting you.'

'I don't need protecting. Why would they even think that?'

Ben shrugged his shoulders. 'You didn't take much time off. Maybe they think you could do without the stress.'

Hannah swigged more wine. 'I can handle stress. It goes with the badge. It's not about that. It's because they think I'm a fuck-up.'

'No they don't.'

'They do. The Suzy Carling thing was just the cherry on a whole cake of fuck-up.'

'That wasn't your fault. You know that.'

Which was another thing she loved about Ben. They'd had this conversation probably a thousand times before, and each time he could have said something like 'Oh, Christ, not this again', but he never did. Although sometimes – right now, for example – a part of her wished he would do precisely that so she could have a damn good argument.

'I know what they put in the official reports, but the force doesn't admit to mistakes unless it absolutely has to. What they write about me and what they think about me privately are two different things.'

Ben pointed to the wine bottle. 'Are you planning to share that?'

She took down another glass. As she filled it she wondered if he'd asked for it just to prevent her drinking it all.

Ben sipped the wine and studied her over the rim of his glass.

'What makes you think they're so against you?'

'Don't ask that like you're a psychologist talking to a paranoid schizophrenic. I'm not imagining things. I look at the cases I used to get and I look at the cases I get now and they're different. I used to work murders. I was right at the forefront on those investigations. Everyone had me pegged for shooting up the ranks.' She waved her glass at him, and some of the wine sloshed over the sides. 'You know what they gave me today? A missing husband.'

'Well, that sounds pretty important to me. I mean, I'd like to think that if I went missing—'

'He disappeared two years ago. Two fucking years. And he'd emptied out his savings account before he went, so it looked like he knew exactly what he was doing. But now the family are kicking up a fuss about it again, and my bosses want to show that they're taking it seriously. So who gets the job? Muggins here.'

'I suppose somebody has to do it.'

There he goes again, she thought. The voice of reason.

'Yes, of course somebody has to do it, and if it was just the once, I wouldn't be complaining. But when it happens again and again – when every shitty meaningless job lands on my desk – then it starts to get pretty tedious pretty damn quickly.'

'Have you spoken to anyone about it? Have you talked it over with your boss?'

'Yes, I had a chat with Ray Devereux.'

'And? What did he say?'

'He said . . . he said I should have a good long think about whether I'm on the right career path.'

The shock was evident on Ben's face. 'What kind of support is that? Shouldn't he be sticking up for you? Jesus! And this is all because some stupid woman tried to outrun a train? That's not fair.'

That's more like it, she thought. A bit of outrage against the bastards I have to deal with. Mild outrage, admittedly, but for Ben it's the equivalent of a volcanic eruption.

'It's . . . it's not just that.'

'What do you mean?'

Confession time. She'd kept this to herself out of embarrassment, but right now she needed support.

'There are other things. Mistakes.'

'What mistakes?'

'Little things. Mostly.'

'Mostly?'

'There was a lad. He came in for a voluntary interview last week. He had information related to a stabbing we were investigating. I led the interview. Only . . . I forgot to caution him prior to questioning.'

She saw how Ben's face dropped. He knew enough about police work to realise how serious this was. It could lead to the collapse of a case in court.

'Oh, shit,' he said. 'What happened?'

'Somebody noticed there was no caution on the recording of the interview, which left the lad's statements open to legal challenge. A stink was raised. I was asked for an explanation.'

'And what did you say?'

'The only thing I could say. I remained adamant that I had issued a caution.'

'Did they believe you?'

'Only when Marcel Lang came to my aid and said he'd heard me do it. He said he was late pressing the button on the recorder.'

'He lied?'

Hannah nodded. This was only one of many things over the years for which she had Marcel to thank.

Ben sighed. 'Come and sit down. Take your coat off.'

They eased themselves onto the stools at the breakfast bar. Hannah could hear the whirring of the fans in the oven and the extractor unit. A smell of goulash wafted across to her, but she had no appetite for it, even though Ben was a great cook. His health regime might consist of drinking beverages that smelled like piss, and tying his ankles together behind his neck, but so far he had resisted crossing the Styx into the darkness that was vegetarianism.

He took her hand. 'Hannah,' he said, 'do you think maybe you *do* need to take some more time off? It's not like you to make mistakes like that.'

She was silent for a moment, but it was only to convince her husband that she was giving it serious consideration.

'I can't sit at home doing nothing. I tried that and it killed me. I need to work.'

'Then . . . then maybe your boss was right. Maybe you need to think about making a change.'

She yanked her hand away from his. 'I don't want a fucking change. I'm good at what I do. What I need is for people to start believing in me.'

She meant her police superiors, but realised it came across as being directed at Ben. He looked hurt.

'Look,' she said, 'I didn't mean—'

'It's okay. You've had a tough time. We both have.' He looked at the oven and got to his feet. 'That goulash is nearly ready. I'll put some rice on.'

She didn't stop him. He also needed to be busy. That was how they lived their lives now: keeping themselves distracted. When she wanted to talk about it, she wasn't sure he did; and she was sure there were also times that he was afraid of bringing up the topic.

It shouldn't be like this, she thought. We can't keep pretending that things are back to normal. They're not, and never will be.

She watched as he put a pan of water on the hob and turned on the gas. He remained staring at the pan, his back to her, as though his gaze was essential to the boiling process.

'I see her,' Hannah said.

Ben turned his head slightly. 'What?'

More confessions, she thought. Seems to be the night for them.

'Tilly. I see her.'

'What do you mean?'

'She keeps appearing to me, and at the strangest times. I'm usually not even thinking about her when it happens. She'll just walk right out in front of me, or I'll see her in the distance. But when I try going to her, she disappears.'

Ben said nothing. Just stood and waited to hear more. Hannah looked at the light bouncing off the surface of her wine as she remembered.

'It happened at Suzy Carling's house. She came out of the kitchen while we were talking. She was in her school uniform. She looked . . . proud. And then afterwards – after the train – I saw her again. She was far away, looking back at me as if she wanted me to follow.'

'You . . . you see her a lot, then?'

'Not a lot. But enough. And I know she's not real. It's just my mind playing tricks. But she's so clear. So solid. She's *there*, Ben.'

His response of silence demanded her attention, and she looked up to see that his eyes were glistening.

38

'Oh, what's the matter?' she asked. 'What's the matter?'

He looked so helpless, so at a loss. 'I don't see her. I never see her. I look, but she's never there. Every time I walk into a room, I think she'll be there. Every time I hear a sound in the house, I expect it to be her. And it's not. It never is. I don't see her, Hannah. I don't see her.'

She went to him then. Held him tightly as his tears flowed.

Sometimes she forgot that she wasn't the only one who needed consoling.

And sometimes she felt that the thing most tightly binding them together was their shared pain.

4

For Scott, working with his son was always beautiful.

Daniel liked to pretend. He would watch his dad working on a car, and then he would mimic the actions on his own invisible vehicle, his eyes constantly roving to his father to check he was doing it right. He would even hitch up his trousers when his father did, or rub his hands at the same time, or sigh and tut in concert.

In those moments, Scott could easily forget that his son was nearly twenty-three.

He was fully aware that his boss didn't approve of Daniel being in the garage. 'It's dangerous,' Gavin would say. 'He could get hurt, or damage something.' But Gavin wasn't working today, and Scott had jumped at the opportunity to spend time alone with his son. No offence to Gemma, but the father–son bond was like epoxy resin: it worked best without a third ingredient.

Right now, Scott was labouring beneath a jacked-up 4x4. He looked across at Daniel, lying flat on his back and staring up at his own imaginary car while making twisting motions with his imaginary spanner. The simplicity and purity of it brought a lump to Scott's throat.

'Daniel,' he called. 'I'm nearly done here. Could you bring over the wheels for this Audi, please?'

Scott came out from beneath the car and stood up, stretching his aching back.

'Here you go, Dad.'

Scott turned. He had expected Daniel to roll one of the wheels over to him. Instead, Daniel was carrying all four of them, two tucked under each arm. Wheels, not just tyres. He might as well have been carrying swimming floats.

'Er, thanks, Daniel. Just put them down there for me, will you?'

Daniel propped his load up against a metal post. 'What else can I do?'

Scott scanned the interior of the garage for a task that would be useful but not hazardous.

'You see that filing cabinet over there? We've made room for it in the office. Would you mind taking all the stuff out of the drawers? Then you can help me shift it.'

Daniel nodded vigorously, then marched like a soldier towards the cabinet, his arms swinging wildly at his sides.

Scott smiled and focused his attention on the first of the wheels. Seconds later, he heard a grunt from behind. He turned and saw that, rather than emptying the drawers, Daniel had simply wrapped his arms around the full cabinet, picked the whole thing up, and was now carrying it into the office.

Scott shook his head in amazement. 'Jesus,' he muttered. 'Where the hell did he get those genes from?'

*

41

The movie was just okay. Scott had sat through enough films like this one to know what to expect. There were a few one-liners aimed at a more adult audience, and there was some amusing slapstick, but the main enjoyment for Scott came from watching the reaction of his son. Daniel was transfixed from beginning to end. He even seemed unaware of his hand mechanically grabbing popcorn and transferring it to his mouth. For a couple of hours, the outside world ceased to exist for Daniel, and even when the closing music thundered in, he insisted on remaining in his seat until the credits had finished rolling.

Scott wanted to hang on to that enjoyment as he drove home. He listened to Daniel jabbering endlessly about the film and tried to absorb some of his exhilaration.

But then he pulled his old Ford into the car park, and the tower block loomed as if to impress upon him that this was, and always would be, the end of the line. His heart sank. The short-lived fantasy was over.

The pair entered the building. Scott wrinkled his nose at the pungent odour of weed, but Daniel didn't seem to notice. He had stopped talking about the film and was now on to television soap operas.

'You mind if we take the lift?' Scott said.

'I don't like lifts. I like the stairs.'

'I know, but I really don't feel like walking all that way up. Come on, Daniel, keep me company.'

Daniel looked up the staircase and then back at the lift doors. 'Oh, okay.'

Scott allowed Daniel the disproportionate pleasure of summoning the lift. While they waited, Scott reflected on how quiet the building was. It could be like that sometimes, the vast structure feeling almost devoid of life.

The lift doors shuddered open. Daniel stepped in with some trepidation and stared at the metal walls enclosing him. He let out a slight murmur of discomfort when the lift jerked into life again and began dragging them upwards.

'It's all right, Daniel. It's perfectly safe.'

'It doesn't feel very safe.'

'I know, but it is. Trust me.'

'I always trust you, Dad.'

The lift slowed and came to a stop.

'This is number eight,' Daniel said. 'We don't live on this floor.'

'No, we don't.'

The doors opened. Facing them was a man who made Scott tense immediately. The man appeared to be in his twenties. Stocky, with coarse stubble and thick eyebrows. He wore a black leather jacket and skinny jeans, and over one shoulder was slung a khaki backpack – much older and heavier looking than the one Scott was carrying. He was chewing gum, and had a cigarette tucked behind one ear. There was something in the way he glared at Scott that suggested he wasn't a person to be trifled with.

The man came forward. Scott and Daniel parted to let him through, Daniel flattening his bulk against the side wall. As the man turned and faced forward, Scott asked him what floor he wanted.

'Ground,' the man said.

Scott really wished he could grant the request, but he knew the lift would insist on completing its assigned journey first.

'Er, we're going up.'

The man narrowed his eyes at Scott, as if to discern whether his command was being challenged. As the doors closed and the lift groaned with its increased load, the man said, 'Right. I'll go up, and then I'll go down again.' He made it sound as though Scott was entirely to blame for this elongation of his journey.

'You must have pressed the wrong button,' Daniel said.

Shit, Scott thought.

'What?' the man said. The single word dripped with a menace that went undetected by Daniel.

'You must have pressed the up button. The lift wouldn't have stopped if you'd pressed the down button.'

'I pressed the down button.' It was said with finality, but Daniel was determined.

'Then the lift must be broken.' He turned to his father. 'Dad, you said this lift was safe.'

'It *is* safe, Daniel.' Scott flashed a weak smile at the third occupant, but it seemed to have no effect.

'You should walk,' Daniel said to the man.

'What?'

'It's better for you. And it's easier going down.'

The man looked at Scott. 'Is he for real?'

'He's got—' Scott began. And then he thought, No, why should I have to tell people he's got learning difficulties? It's their damn problem, not his.

He worked his jaw, not knowing what he should say instead. He thought he was saved when the lift halted suddenly.

But that's when it all went wrong.

Later, he would delve into chaos theory without even knowing he was doing so. He would wonder about how things could be so finely balanced that the most inoffensive of words, the briefest of glances, the tiniest lapse of concentration could alter lives so profoundly and irreversibly. A touch that could start an avalanche.

Perhaps it wasn't the jolt of the lift stopping – perhaps it would have happened anyway – but it was in that moment that the strap on the man's backpack came loose, and the bag slipped from his shoulder and fell to the floor and the flap flew open and some of the contents spilled out and Scott saw the plastic bags of white powder and the wads of money and the semi-automatic pistol.

'Fuck!' the man said as he squatted to retrieve his possessions.

Scott looked away. He saw that Daniel wasn't looking away but instead staring wide-eyed at the items, and he thought, No, Daniel, look at me, not him, don't see those things, don't say anything, and why the hell aren't these doors opening, why can't we get out of—?

The doors opened.

Scott grabbed Daniel by the wrist and pulled him into the corridor. He wanted to move faster, but Daniel was dragging his feet, his eyes still on the man. Scott pulled harder, his own gaze on the fire doors ahead.

'Wait!'

Scott halted.

Shit.

The man followed them out of the lift, walked directly up to Scott and locked eyes with him. 'What did you see?' he asked.

'Nothing,' Scott said. 'I didn't see anything.'

'Right answer.' He turned to Daniel. 'What about you? What did you see in the lift?'

Say what I said, Scott willed. For once in your life, tell a damn lie.

'I saw my dad, and I saw you, and I saw some money and a gun.'

Shit, shit, shit.

The man moved into Daniel's personal space. 'Have you got a fucking death wish or something? I'll ask you again, dickhead. What did you see?'

Daniel seemed puzzled, but then his face brightened.

'Oh yeah. You've got some bags of white stuff in there too.'

Scott hastened forward. 'He doesn't understand. He's got learning difficulties.' As soon as the words left his mouth, he hated himself.

The man gave him a withering look. 'I'm not asking him to win the Nobel Prize. I just want to know if he can keep his mouth shut.'

'He will. He won't tell a—'

'Shut it.' He turned to Daniel again. 'So what about it? What're you going to say if anyone asks about me?'

Daniel looked helplessly at his father.

'It's okay, Daniel. Just tell him what he wants to hear, and then we can go home.'

'Yeah, Daniel,' the man said. 'You heard him. Tell me.'

'Tell you what?'

'Tell me what I've got in this fucking bag.'

Daniel looked again at his dad, and then at the man. 'I don't know,' he said.

The man nodded. 'That's more like it. Now you've—'

'I didn't see everything. I only saw the money and the gun and the white stuff.'

Scott moved forward again. He said, 'Look, he's not being funny with you. He doesn't know how to lie, that's all. He's not going to talk to anyone about this.'

And then he made the mistake of putting his hand on the man's shoulder.

The man whirled and slapped Scott's hand away.

'What the fuck do you think you're doing?'

Scott stepped backwards, but the man followed, jabbing Scott in the chest.

'What kind of fucking game are you two trying to play?'

'No game,' Scott protested. 'We just want to go home, okay? Leave now, and we won't say a thing.'

'I know you won't, because you'll be dead in a fucking ditch if you do. Do you understand?'

Scott nodded furiously.

'And what about the fucking retard over there?'

Even for Scott, who had heard every insult invented, the word sent shockwaves through his body. It pressed a button within him that electrified his limbs. He lashed out, pushing the man away.

'Don't call him that!' he yelled. 'He's my son!'

But the man was already shaking his head and clenching his jaw and bunching his fists and advancing towards Scott. There was a glint in his eye that told Scott he was about to show no mercy and he was going to enjoy it, and Scott tried to ready himself for a fight that he knew he wasn't going to win, and he

47

wondered what it would be like to have broken teeth and bones, and he could feel his legs turning to jelly and his chest panting for air, and he hoped that he could at least put on a decent show in front of his son before ending up in hospital ...

And then the man was gone.

He was whisked off his feet as if by a whirlwind, and that whirlwind was Daniel, who now had a meaty hand clamped around the man's neck and was pushing him further and further up the drab grey wall and saying through his tears, 'Leave my dad alone, leave my dad alone, leave my dad alone ...' And as the man's dangling legs twisted and kicked out for purchase, Scott grabbed his son's arms and yelled at him to stop, stop it now, Daniel, put him down ...

When the message finally penetrated, Daniel obeyed his father and released his grip, and the man fell in a heap on the floor. Scott went to the man as Daniel retreated, whimpering, to a window in the corner of the gloomy corridor, but it was obvious even to Scott's untrained eyes that nothing could be done, that even such a small fragment of time was impossible to reverse.

The man was dead.

5

Scott had never seen a corpse before. For some reason he had expected them to look like they were sleeping, and was shocked at how wrong he'd got it. He wasn't sure he could explain it to anyone in words, except to say that there was an *absence*, an emptiness to the body that could never be detected in someone still clinging on to life. What lay before him was just a shell, its previous aggression now completely wiped away.

'Is he dead?' Daniel asked. 'Is he like Perry?'

Scott didn't answer. He was trying to think.

I should call the police, he thought. Police and also ambulance, just in case he isn't really dead, even though I know he is. That's what you do in situations like this. When you get in a fight and someone drops dead at your feet, you can't run away from it. You have to face up to it and call in the experts, let them sort it out.

And yet . . .

Other thoughts were intruding, complicating the situation, muddling his brain. Thoughts that began with 'But what if . . .'

Adrenaline was flooding his system. There was a time pressure here. At any moment, someone else might appear and then it would be too late, the decision would be taken out of his hands.

'Dad, is he—'

'Come here.'

'W-What?'

'Come here, Daniel. We need to move him. Pick him up for me.'

Daniel shrank further into his corner. 'I don't want to pick him up.'

'Daniel, please. We need to— we need to get help for him.'

It was a lie. The man was beyond help. He was no longer Scott's number-one concern.

The lie did the trick. Chewing one of his fingers, Daniel shuffled over. He stared down at the body.

Scott clapped his hands to emphasise the urgency. 'Now, Daniel. Pick him up.'

Daniel bent down, scooped up the corpse like it was a large pillow. The dead man's head drooped and his tongue lolled out of his open mouth. Daniel looked down at it with distaste and fear.

'He *is* like Perry. Perry's tongue did that too.'

'This way, Daniel. Move.'

Scott picked up the man's backpack, then opened the fire doors and ushered his son through. As they passed each apartment, Scott willed its inhabitants not to appear.

They reached 1204. Scott dug out his keys and unlocked the door. 'Go in, Daniel. Hurry!'

As Daniel headed inside, Scott took one last look along the corridor. There was no sign of anyone. No obvious indicators that a killing had just taken place.

He closed the door. Daniel was still in the hallway, clearly wondering what on earth he was supposed to do with the corpse he was carrying.

'Bring him in,' Scott told him. 'Put him on the sofa. That's it.'

Scott put the man's backpack down on the floor, then took off his own and tossed it across the room. He wiped sweat from his brow and tried to breathe again. Tried to gather his thoughts.

'Scott?'

Gemma. Coming in from the bathroom.

'What's going on? Who the hell is that?'

He turned to see her pointing, her expression a mixture of puzzlement and worry.

Scott turned to his son. 'Daniel, go to your room, please.'

'Dad, I—'

'*Now*, Daniel. Please.'

'Scott,' Gemma said again. She was still staring at the occupant of her sofa. 'What's wrong with him?'

'*Daniel*,' Scott said.

Daniel sloped off to his room. As he went, Scott held up a finger to Gemma, advising her to wait a moment. After Daniel's bedroom door had been shut, Scott closed the living-room door too.

Gemma had moved closer and now had a hand to her mouth. Her gaze was locked in disbelief and horror on the unwanted guest.

'Scott, who is this? What's wrong with him? Is he drunk? A druggie?'

Scott went to her, put his hands on her shoulders. 'Gemma, listen to me . . .'

Her eyes searched his face, and he could see fear there now as the truth began to seep in.

'What?' she said. '*What?*'

'He's dead.' He felt he should offer more, but all he could do was repeat himself. 'He's dead.'

Gemma glanced at the unmoving figure. 'I don't understand. What do you mean, he's dead? Why have you just put a dead man on our sofa?'

Scott struggled to find the right answer. It was such a simple concept and yet so difficult to do it justice with mere words.

'Oh, God, Gemma . . .' He began to cry.

'Scott, stop it!' she yelled. 'Explain this to me! What the hell is going on?'

'He . . . he attacked me. When we got out of the lift. And . . . and Daniel . . .'

'Daniel what? What about Daniel?'

'Daniel was trying to protect me. He came to my rescue, and . . . and . . . and he killed him.'

'Killed him? What do you mean, Daniel killed him? How did he kill him?'

'He didn't mean to. He grabbed him. By the neck. And that was it. It wasn't his—'

'Scott, stop. You're going too fast. I don't understand any of this. Why . . . why did you bring him in here?'

'He's . . . I don't know . . . I thought maybe . . .'

'Thought what?'

'I don't know. I panicked. It seemed the right thing.'

'How? How could it possibly be the right thing? What were you thinking?'

She pulled away from Scott and moved closer to the body. She started to reach a hand out towards the man's face, then withdrew it.

'You're sure he's dead?' she asked.

Scott simply nodded. He could tell she was in no doubt of it herself.

Gemma took a deep breath and let it out again. 'Then there's only one thing we can do. We have to call the police. You need to explain to them exactly what happened.'

Scott shook his head. 'I can't.'

'What do you mean, you can't? The man is dead, Scott. We have to tell someone.'

'It's not that simple.'

Something dawned on Gemma then. Her face changed, filling with dread.

'Why?' she asked. 'Why isn't it that simple, Scott? You said the man attacked you, and that Daniel saved you. He *did* attack you, didn't he?'

Scott hesitated. 'Kind of.'

'Kind of? What does that even mean? What happened, exactly?'

'He pushed me. And then I pushed him back.'

'And then what?'

'That was it. He started coming towards me again, but Daniel stopped him.'

Gemma lowered her head and took another deep breath.

'Please tell me I'm missing something here. He pushed you?

How? How did he push you? Was he trying to throw you down the stairs or out of the window? Or was it a push like this?' She thrust a hand into his chest, and Scott got the feeling she was doing it for more than demonstration purposes – that she really did want to vent some of her frustration on him.

'Yes, more like that.'

'And then you shoved back at him.'

'Yes.'

'Like two fucking kids in a playground? Is that what you're telling me? Two immature boys getting a bit rough with each other and then suddenly it turns into World War Three? What the hell, Scott? What the fucking hell?'

'You don't understand. He was threatening us. He had a gun.'

She blinked. 'A gun? Un-fucking-believable. And at what point were you planning to let me in on this crucial piece of information? He pulled a gun on you?'

'Not exactly. It was in his bag. He dropped his bag and we saw it. That's how the argument started. He wanted us to promise not to say anything, but Daniel being Daniel . . .'

Gemma thought for a moment, then turned and walked away. She picked up her mobile phone from the table next to the sofa.

'What are you doing?' Scott asked her.

'I'm calling 999. They need to sort this mess out.'

He moved towards her. 'No.'

'Scott, we have a dead body on our hands. You can't hide something like this.'

'I . . . I'm not trying to hide anything. I just want us to think about our options.'

'What options? We don't have any options. What's happened has happened.'

She began to raise the phone again, but Scott grabbed her wrist. 'No!'

She stared at him.

'No,' he said again. 'Think about Daniel.'

'I *am* thinking about Daniel. This was just a tragic accident. The police will understand that when you explain it to them.'

'Will they?'

'Of course they will,' she said, but Scott could already hear the doubt. 'This guy was up to no good. He had a gun, for Christ's sake. And Daniel is . . . well, they'll understand. Daniel doesn't have an evil bone in his body. He was just trying to protect his dad.'

Scott shook his head. 'They'll crucify him, and you know it.'

'No. Why do you say that?'

'Do I have to spell it out? Two blokes name-calling and pushing each other. You said it yourself: like kids in a playground. And then along comes this much bigger kid and snaps the neck of one of them. Does that sound like a reasonable response to you?'

'Not reasonable, no. But reason doesn't apply in Daniel's case. He's not like most people. They'll treat him as a special case.'

A wave of immense sadness suddenly overwhelmed Scott. In a shaky voice he said, 'I'll tell you what will happen. The police will come here, and when we tell them what happened they'll arrest Daniel because they'll have no other choice. And it won't matter how much we try to reassure Daniel, he won't understand. He will hate being touched, because it breaks The Rule, and there's a good chance he'll lash out, and maybe an officer or two will get hurt, and then they'll get rough with him. Maybe they'll taser him or something – I don't know.'

'Scott, no. It won't be as bad as—'

'They'll put him in a cell, and they'll question him endlessly, and they'll bring us in for questioning too. Daniel will be afraid – more afraid than he's ever been in his life – but the one thing we can be certain of is that he will tell the truth. Even if we ask Daniel to say that the man put a gun to my head, Daniel won't play that game. He doesn't know how to. He will tell the police exactly what he saw and did.'

'But surely that won't matter? His difficulties are all on record. They'll realise that he didn't—'

'What they'll realise, Gem, is that he's a danger to those around him. Doesn't matter what was going through his head, if he poses a risk to the public they'll lock him up.'

'They wouldn't put him in prison. Not someone with his problems.'

'Happened before. "Diminished responsibility" they call it in court. They've still ended up in jail. I looked it up last time.'

'Last time? What do you mean, last time?'

'Well, that's the other thing, isn't it? Daniel's got form.'

'He hasn't got form. Stop talking about him as though he's some kind of hardened criminal.'

'He killed Perry, didn't he?'

'That wasn't his fault. The stupid dog went for him.'

'That's not what the owners said. They said he was just being playful.'

'Daniel wasn't to know that, was he? Whose side are you on, anyway? They got a new puppy out of it, didn't they?'

'And then there's Ewan Rogers.'

'Ewan was a bully. He deserved a good smack.'

'A smack, yes. But a broken arm?'

'I'll ask you again: whose side are you on?'

'Ours, of course. I'm just trying to show you what others will say. Can you imagine what will happen if this goes to court? They'll all come out of the woodwork. They hated us at the old place. They were practically on the verge of forming a lynch mob. I thought we'd managed to escape from all that, and now . . . and now . . .'

The stress of it all became too intense and tears formed again. Gemma came to him.

'Do you really think it would be that bad?'

'I don't know, Gem, I really don't. Maybe that's just a worst-case scenario. But even if they didn't put him in prison, they'd probably want to put him somewhere secure.'

'You mean like a mental hospital?'

'I don't know. But somewhere that's not his home. Can you imagine what that'll do to him?'

Gemma chewed her lip. She turned to look at the body again.

'So what do you suggest?'

6

'I don't know.'

'What do you mean, you don't know? Why did you bring him in here if you don't know?'

'Like I said, I was panicking. I needed time to think. Talk it over with you.'

'So now we've talked it over, what do we do?'

'I still don't know.'

They stood staring at the body, not speaking for a full minute.

'Oh, God,' Gemma said. 'I can't believe we're doing this. I can't believe we're standing here discussing what we should do about a dead body lying on our sofa. Who the hell is he anyway, this guy who carries a gun around with him?'

'That's not all he's got,' Scott said. He knelt on the carpet and opened up the backpack. 'Look at this.' He showed her the money and the bags of white powder.

'Is that what I think it is?'

'Well, I don't think it's flour. He doesn't strike me as someone who did much baking.'

'Jesus.'

'Yeah. And that's another thing. This guy is no low-level druggie. He'll have friends in low places. Friends who won't take kindly to someone bumping him off. If they ever hear about what Daniel did to him—'

'All right! Stop it, Scott! I get the idea. But I still don't know what you think we can do about it. He can't stay here.'

Scott went to the body and started patting it down.

'What are you doing?'

'Trying to find out more about him.'

One of the jacket pockets seemed full. Scott reached into it and pulled out a wallet and mobile phone. He opened up the wallet and took out a bank card.

'His name is Joseph Cobb. Mean anything to you?'

Gemma shook her head.

Scott pressed a button on the phone. The screen flared into life.

'It needs a passcode. There's no way we'll ever—'

He almost dropped the phone when it rang in his hand. The caller was 'Timely Taxis'.

'Who is it?' Gemma said.

'Taxi firm.'

'Answer it.'

'What?'

'He must have called for a taxi. Tell them you've already left.'

'What?'

'Just do it!'

Scott thumbed the answer button.

'Hello?' he said.

'Mr Cobb? Taxi here for you.'

'Oh. Sorry, I don't need one now. Mate of mine gave me a lift.'

'For fuck's sake.' The driver ended the call.

'What was that about?' Scott asked his wife.

'Put them off the scent.'

'Who? What scent?'

'I don't know. It's what you do, isn't it? I've never covered up a crime before.'

It struck Scott how far out of their depth they both were. They were a law-abiding family, and he was plunging them into an alien world. He began to doubt they could survive for very long here.

'Gem . . .' he began.

'Give me the phone.'

'What?'

'The phone!'

He handed it over. Gemma tried removing the back cover, then gave up and took the phone to the kitchen counter, where she used a rolling pin to accomplish the task in an instant.

'What are you doing?'

'Taking out the battery and the SIM card.'

'Why?'

'They do it on television programmes. Stops the phone being traced, I think.'

She pulled out the guts of the phone, then hit it a few more times with the rolling pin before tossing the pieces into the pedal bin.

'Gem,' he said when she came back to him, 'are we doing the right thing?'

'What? You've just been telling me—'

'I know. But maybe I'm wrong. Maybe we should come clean, like you said. Face the music.'

Gemma brought her hands to her cheeks. She was clearly floundering too.

'We need to mull it over,' she said. 'We can't rush into anything. Whatever we decide, we have to be sure it's the right thing. Where did all this happen, anyway?'

'By the lift. Cobb came up with us from the eighth floor.'

'He was coming up to this floor?'

'No. Daniel had a conversation with him. Cobb said he wanted to leave the building, but he must have pressed the up button by mistake.'

'Then ... that's good. If there was no reason for him to come up to this floor, nobody will come looking for him here. And now if anyone asks the taxi firm, they'll say he left the building.'

Scott watched as his wife's eyes darted, her brain frantically working through the possible scenarios, just as his own had done in the corridor. She was on side, but a part of him still wished that she wasn't, and that instead she would insist on going to the police and throwing the family on their mercy.

'We can't tell Daniel,' Gemma said. 'The less he knows, the better.'

Scott looked at the closed door. 'He'll be worrying about it now. He already believes he's killed a man. Even Daniel understands how bad that is.'

Gemma suddenly marched towards the door.

'Where are you going?'

'I'll be right back.'

She returned with a folded sheet in her hands. She unfurled it and draped it over Cobb's body.

'Why are you doing that?' Scott asked.

'Because I don't want to stress Daniel out any more than he already is. Let's get him in here, give him his tea, and then put him to bed, just like we do every night. We have to behave like this is just another normal day.'

'Gemma, it's hardly a normal—'

'I know that! But if we're going to get through this, we have to keep Daniel in the dark. Get him in here. And try to act casual.'

Acting anything other than terrified seemed one hell of a feat at the moment. Scott took a deep breath before rapping on Daniel's door and then breezing in. He found his son moping on the bed.

'Time to eat,' Scott said. 'Hungry?'

Daniel lifted large, sad eyes. 'Dad?'

'Yes, son?'

'Who's that man?'

'He . . . His name's Joseph Cobb. He just told me.'

A flicker of brightness. 'He told you? You mean he's not dead?'

'Dead? No, of course not. He was unconscious, that's all. You knocked him out.'

'Unconscious?'

'Yeah. You've seen Adam-9 knock people out before, haven't you?'

Daniel nodded. 'But now he's okay?'

'Kind of. He's gone back to sleep. He needs to rest for a while. Anyway, food time. Coming?'

Daniel stood. He shambled after his father. As he entered the living area, he stopped and looked down at the sheet-covered mound on the sofa.

'Why's he all covered up if he's not dead?'

'I told you, he needs to sleep. We had to cover his face because it's so bright in here. Isn't that right, Gem? He needs to sleep after Daniel knocked him out.'

'Y-yes,' Gemma answered. 'That's right. Don't worry about him. He'll be fine in a few hours. Come and sit at the table so we can eat.'

Daniel moved towards the dining table near the window, but all the time he kept his eyes on the sofa. He ended up crashing into the table and almost upending it.

'Careful,' Scott said, shifting everything back into its rightful place. 'Come on, lad. Sit down.'

They all took their seats. Gemma began ladling out thick stew onto their plates. She glanced worriedly at Scott and he returned a subtle shake of his head.

'Help yourself to bread,' Scott said. 'You must be starving.'

They ate in near silence. Scott gave up trying to chivvy Daniel along, and instead sank into his own dark contemplation. He guessed that Gemma was doing the same. Every so often, he found his gaze drifting to the corpse at the far side of the room. He did it so frequently that Daniel noticed and turned to look too. When he faced forward, Scott flashed him a fake smile of reassurance and swore to himself not to glance that way again.

Scott struggled to get any food inside him. Each mouthful objected to being forced down his gullet; it just squatted there, filling his cheeks and making him want to heave. He side-eyed Gemma's plate and saw that her chunks of meat and vegetables were also being herded around in slow circles.

A minute later, Gemma yelped and jumped out of her chair. Scott immediately followed her line of sight to Cobb's body. One of Cobb's arms had slipped from the sofa, and his pale hand was now resting on the carpet.

'Maybe he's coming round already!' Scott said, the falsity of the optimism in his voice so pronounced it was embarrassing. 'I'll check on him, shall I?'

As he stood up, he gestured to Gemma to retake her seat and stay calm. He went to the sofa, feeling Daniel's eyes burning into his back. Using his body to block Daniel's view, he raised the sheet from Cobb's head and quickly replaced it again, before tucking the man's arm back into position.

'Not quite,' he announced, coming back to the table. 'Another couple of hours, I think.'

He couldn't face Daniel as he said this. He didn't enjoy lying to his son, let alone perpetrating such an immense charade. He had the uneasy feeling that Daniel could see right through him, and that his disappointment in his hero was intensifying with every painful second.

Silence descended again. Scott gave up even the pretence of enjoying his meal. He returned his thoughts to their predicament, and he hunted frantically for solutions. He wanted to pray for a guiding light, while knowing that any appeal to a higher presence would result in advice he didn't want right now. He needed an escape – a simple and effective means of airbrushing this whole unsavoury episode out of their lives.

And, as time ticked away, he became more and more certain of one thing.

Neither he nor Gemma had any intention of going to the police.

He knew this without even asking his wife. Knew her mind almost as well as his own.

It was as though the passage of time had closed that avenue off to them. It had been a now-or-never moment, a once-in-a-lifetime offer, a ship that had sailed.

So, he thought, the decision is made. We are where we are.

Joseph Cobb must disappear.

7

They waited patiently while Daniel finished his meal. They waited patiently while he watched a little television. They waited patiently while he washed and undressed and climbed into bed. They patiently answered all his questions about the dead man who was, according to them, very much alive.

They could have speeded up the process by sending Daniel straight to bed after dessert, but it would merely have seeded more doubt in his already suspicious mind.

So they waited. And when they were alone and the quietness became unbearable, they spoke.

'He's a drug-dealing, gun-carrying, violent piece of shit,' Gemma said.

'Yeah,' Scott said, 'but he's got his bad points too.'

Gemma didn't laugh, and Scott wondered why he'd even tried to inject humour into this situation. He guessed his mind had endured enough of the grimness of reality.

'He doesn't deserve better,' Gemma continued. 'Why should our Daniel suffer because of this worthless scum?'

Scott realised that she was attempting to make peace with her decision.

'Then we're agreed?' he asked.

Gemma looked into his eyes. 'I don't think we have a choice, do you?'

'No.'

'This man started it. He picked a fight with the wrong people, and now he's paid for it. Daniel has been through enough. We have to protect him now. We have to save him.'

'Yes.'

'I'm right, aren't I? I mean, we're doing the right thing?'

'Yes.'

She threw her arms around him, pressed her face into his shoulder.

'So . . .' she said, 'what happens now?'

He pulled away so that he could look her in the eye. 'What happens now is that you get washed and you have an early night.'

She looked puzzled. 'What?'

'You heard me. Take a bath and try to relax, then go to bed.'

'Scott? I don't—'

'I'll sort it. Okay? Just stay in the bedroom and leave it to me. By the morning he'll be gone. It'll be as if he was never here.'

She shook her head. 'No. We're in this together now. You can't manage this alone.'

'I can. Trust me. I've come up with a plan. It'll work.'

Gemma glanced at the shrouded corpse. 'What will you—?'

'You don't need to know. It's best if you don't know.'

He watched her try to read his mind. After a few seconds, he sensed a jolt of understanding.

Gemma nodded, then stepped away from him. She seemed suddenly very small and frightened.

'I'll do that,' she said. 'I'll take a bath. I . . . I always sleep better after a bath.'

She walked towards the bathroom, then halted and turned.

'You'll be careful?' she said. 'You won't do anything stupid?'

'No. I promise.'

He watched her leave the room. When he heard the bath taps running, he sat down and stared at the body.

What he had decided was that Gemma shouldn't be involved any more than she already was. If this all went wrong, he'd like to be able to say that it was all his doing, that Gemma tried to talk him out of it, and that she had no idea he was planning to dispose of the body.

He put on the television, keeping the sound low. He saw a blur of images that meant little to him, but they helped to kill time.

Gemma came back into the living room, wrapped in a thick bathrobe. She sat on the arm of his chair and kissed the top of his head. She smelt lovely. She smelt of life.

'I've been thinking,' she said.

'What about?'

'You said you're going to make it all go away.'

'Uh-huh.'

'All of it.'

'Yes. What are you—?'

'It's just that . . . there's a lot of money in that bag.'

'Gemma—'

'I mean there must be thousands there, right?'

'Gemma, no.'

'I just—'

'No. We can't. It wouldn't be right. It's dirty money. Drug money. We can't profit from what happened. Besides, it might be traceable. Every time we spent one of those notes we'd be looking over our shoulder.'

She nodded slowly. He didn't blame her for thinking that way. It had crossed his own mind too. A sum of money like that could solve a lot of their problems.

'How long are you going to stay up?' she asked.

'I don't know. A few hours. I have to make sure I'm not seen.'

'You're going out, then?'

'Yes.'

'Where?'

'Somewhere. It doesn't matter.'

She nodded. 'Would you like me to stay up with you for a while?'

He stroked the back of her hand. 'No. You go to bed. Get some rest. Like I said, tomorrow this will all seem like a dream.'

She kissed him again. As she walked away, he said, 'Gemma?'

'Yes?'

'Take a sleeping tablet and put in some earplugs. And if you hear anything, don't get up. Do you understand?'

She opened her mouth to question him, then thought better of it. But she looked frightened again.

And when she left the room, she almost seemed relieved to get out of there.

8

The garage seemed eerie at two o'clock in the morning, but Scott had no plans to stay very long. He put on as few lights as possible to avoid attracting unwanted attention. If the police did come knocking, he would tell them he had been out with friends and had left his house keys here. He had it all worked out, and he hated that he had been forced into thinking like a criminal.

The Audi 4x4 he had worked on with Daniel was still here, but he rejected it as being too new and flashy – its owner would probably notice if he left even the tiniest mark on it. Like a speck of blood, for example.

He went outside to the fenced-off compound at the rear, and played a torch over the customer vehicles awaiting work. The choice came to a grand total of two cars. The Fiat 500 was far too small, which left only an old silver Toyota Avensis. It had been towed in with a wrecked gearbox, but that had now been fixed.

Scott turned his torch onto the registration plate. It would have to do.

He went back inside for a while, then returned with the key to the Toyota, some black insulation tape, a pair of scissors, and a rag coated with a mixture of old engine oil, axle grease and brake dust. A few minutes later and the car had a new registration: a 1 turned into a T, an F into a P, a 3 into a B. Then he dabbed the rag on and around the registration plates, blurring the characters. It wouldn't stand close inspection, but with any luck that would never happen.

He unlocked the gates of the compound, then drove the car out onto the street. He left it there while he closed and locked the garage up again, then drove home. It was only a ten-minute journey, but for every second of it he dreaded the blue flashing lights of the police, pulling him over for having dodgy plates.

He parked as close as he could get to the rear door of the block of flats. The short walk to the door felt more like a marathon, his heart now hammering in his chest. He prayed that Biggo and his mates hadn't assembled here while he'd been gone, then cursed himself for having planted his image so firmly in their minds.

But the lobby was empty. Scott summoned the lift and travelled back up to the top storey. As he passed the eighth floor, the memories of what had happened only hours ago came crashing back in waves that made him nauseous.

The lift reached its destination and its doors opened. When Scott stepped out, he paused in the corridor for a moment while he scanned it for any signs of the extreme violence that had taken place. He could see nothing. Not a trace.

Maybe it was all a dream, he told himself at his front door. It's too weird to be real, so maybe I'll go in and he won't be there. There won't be a dead body lying on my couch, because that would be crazy.

But the body was there, all right. Scott stood looking at it for a good two minutes while he tried to convince himself otherwise, but his brain was having none of it. This was reality, and it wasn't about to go away without some assistance.

He went to Daniel's bedroom. Eased the door open and sneaked across to the bed. Daniel was fast asleep, the earmuffs he was wearing cutting off all outside noise. He had worn earmuffs in bed ever since he was a child, when every sound had made him fearful of monsters.

They were something to be especially grateful for tonight.

Back in the hallway, Scott opened the cupboard. The boiler was in here, along with the gas and electric meters, the vacuum cleaner, tools, paint and decorating equipment and a whole host of other items. That was another problem with living in a tiny flat: there was hardly any room to store anything.

He tried to keep his noise to a minimum while he searched the boxes and shelves. Eventually he found what he was looking for.

A set of plastic decorating sheets.

Some masking tape.

And a saw.

He stared for some time at the saw. It was a little rusty, but its teeth looked sharp. He touched his finger to them and felt their bite. They could still cut well.

Yes, they could cut. They could sever.

He gulped.

He closed the cupboard, then grabbed some other things from the kitchen before going into the bathroom. There, he began to spread out the plastic sheets. He covered everything with them. He even taped them to the walls. He stood and surveyed his handiwork. There was one other thing he needed.

The body.

He returned to the living area. Stood over the man called Joseph Cobb and tried to tell himself that what he was looking at was no longer a man. He was meat. Just meat.

I'm wasting time, he thought. Let's get this over with.

He reached for the sheet and pulled it away from Cobb's face.

And then he yelped and leapt backwards.

Cobb was staring at him. His eyes *had* been closed – Scott was certain of it – but now they were wide open, accusatory.

Scott felt suddenly terrified. He knew nothing about death and what could happen afterwards. Could the dead open their eyes? Was it possible that Cobb wasn't properly dead when they brought him in here?

He approached the body again, watching the eyes. They didn't follow him.

The sheet. When the sheet was pulled across his face, that's when it must have happened. The cloth must have tugged his eyelids up. It was the only explanation.

Scott could feel his heart pounding again. This was getting too stressful.

Calm down, he told himself. It'll be over soon. Just do what you have to.

He placed his index finger and thumb on the eyelids. Tried to lower them.

They wouldn't move.

'Fucking close, will you?' he rasped.

But it was as if Cobb's eyelids had been sewn open. And the more Scott tried, the more his fingers slid across the cold eyeballs. The sensation made him want to retch.

'Shit!'

Just do it. Forget the eyes. He's not looking at you. He can't look at anything now. Shift him!

Scott took the sheet away completely, then grabbed one of Cobb's arms. It didn't want to move away from his body. Scott pulled harder, dragging the body from the sofa and onto the floor. He had expected it to flop onto the carpet like an octopus out of water, but instead it remained rigid like a mannequin.

They do that, he thought. I read about it somewhere. Rigorous mortem or something.

Scott grabbed the man's ankles and slid him across the floor, out into the hallway (*Daniel and Gemma, do not come out now!*), and then into the bathroom. He closed the door and locked it.

He was breathing heavily, and had to take a minute to recover. *Enough time-wasting. It'll be daylight soon. Get on with it.*

He kneeled down next to the body. Picked up the saw. Took a deep breath. Touched the saw to the point where Cobb's right arm joined his shoulder.

There'll be blood, he thought. Lots of it, probably. But it doesn't shoot out as quickly when the heart's not working, does it? And it's probably gone all gooey by now. Maybe it'll just ooze out.

He looked at the bath and thought about manhandling

Cobb into it. But the bath was in an alcove, and he didn't think he could properly manipulate the saw in that cramped space. Chances were he'd end up sawing through the bath.

He had brought plenty of cloths and a bucket. He would mop up as he went. It would be fine.

But still . . .

Scott undressed, then tied up his clothes in a bin-bag and put it on top of the cistern. He didn't feel comfortable standing naked under the gaze of another man, even a dead one, but needs must.

He positioned the saw again. Took another deep breath.

Cobb's jacket. It was made of thick leather, and wasn't going to make this job any easier.

Scott put down the saw, then spent the next few minutes struggling to divest Cobb of his jacket. No simple task when the man's arms refused to bend.

Panting, Scott picked up his saw and leant over the body again.

The eyes. Cobb was staring at him. How can you dismember someone who insists on glaring at you while you do it?

He picked up the jacket and wrapped it around Cobb's face. And then another thought occurred to him.

Get the worst of it over with first.

Do that, and the rest will be a walk in the park.

He's not looking at you now. You can do this.

Can I? Can I do it?

Scott brought the saw to Cobb's neck. He took long deep breaths – in through the nose, out through the mouth.

And then he closed his eyes and began to saw.

He sat on the lavatory, staring at his handiwork and finding it difficult to believe he had managed to get through it.

He had puked during the process. He wasn't sure when, exactly. He just remembered a sudden dive to the toilet. Everything was a blur, as though he had somehow disassociated himself from the abominable act.

But it was done. All the pieces tied up in neat black plastic bundles. The room scoured and bleached, gleaming innocently.

He had showered and dressed, and now he was exhausted.

He checked his watch. Four in the morning. Plenty of time to finish what he'd started.

He carried several of the bags out of the flat, then summoned the lift. When it arrived, he put most of the bags into the lift, leaving one to jam the doors open. Then he went back to the flat for the remaining bags. When he had everything in the lift, he took it down to the ground floor, praying that it wouldn't be stopped on its descent.

The doors opened to silence.

He unloaded the bags, then lugged them out to the Toyota as quick as he could. Only when he had locked the vehicle and returned to the flat did he breathe a sigh of relief.

He hadn't been seen – he was sure of it.

That meant he was almost home and dry.

He sneaked into the bedroom, undressed and climbed into bed. He thought at first that he had done so without disturbing Gemma, but she spoke to him with a clarity that suggested she hadn't slept a wink.

'I thought you were never coming to bed,' she said.

'There was a lot to do,' he answered.

'But it's finished now, right? We're in the clear?'

'Yes.'

'Then promise me something.'

'Anything. What is it?'

'Never tell me what you did tonight. Can you do that?'

'I can do that.'

'It's not that I don't want to be there for you. It's just that . . . I can't cope with hearing the details, Scott. I can't.'

He slipped his arm around her. 'You don't have to. I promise.'

He pulled her close to him and tried to absorb her warmth. Tried to force out the chill that seemed to have settled in his core.

9

Ronan Cobb's heart sank when he pulled up at the old sandstone farmhouse. It looked worse every time he turned up here. His mother's dilapidated Land Rover was parked on what used to be a lawn and was now just churned-up mud. It stood in front of a line of other rusting vehicles that his now-deceased father had bought to renovate and never bothered with. Hedges were overgrown. Paint was peeling. Roof slates were missing. A length of guttering had broken away and was angled downwards, so that when it rained it would channel water onto the roof of the dog kennel, sadly no longer inhabited. This place had been picture-postcard beautiful once, and his mother had sparkled. Now, both were wretched shadows of their former selves. His father, a man who had demanded and received respect, would have been horrified to see how his legacy had been allowed to perish.

Myra Cobb was where Ronan expected her to be: at the kitchen table, watching one of the shopping channels on television and swigging gin. It was early on a Sunday morning, and already she had downed much of a bottle. He wondered if she had even been to bed last night.

She accompanied the gin with plenty of tonic and bowlfuls of dry-roasted peanuts. The combination had the most unfortunate effect on her digestive system, and the room stank.

Ronan studied the labels on some of the numerous unopened boxes dotted around the kitchen. One contained a fondue set; others contained a brass oil lamp, a pair of bookends shaped like horse's heads, a year's supply of bird food, a beer-making kit, a set of Disney character pastry cutters . . . His mother had a habit of ordering stuff when she was drunk and then not doing anything with it when it arrived. It was a complete waste of money, but Ronan guessed she wasn't running short of that. She had paid outright for his flat and Joey's, and he imagined that one day her two sons would come into a decent inheritance. Sooner rather than later if her appearance was anything to go by. Ronan had often been tempted to suggest that she spend some of it on a new house for herself, but what was the point? She was not yet fifty, but she was already knocking on death's door, and any place she bought would simply be turned into another shit-heap.

He gave her a peck on the cheek and made the mistake of breathing in her alcohol fumes. He liked a drink as much as the next man – the occasional bit of weed, too – but not at this hour of the day.

'What's for breakfast, Mam?' he asked.

'What do you mean, breakfast? Doesn't she feed you, that tart of yours?'

'Donna's not a tart, Mam. She's a good lass.'

'Then tell her to get off her fat arse and rustle up some breakfast for you. I'm not having my lads starting the day without a decent meal inside them.'

Ronan bit his tongue. The last time she had prepared a proper meal for either of her children was long before they had left home.

'I'll make us a cuppa, shall I?'

'You have one, if you want,' she said, raising a tumbler covered in greasy fingerprints. 'I've got this.'

Ronan glanced at the kettle and saw a white stain running all the way down its side. He decided not to bother with tea.

'So,' he said. 'What's got you dragging me out here so early on a Sunday?'

'It's not that early. Besides, I shouldn't have to drag you. If you came here more often . . .'

Here we go, Ronan thought.

'. . . instead of spending all your time with that tart of yours—'

'I've told you, Mam. Don't call her a tart.'

'I'll call her what I bloody well like. Anyway . . . what was the question?'

'I was asking about the fire.'

'What fire?'

'Exactly. What's the big emergency?'

She went silent for a few seconds while her brain caught up. 'I had a call this morning.'

'Oh yeah? Was the vicar missing you at Sunday service?'

'Don't get funny with me, lad. You're never too old for a smack. For your information, the call was from Mental Micky.'

Ronan's face dropped. A call from Mental himself, rather than one of his subordinates, was never something to gladden the heart.

'What did he want?'

'Ah, now that's wiped the smile off your face, hasn't it?'

'Mam, what did he want?'

'He wants your brother. Says that Joey didn't turn up for an important meeting last night, and that he's got some things that don't belong to him. Things that Mental wants back.'

Ronan could guess the nature of those things. What he couldn't guess at was why on earth Joey would do anything that might upset Mental.

'Well, have you tried phoning Joey?'

Myra slammed down her tumbler, slopping some of her precious gin over the sides. 'Do I look like I'm bloody thick? Of course I've tried phoning him. I've called him a dozen times today. He's not answering.'

'Do you think something's happened to him?'

'Something *will* happen to him when I get hold of him, I can tell you that much. I'm not having him put me in Mental's bad books. I've got enough on my plate without that bloody lunatic giving me grief.'

Ronan took out his own phone and speed-dialled his brother. It went straight to voicemail.

'His phone must be off.'

'Joey's phone is never off. He always answers my calls.'

This was true. Life wouldn't be living for Ronan or Joey if either of them avoided their mother for too long. Besides, there was the little matter of their inheritance.

'All right, Mam. What do you want me to do about it?'

'Find him.'

'How am I supposed to—'

'I don't care! Go to his flat. Ask around. If he's left the country with Mental's property, it'll be your hide that gets tanned.'

'What do you mean, *my* hide? What's it got to do with me?'

'Tweedledum or Tweedledee. Makes no difference to Mental.'

Ronan recoiled at the insult. There was no need for that comparison.

Even though he and Joey were identical twins.

10

Scott was awakened by a knock on the bedroom door. He glanced at the alarm clock, saw that it had gone ten o'clock.

Shit.

'Come in,' he called. Next to him, Gemma grunted and her eyes flickered open.

Daniel came into the room. He seemed uncertain, as if expecting something to jump out of the wardrobe.

'Nobody's getting up,' he said. 'Is something the matter?'

'No,' Scott answered. 'Nothing's wrong. Is everything okay with you?'

Daniel nodded. 'The man. In the other room.'

Scott's heart was suddenly at full speed. Was his night-time activity all a dream – had he not disposed of the body? Gemma turned to look at him, fear in her eyes.

'What about him?' Scott asked.

'He's gone.'

Phew.

'Uhm, yes. He went home after you'd gone to bed.'

'Is he all right now?'

'Yes, he's fine. Like I said, he was just knocked out for a while.'

'Will he tell on me? Will he tell the police?'

'No. I don't think he'll be doing that.'

Daniel nodded again, although he didn't seem entirely satisfied.

'Can we have breakfast now? I'm starving.'

'Yes,' Gemma said. 'Of course. We're getting up now. Go and put the kettle on.'

Daniel left the room and closed the door. Gemma and Scott looked at each other.

'You weren't lying to me, were you?' Gemma asked. 'We can stop worrying?'

'I wasn't lying. Go and see for yourself. Make some breakfast. I need to go out.'

'Out? Out where?'

'Just out. Some things I need to tidy up.'

'Scott, you said it was over. You told me—'

'It is! It's over. I'm just tying up some loose ends, that's all.'

'What kind of loose ends?'

Scott chopped the air in front of him. 'Gem! Stop, okay? It's all in hand. Trust me.'

There was a heavy silence, and then Gemma swung her legs out of bed.

'I need the bathroom,' she said.

'Oookaay.'

'What I mean is . . . is it safe to go in there?'

Scott realised she must have heard some of what went on in that room last night. The walls were hardly soundproof. It made him wonder if Daniel had heard any of it too, even through his earmuffs.

84

'It's perfectly safe. I'm sure Daniel's already been in there.'

Gemma stood up. Put on a dressing gown and slippers. Shuffled off to the bathroom. Scott remained seated on the bed for a while. She had sneaked doubt into his mind: doubt that he had been thorough enough, and that any second now he would hear her scream at the sight of a blood stain or a gobbet of flesh.

He relaxed a little when he heard the shower come on.

He dressed swiftly and went into the living area. Daniel was seated at the dining table, his eyes turned towards the sofa. Scott looked too, and was reassured that there was nothing to see. He had even disposed of the sheet and plumped up the cushions. But still Daniel stared.

A line from a movie flashed through Scott's mind: *I see dead people.*

'So,' he said, too loudly, 'where's that cup of tea?'

Daniel dragged his gaze towards the kettle. 'Oh. I forgot.'

Scott smiled. 'Doesn't matter.' When he saw Daniel returning his attention to the sofa, he went and sat on it, hoping to crush whatever image Daniel might be seeing. He bent to retrieve a pair of trainers from alongside the sofa and began to pull them on.

'Are you going out?' Daniel asked.

'Just for a few minutes.'

'Where are you going?'

'Er, I left something at the garage. I need to go back for it.'

'Can I come? I like the garage.'

'No. You stay and have your breakfast. I'm not doing any work today. Later, we could go out for a pub lunch, if you fancy it.'

Scott realised he was over-compensating, but he couldn't help himself. The prospect of a Sunday carvery always made Daniel jump for joy.

Not today, though. Daniel's voice remained flat as he said, 'Yes, that would be nice.'

Scott left quickly. The return to normality he had hoped for hadn't yet materialised.

I'm expecting too much, he thought. Give it time. When I get this final bit done I'll be able to relax. And when I'm relaxed, they'll calm down too. We're in the home straight now. Just one more little job.

When he exited from the rear of the building, he checked to make sure nobody was watching, then marched straight to the Toyota, climbed in and started the engine. He was breathing rapidly again, terrified of something scuppering his plans at this late stage.

He flipped down both sun visors on the car to make it more difficult for cameras to pick up his face, then drove out of the car park and headed south, away from town. Ten minutes later he saw the sign for the council refuse site. He took the turning onto the winding lane, and then into the site itself.

Being a Sunday, it was busy. Mostly men with trailers and large estate cars stuffed with junk. He had to wait for a parking spot to become free next to one of the massive containers for non-recyclable rubbish. He wanted the walk with his cargo to be as brief as possible.

He got out of the car, opened up the boot, stared at the array of black bin liners sitting there waiting patiently. He grabbed a couple and heaved them out, then made his way over to the container. He waited while a man threw in some stuff that included a toaster, even though there was a separate container for appliances, and he thought to himself, What if they spot it after I've thrown my stuff in? What if they see that there's a toaster in there and they stop the machine and they climb in to look for other things that might have been dumped by mistake? What then?

Don't be stupid. They're not going to do that. The people who work here don't give a shit. Besides, they're hardly going to start ripping open bin liners.

Toaster man smiled as he made way for Scott, and Scott simply nodded. Starting an argument was the last thing he needed right now.

He chose not to toss the bags in for fear of them bursting open, but instead reached out as far as he could and gently lowered them into the morass below.

Two down.

He repeated the process. Two bags at a time, spread across several containers. Calmly and carefully. Just another bored husband carrying out his weekend chores. Nothing to see here, folks.

And then it was done. The car boot was empty. He closed it and clambered in behind the wheel again. Despite the queue of cars jostling for spaces, he remained where he was. Waited for the council refuse worker to move from container to container, pressing the big red buttons that woke up the dormant monsters and caused them to compact the garbage into their metallic stomachs.

Only then did Scott drive away.

11

She wanted an update, and she wanted it in person.

Ronan wanted simply to be allowed to get on with the job. He felt he was making some progress, but he still had plenty of other people he could talk to, and being dragged back to the farmhouse was an unnecessary hindrance.

But Myra Cobb always got her way.

There was a time when Ronan would not have been asked to comb the streets like this. But that was back when his dad was alive. Patrick Cobb wouldn't have allowed one of his sons to perform such a menial task. If something needed doing, he would have clicked his fingers and it would have been carried out immediately by a squadron of his goons.

But all the soldiers had gone. With Patrick out of the way, the challengers crept out from under the rocks. They took bites out of the Cobb empire like hyenas nipping at the limbs of prey. Anyone with any sense traded in their membership cards.

So now it was just the twins and their mother. They survived on their reputation more than anything, but even that was dwindling.

In the kitchen, Ronan saw that there was a newly opened bottle of gin on the table, and his mother had that glassy look that told him she had entered a state of unpredictability. Next to the bottle were her phone and credit card. He wondered what wondrous trinkets she had purchased since this morning.

'Found him yet?' she demanded.

'I'm making good progress,' he said.

'What the fuck does that mean? You've either found him or you haven't. And if you haven't, you need to get a bloody move on, you lazy bastard.'

'Mam, it's not that easy. Joey doesn't always tell me what he does or where he goes. I'm doing all my own detective work here.'

'Detective? Pah! You couldn't detect your own arse with both hands. He's your twin brother, for Christ's sake. You're supposed to know what the other one is thinking.'

'We're not telepathic, Mam.'

'You certainly aren't. Tele-pathetic, more like. So what have you managed to deduce so far, Sherlock?'

Ronan ran through the list of people he'd spoken to, and what he'd learnt about their last contact with Joey.

'Is that it?' his mother asked.

'I thought it was quite a lot.'

'Well, you thought wrong. You've talked to a set of druggies and pond life who'd tell you anything you want to hear if it keeps them out of trouble or in with a chance of getting high. I wouldn't trust any of those maggots as far as I could throw them.'

'Give us a chance, Mam. I've only just started.'

'How hard can it be? I could do better myself.'

Yeah, Ronan thought. Maybe you could if you weren't pissed all the time.

'Any other earth-shattering news to report?' she asked, her question dripping with sarcasm.

'There's this,' he said, reaching into his pocket and handing over a piece of paper.

Myra squinted at the squiggles. 'What is it?'

'Joey had a second phone. A burner. That's the number.'

'And have you tried ringing it?'

'Course I have. No answer.'

'So this is also useless.'

Ronan wanted to scream his frustration. 'Give it back here, then. I'll keep trying.'

She pulled the paper out of his reach. 'No, I'll try it. You've obviously got more important things to do, like prancing around town pretending you care about your missing brother.'

'I'll see you later, Mam,' he said, and stormed out before he throttled her.

Reggie Billings felt under-appreciated.

He had gone on a blind date last night. The first since his wife had died. He thought it had gone well until she asked him what he did for a living.

'So, you dig holes,' she'd said. 'And then you put rubbish in them. And then you cover them over?'

And that, in a nutshell, was the problem he always faced. This massively over-simplistic view of what went on at a land-fill site.

They just don't realise the expertise involved, he thought. The science of it. The care for the environment.

They don't know that you can't just dig any old hole in the middle of nowhere. The geography has to be right. The right sort of clay to make a base, for one thing. You have to build in a drainage network to remove the leachate. You have to install pipes to siphon off the methane. But you can't just release gases like that into the atmosphere, oh no. You burn it in a generator to produce electricity. Megawatts of precious power being pumped into the National Grid.

And then there are the schemes to minimise the impact on the surroundings. A system of nets to catch stray litter. Gas guns and even birds of prey to frighten the seagulls and other scavengers away. Baiting and traps for rats and other vermin.

And then there's the monitoring. The constant testing of the groundwater. The cleaning of it to remove iron and other pollutants before it's allowed to go off-site.

No, they don't understand. They don't appreciate what we do here.

Reggie sighed and ate the last mouthful of his sandwich, then fired up the van assigned to him as foreman. He navigated slowly around the site, inspecting, checking, approving, noting.

Ahead, he saw one of the compactor drivers next to his colossus of a machine, enjoying a cigarette break before crushing the next layer of detritus into oblivion.

Reggie pulled his van in next to the man and got out. 'Denzil.'

'Reggie.'

Reggie found a cigarette of his own. Denzil snapped his lighter on and held it out for Reggie. A small but significant gesture of comradeship. They stared out across the sea of rotting garbage as though it concealed sunken treasures. Which perhaps it did.

'Go out last night?' Reggie asked.

'Natch,' Denzil said. 'Saturday night, weren't it? Can't let the lads down on a Saturday night.'

Reggie felt a stab of irritation. Most of his own Saturday nights now consisted of sitting in front of the television with a microwave meal.

Go on, he thought. Ask me. Ask me what I did last night.

'What about you?' Denzil said.

Reggie puffed himself up. 'Had a date, didn't I?'

Denzil turned his head slightly. Reggie was convinced he detected a tiny smile of admiration.

'Oh yeah? You've been keeping that quiet. Who is she?'

'Her name's Julie. It was a blind date.'

'Lucky for you, that.'

'How d'you mean?'

'That she's blind.'

Reggie studied the man for signs that he was teasing. Saw nothing. But then Denzil cracked a broad smile.

'Only joking, man. How did that come about, then?'

Reggie didn't feel like telling him now. He felt instead like reporting him to management for being an idle bastard who took too many smoking breaks.

'My sister set it up. Someone she works with.'

'Gotcha. How did it go? Did you get your leg over?'

Reggie suddenly wished he hadn't begun this tale. Not only had he not managed to get his leg over, he hadn't even reached first base. In fact, to continue the baseball analogy, he'd been stuck on the bus on the way to the stadium.

'She's not a girl for rushing into things,' Reggie said. Then, when he noticed the knowing look on Denzil's face, he quickly added, 'To tell you the truth, I'm not sure I want to see her again.'

'Yeah? Why's that, then?'

'She was dissing the job we do. To be honest, I don't think she really got it.'

Denzil shrugged. 'What's to get? We dig a hole, we put rubbish in it, we cover it over again. It's not rocket science.'

And now Reggie wanted to throw Denzil in front of one of his compactor's massive spiked wheels and drive it over him.

His homicidal thoughts were interrupted by a muffled blast of music.

'Is that you?' he asked.

'Not me,' Denzil said. 'Maybe it's Julie.'

Reggie realised the noise was coming from one of the bags lying in front of them. Realised too that this was an opportunity to exact a tiny revenge.

'It's coming from there. In you go.'

The speed at which the smile evaporated from Denzil's face was satisfying.

'Who, me?'

'Hurry up. This might be your opportunity to return some poor old lady's lost phone.'

Denzil sighed and waded in. Reggie smiled inwardly at the comical sight of Denzil pulling out bags and listening to them.

'It's this one,' Denzil announced, just as the ringtone ended. 'Open it up, then.'

He waited with glee for Denzil to start pawing through mouldy vegetables or used nappies. But all that fell out as Denzil ripped open the bag was a balled-up item of clothing. A jacket, by the looks of it.

Reggie took a drag on his cigarette. 'Search the pockets,' he said.

Denzil reached down and opened up the jacket, and it was as if the act released a shockwave that sent him back-pedalling with a yelp.

Reggie sniggered as Denzil fell backwards into a layer of crap, but a voice in his head warned him that the man might be up to something.

'What's the matter?' he asked.

Denzil clambered to his feet, pointing and jabbering. 'L-look! C-come and see!'

Reggie tossed his cigarette aside and began to climb the mound in front of him. He thought, If this is a practical joke...

And then he saw the new face staring back at him, a face without a body, and he realised this was no laughing matter.

12

It occasionally entered the mind of Detective Chief Inspector Ray Devereux that his wife might be having an affair.

The notion always dissipated as swiftly as it arrived, though. The real reason she was always pushing him out of the house was ambition. Hers, rather than his. She wanted him to rise up through the ranks like a moon rocket. The very fact that he had reached the level of DCI was largely down to her, constantly pushing him and bolstering his ego and telling him how he needed to 'fulfil his potential'. She was like a motivational speaker on steroids.

Yes, that's the real reason I'm here, he told himself. Not an affair. No one else would have her.

He was in the plush surroundings of the Blackstone Private Members' Club. All oak panelling and leather chesterfields and shelves of musty unread books. He wouldn't mind the eye-watering membership fees if he loved coming here, but the truth was that enclaves like this made him feel uncomfortable. He experienced the same lack of enthusiasm about golf – knocking a small ball into a hole with a stick while walking in the rain for miles held little appeal – but it was something else he had taken up recently.

'It's where the real business is done,' his wife had told him. 'Not at the station. It's not *what* you know, it's *who* you know. Mix with them. Do what they do. Show them you're one of the gang. That's how it works. That's how everything in life works.'

He had no idea where Fiona had picked up these shiny nuggets of wisdom, but he was willing to play along. To an extent.

He glimpsed Peter Fletcher sitting in an armchair in front of the roaring fire, his head buried in *The Times*. Ray could almost feel Fiona at his elbow, nudging him to go and speak to the man.

Although younger than Ray, Fletcher was already a chief superintendent. Rumour had it that he was lined up to be the next assistant chief constable. He was clearly a go-getter, a man who knew better than most how to exploit the system. Probably the sort of man with whom Fiona would love to have an affair.

Ray sidled up to him. Coughed discreetly.

'Ray!' Fletcher said, putting out his hand.

Ray shook it. 'Evening, Peter.' He gestured at the newspaper. 'Catching up on all the misery in the world?'

'I get enough misery at home. Why do you think I come here? Cheers!' He raised his glass of red wine, and Ray clinked his own glass against it.

'Have a seat,' Fletcher said. 'Tell me what brings you to this neck of the woods on a Sunday evening.'

You, mainly, Ray thought. You and all the other top brass getting pissed prior to breaking the law driving home drunk.

'I needed to wind down,' Ray said.

'Tough day in the trenches?'

'You could say that. Not the day of rest a Sunday is supposed to be.'

'What's on the books, then?'

'Where do I start? Several stabbings. A couple of shootings. More drugs than you can shake a stick at. An armed robbery at a jeweller's. And this afternoon we've just topped it off with a juicy murder.'

'Juicy?'

'Yes. Chopped into bits and dumped. Workers came across his head at the landfill site. We've had to shut the place down while we search for the rest of him.'

'Need a hand? Perhaps some additional leg work?' Fletcher said, then laughed.

Ray tried to make his own laugh sound convincing. 'Now you mention it, staff shortages are a big problem at the moment.'

'Aren't they always?' Fletcher said, curtailing what Ray was hoping might be a fruitful discussion about additional assistance. 'Managed to identify the victim yet?'

'We have. It's Joey Cobb.'

Fletcher raised an eyebrow. 'Joey Cobb? Well, I'll drink to that.' He raised his glass again and took a good swallow. 'Gangland execution, I assume?'

'Probably. We still have to look into it, though.'

'Well, my advice would be not to put too much effort into that one. He's not worth it. In fact, if you find the guilty party, give them a pat on the back from me.'

'We still have to put on a show, though. Cobb's mother is already threatening to ring the tabloids and kick up a fuss.'

'I'm not surprised. She's worse than her evil twins. She'll do anything for a fast buck. I wouldn't be surprised if she murdered her own son because she found a way of making money out of it.'

'True,' Ray said. 'But you see my problem?'

'Hmm,' Fletcher said, and for a moment Ray believed he might actually be considering ways of sending more staff his way. But then Fletcher added, 'How's Hannah Washington getting on now?'

'Hannah? She's . . . fine.'

'I like her. Always struck me as someone heading through that glass ceiling. Promoting people like her sends out all the right signals.'

Ray cringed a little at the suggestion. Fletcher would undoubtedly have said something similar if Hannah had belonged to an ethnic minority or been disabled.

'Yes,' Ray said.

'Does she have her hands full at the moment?'

'Well . . . not quite. I've kept her on light duties since . . .'

'Since the train incident.'

'Yes.'

'Hmm. Remind me of her story again.'

'She lost her daughter not so long ago. Meningitis.'

'That's right. I imagine something like that could affect a mother quite badly.'

'Yes, I think it has. She . . .'

'Go on.'

'I'd say she's lost focus. Not quite as sharp as she was.'

'But you're not saying—'

'No. I think she'll be fine, given time.'

'And yet she's back on full duty, yes?'

'Yes. She's keen enough.'

'And she's a DI, correct?'

'Yes.'

'Acted as SIO on murder cases?'

'Yes. Good clearance rate, too.'

'Well, there you go then. Problem sorted.'

'Sorry?'

'The Cobb case. Give it to Hannah.'

'Hannah? Well, I'm not sure that—'

'You said it yourself, Ray. You need to put on a show. Your spin on this is that an experienced and senior detective with an excellent clearance rate has been assigned to the case. If she solves it, then good for her. On the other hand, if she cocks it up, then it's no great loss, is it? You and your team will be free to concentrate on all those other cases you mentioned. Meanwhile, Cobb will be six feet under where he belongs, and the world will be a happier place.'

Not for Hannah, Ray thought. The stress of a case like this will be bad enough. Failing to solve it could finish her.

'Another glass of Merlot?' Fletcher asked.

'Um . . .'

'And by the way, if you're not too snowed under, I'm looking for an opponent to thrash at golf next weekend. Fancy it?'

Ray smiled.

Fiona would be proud of him.

*

The phone call was brief and to the point, with no doubt left in Hannah's mind that Devereux was not asking her but telling her. When she re-entered the living room, Ben looked up inquiringly from where he was lounging on the sofa. He was already in his dressing gown and his ridiculous fluffy mouse slippers.

'Well?' he asked. 'Are you going to tell me, or will you have to kill me if you do?'

'Don't tempt me. I'm in the mood for killing someone.'

'Ah. One of those calls. Devereux?'

'Yes, Devereux. He's just made me SIO on a murder that landed this afternoon.'

Ben looked understandably puzzled. 'That's good, isn't it?'

'It should be, but it isn't.'

'Now I'm really confused. Sit down and explain it to your simpleton of a husband.'

He budged up and she plonked herself down next to him.

He said, 'You've been complaining for ages about the crap cases you've been getting. And now you've just been made the senior investigating officer on a murder case. So what am I missing?'

'The victim is a man named Joey Cobb. Local villain and all-round dirtbag. Drugs, guns, prostitutes – you name it, he had a finger in it.'

'He had a finger in prostitutes?'

She frowned at him. 'Don't make a joke out of it, Ben. I'm not in the mood.'

Ben dropped his smirk. 'Sorry. You were saying.'

'Cobb's body had been chopped into pieces and dumped in the rubbish.'

'Nasty.'

'Yeah. Not a surprising end for someone like that, though.'

'So it's a gang thing, then?'

'Very probably, but that's not my point.'

'Okay, so what is?'

Hannah took a deep breath. 'Up until a few hours ago, they wouldn't have let me within a mile of a murder investigation, and now they've suddenly decided I'm the ideal SIO. Don't you think that's a little suspicious?'

'No. Should I? What could possibly be underhand about it?'

'They want to use it to get rid of me.'

'What? Don't be ridiculous. Why would they—'

'I'm not being ridiculous! It's the opportunity they've been hoping for. They're waiting for me to balls this up so that they can chuck me out.'

'No. That's crazy talk. This is murder we're talking about. They need to find a killer. They need someone they can trust.'

Hannah shook her head. 'There's a saying in the police. They call this a shit-on-shit crime. If it decreases the population of scumbags then that can only be a good thing. If I cock up the case, nobody in the force will lose sleep over it. They will, however, have a scapegoat and a ready-made excuse for getting rid of me.'

Ben was silent. Then he said, 'I think you're being too hard on yourself. Reading things into the situation that aren't there.'

Anger flashed through her. 'For God's sake, Ben, you don't work with these people. You have no idea. The internal politics, the backstabbing, the sucking up to bosses, the sexism, the bullying. It's a fucking cesspit.'

Ben's response was typically anti-inflammatory. He took her hand and squeezed it. 'Then it's just like any other large organisation. That's why I could never cope with working for one. But you're different. You're stronger.'

'I don't know if I am anymore. Maybe I should leave. Jump before I'm pushed.'

'And let the bastards win? No, you're better than that.'

She pushed herself back into the soft cushions. 'I used to believe that. I used to have tons more self-confidence. I didn't make stupid mistakes like I do now. Maybe I should just accept that things have changed, and that I'm not the copper I used to be.'

He placed his other hand on top of hers, cupping it in his warmth. 'After what we've been through, neither of us is the same. Tilly has changed us for ever. When she went out of our lives, she took huge pieces of us with her. But we're bigger and better and stronger and richer for having known her, and it far outweighs the loss. That's what we have to remember.'

Hannah couldn't stop the tears. 'Then why am I so unhappy, so afraid?'

'Maybe . . . maybe it's because you haven't let her go yet.'

She turned glistening eyes on him. 'I can't, Ben. I'm not ready to let her go. Not yet.'

'Then show her the mother she knew. Prove to her that she can rest in peace, knowing that the memory of her will be in safe, strong hands.'

Hannah bowed her head. She felt destroyed.

But she knew what she had to do.

Tomorrow she would rise up again.

13

In Devereux's office, Hannah zoned out. There was no point listening. Everything he was saying to her was complete bollocks. All that flannel about her being the best detective for the job. Crap.

She played the game, though. Nodded along to his droning voice, hiding her contempt.

Watch me, she thought. Watch how I run this investigation. Worthless victim or not, I will find Cobb's murderer if it's the last thing I do as a police officer.

It was when he led her back out to the CID room that the butterflies took flight. It was like being a kid getting introduced to her new schoolmates by the teacher. She stood at the front, facing a squad she had led many times but still feeling as though she didn't know them.

When Devereux announced that she would be lead detective on the Cobb case, she noted the surprise, even on Marcel's face. That was to be expected. What was less reassuring was the palpable sense of unease that rippled through the room. She saw the exchanges of glances, the raised eyebrows. She was convinced she even heard someone tutting.

When Devereux handed over to her, she began to speak, but her words came out in a strangled squeak. She tried again.

'The first thing I want to say to you is to forget what a nasty piece of work Joey Cobb was. The fact is, somebody has committed murder, and we don't turn a blind eye to murder, no matter who the victim. We are going to catch whoever did this, and I personally will devote one hundred per cent of my efforts to achieving that aim. I hope that you will give me a similar level of dedication. If you have any qualms about that, come and talk to me. If I make any decisions you don't like, come and talk to me. I won't bite your head off, and if you make a good point, I promise to take it on board.'

She scanned the room for a reaction. It felt like a good start. She noted that Devereux was still hovering, and was glad of it. Although she suspected that he would continue to watch her like a hawk, waiting for her to misstep, she wanted him to hear that if she was going down, it wouldn't be without a fight.

'Right,' she said. 'Where are we up to?'

Marcel – good old dependable Marcel – was the first to speak.

'It looks like the phone was a burner. We're getting it analysed now. We've also asked the mobile operator for tracking info.'

'Okay. Stay on their backs. Let me know as soon as you have anything. What else?'

DC Trisha Lacey added her voice. 'We're still looking through the rubbish at the landfill site. There are still some body parts missing, but they may never come to the site. Even if they do, it's a bloody big place. It's possible we may never find them.'

'Any chance of working out where the parts were originally dumped?'

'We're talking to management at the site. They're analysing their logs and checking their cameras. We're hoping they can narrow it down to just a few trucks that could have unloaded their contents there before it got compressed, and then trace it back to the pick-up routes. We're also sifting through all the crap in the proximity by hand, hoping we find something with an address on it.'

'That's a lovely task. Please tell the officers involved that it was on DCI Devereux's orders, before I took over.'

She got a laugh at this, and even a twinkle in the eye of Devereux, who then turned away and left her to it.

'Who attended the post-mortem?' she asked the room.

Another hand shot up. 'That was me. The pathologist is reserving judgement on that one. There's extensive bruising to the neck, with damage that looks to have been inflicted while Cobb was alive. There's also a cervical fracture and pronounced injury to the spinal cord. It looks like he was grabbed hard by the throat, but in the absence of a complete body it's difficult to be definitive about cause of death.'

'All right, but whatever the cause, it's clear that Cobb really pissed somebody off – someone who went to a lot of trouble to cover their tracks. Start working up a list of Cobb's known associates and gang contacts. Find out what toes he may have stepped on.'

Hannah continued to issue instructions and take suggestions, and by the end of it she once again felt comfortable being at the helm. When she eventually retired to her office, she sat and released a long, slow breath of relief.

Marcel Lang came to her within the hour.

'Marcel,' she said. 'Everything okay?'

'News just in,' he said. 'Following your little speech, I thought you'd want to hear it ASAP.'

'Go on.'

'We've had sniffer dogs at the landfill site. They found something.'

'More body parts?'

'Better than that. A backpack.'

'Cobb's?'

'We think so. We'll get it checked for a DNA match. More interesting is what it contains.'

'Which is?'

'Among other things, nearly ten grand in cash and about fifteen grand's worth of cocaine.'

'What?'

Marcel nodded. 'Exactly.'

Hannah gave herself a moment to allow the ramifications to sink in. This was big. Big and heavy enough to turn the world upside down.

'I don't get it. We've been assuming this is gangland. A revenge attack, or part of a turf war. That's the world Cobb lived in. It's the way that people like Cobb exit that world. Kill him, yes. Dismember his body, yes. Dump him in the rubbish, yes. But what gang member worth their salt would throw away twenty-five grand in cash and drugs? How does that make any sense?'

'Exactly,' Marcel said again.

14

Hannah didn't think they'd get much out of the Cobbs, but she went through the motions nonetheless. They all sat together in the kitchen, she and Marcel Lang on one side of the table, Myra and Ronan on the other. Myra had a bottle of gin in front of her, and was already very drunk. The fact that she was wearing a black armband seemed darkly comical to Hannah. Much more unnerving was Ronan, partly because of his uncanny resemblance to his dead twin, but also because of the way he kept staring so intently at Hannah. It was like having the eyes of a ghost on her.

It could have been worse. If Patrick Cobb were here, he'd probably have instigated a riot by now. When he was alive, he and Myra had been a formidable team. The police had never managed to make a charge stick on Myra, although they'd tried several times. It was one reason she hated the cops. Another was that they'd had the temerity to put her beloved Patrick behind bars, where his days were ended when his throat was opened up by another prisoner. In Myra's eyes, that made them just as culpable as the convict who had wielded the razor blade.

Myra's influence gradually faded after the loss of her husband, as she sank into her misery. Her sons had followed in the family tradition, although it was rumoured that Ronan had found himself a girl and pulled back a little from his criminal enterprises. Joey – always the more merciless of the twins – was active right up to his death, save when he was detained at Her Majesty's pleasure, and perhaps even then.

'So,' Myra said. 'What do you want?'

'As I said,' Hannah began, 'I've been appointed to lead the investigation into the death of your son, and—'

'Murder,' Ronan interrupted. 'My brother was murdered.'

'That's right,' said Myra. 'He was fucking murdered. What are you lot doing about it?'

'What we're doing is pulling out all the stops to find his killer. I can assure you of that. I hope we can count on your support.'

'What do you want us to do, give you a round of applause?' Myra raised her glass. 'Hooray for the police!'

Hannah wanted to tell her to stop being such an awkward bitch. 'No,' she said. 'We just want you to help us out with our inquiries.'

'I can't tell you anything. I don't know anything.'

Hannah pressed on. 'Your son Joey—'

'God rest his soul.'

'—had a phone in his possession. An unregistered pay-as-you-go phone.'

'So? What's wrong with that?'

'Nothing. What we're wondering is if he also had a second phone? One that you might have called him on.'

'Why would he have two phones?'

You know very well why, Hannah thought. He was a drug dealer.

'Lots of people do. One for business and one for personal use. I have two myself.'

This seemed to mollify Myra. 'Maybe he did.'

'Could we have the number of his other phone?'

'Why?'

'It could be a big help to us in tracking where he went and who he spoke to.'

Myra thought about it, then looked towards her son. 'Give it to them.'

Marcel pushed his notepad and pen across the table. Ronan glared at him, but then scribbled down the number.

'As you know,' Hannah said, 'this was a particularly brutal attack. Do you know of anyone who might have a reason for doing this to Joey?'

Myra laughed uproariously. A humourless laugh that ended in tears of drunken anguish rolling down her cheeks.

'No,' she said finally. 'Everyone loved Joey. He was a good boy. The best. And anyone who says different is a twat.'

The pre-emptive insult was laid out as a barrier against any attempt by Hannah to challenge Joey's angelic credentials.

'Have we met before?' Ronan asked suddenly.

A bad feeling scurried across Hannah's shoulders. 'Not that I recall.' At any other time she might have said it was likely because of all the police stations that Ronan had been dragged into, but right now that didn't seem appropriate.

'You look familiar,' he said. 'What was your name again?'

'Detective Inspector Hannah Washington.'

'Right.'

He didn't pursue it. Hannah exchanged glances with Marcel before continuing.

'So you're not aware of any altercations he might have been involved in, any threats made against him?'

'No,' Myra said.

Hannah was on the verge of giving up and leaving, but then Marcel added his voice.

'Any idea where Joey might have gone over the weekend? Who he might have visited?'

'Joey was a big boy. He didn't need to check in with me every five minutes.'

'So that's a no, then?'

The sarcasm penetrated even Myra's drunken aura. 'I don't like your tone, lad.' She slapped her armband. 'My son has been cut up into tiny pieces. He was everything to me. So don't you go—'

'Got it!' Ronan said, snapping his fingers. 'You're the one who put Tommy Glover away.'

Hannah's insides tightened. 'I worked on the case. I didn't make the arrest.'

'That's right. They took you off it, didn't they? After you threw his girlfriend under a train.'

Heat blazed in Hannah's cheeks. 'That's not what happened. Now, if you don't mind, I'd like to—'

'What?' Myra said. 'It was *her*? She's the copper who—' She rose suddenly, jettisoning her chair backwards. 'Get out! Get out of my house!'

'Mrs Cobb, if we can be sensible about—'

'Get out! NOW!'

Hannah and Marcel stood up and gathered their belongings. They headed for the door, closely herded by Myra, who was still screaming in their ears.

'How dare you come here? How dare they send a killer to my door? Why don't I get a proper copper like everyone else, eh? What is it, are we not good enough, is that it? Bloody murdering bitch. You shouldn't even be allowed to direct traffic. I can't believe you've still got a job...'

Hannah marched as quickly as she could back to the lane where the car was parked. She needed the words to fade into the distance. She wanted to scream to drown them out. She needed to get in the car and drive away and never come back again, not to this house or the police station or anywhere people knew her.

She reached the car and grabbed the door handle. Found it wouldn't open.

'Boss—' Marcel said.

'Unlock it.'

'Are you okay?'

'Unlock the fucking door, will you?'

He blipped his key fob and she yanked the door open and jumped in and ordered him to get her the hell out of there.

15

Alone in her office, the ability to focus on work gambolled beyond her grasp. Her door was partially open, and from the CID room across the corridor came the ringing of phones and the slamming of file cabinet drawers, which were fine, but also the buzz of conversation punctuated by laughter, which was not. Were they talking about her? She kept telling herself that Marcel wouldn't have said anything about her behaviour at the farmhouse, and yet she could just imagine them making jokes at her expense.

First day on the case, she thought, and already I'm a laughing stock. They think I'm useless. And maybe I am. Why did I let Myra Cobb get to me like that?

She thought about Devereux, and the brass above Devereux. About how big their smiles would be if they knew about this.

First day in, and already it's going to shit.

A knock on her door, and Marcel poked his head round. She told him to come in and close the door. She started speaking before giving him a chance.

'About what happened earlier—' she began.

'Boss, there's no need. Honestly.'

He was trying to help her, but it irritated the hell out of her. She needed to get this off her chest.

'Let me speak, Marcel. I want to apologise.'

Marcel squirmed in his seat. He had a heart of gold and unbounded loyalty, but touchy-feely stuff always made him uncomfortable.

'I allowed the Cobbs to get under my skin,' Hannah continued. 'I shouldn't have. And then I got snappy with you, and I shouldn't have done that either. So I'm sorry.'

Marcel shrugged. 'No worries, boss. I get a lot worse from the wife.'

Hannah smiled. 'If I do it again, you have my permission to give me a bollocking.'

Marcel shook his head. 'Definitely not like the wife.'

Hannah felt suddenly brighter. I can do this, she thought. I need to start trusting my team.

'How's it going?' she asked.

Marcel seemed to realise why he'd come in. 'Oh yeah. I think we've hit on something. Got a minute?'

Hannah followed him into the CID room. Marcel guided her over to one of the desks, where DC Trisha Lacey was tapping away at her computer.

'What've we got?' Hannah asked.

Trisha opened up a map on her screen. It was overlaid with a number of circles. 'This is tracking information given to us by Cobb's mobile phone provider.' She pointed at one of the circles. 'From Saturday evening right through to Sunday morning he was somewhere here. Then the signal moves south to here. Later on Sunday it moves again, ending up at the landfill site.'

Hannah studied the pattern. 'Each of those circles has a pretty big radius. Any chance we can narrow it down?'

'Not from this data. But look . . .' Trisha zoomed in on the map until one of the circles filled her screen. 'Notice anything?'

Hannah stared for a few seconds, and then her eye caught it.

'Communion Road. The tip!'

'Yup. Body had to have been dumped there, along with the phone.'

'Can we be sure?'

'Couldn't have been anywhere else, not in this area. Yesterday was a Sunday, remember. No bin collections. The tip was open, though.'

'Of course.'

'We contacted the company that runs the landfill site. Their logs confirm that deliveries were made from that tip yesterday.'

'Excellent. Good work.'

'That's not all,' Marcel said, a gleam in his eye.

Trisha Lacey opened another window on her monitor. 'This is a list of calls made to and from Cobb's burner phone. A lot of the more recent ones are from his mum, but this other number crops up a lot.'

'Do we know who it belongs to?'

'It's another unregistered number, but what we do know is that its usual location is also in the area that Cobb stayed in on Saturday night. Then there's this . . .'

Another window, another list.

'This relates to calls on Cobb's other phone – the number his mum gave you.' She touched the screen with her biro. 'This one is a call to a local taxi firm. Cobb was banned from driving, so he's been getting around by cab. We contacted the firm and asked about the call. They told us exactly where they took him on Saturday.'

'Where?'

Trisha shifted her pen back to the map. 'Here. A block of flats called Erskine Court.'

'Did they take him home again?'

'That's the funny thing. Cobb had arranged for the firm to pick him up again at six, but there was no sign of him outside the flats when the taxi pulled up. The driver says he gave Cobb a ring, and Cobb told him he was getting a lift and didn't need the taxi anymore.'

'Do we know it was Cobb who did the talking? Maybe he was already dead.'

Trisha shrugged. 'We know it was a male, but the driver didn't record the call, so we've nothing to go on. That said . . .' She double-clicked to open another file. 'This is a list of known associates of Joseph Cobb. It's a work in progress, but it's already quite the rogues' gallery. At the top of the list is a very familiar name.'

Hannah craned forward to read the tiny text. She had recently started to think she might need glasses.

'Ah, yes. Barrington "Drugs R Us" Daley. Why am I not surprised he rears his ugly head in this?'

'Right,' Trisha said. 'But have you seen his address?'

Hannah squinted again, and it was as if the characters jumped out at her. '801 Erskine Court! Well, fuck me sideways!'

'Is that an order, ma'am?' Trisha asked, grinning.

Hannah laughed. Straightened up. 'Right. Get down to that tip. Talk to the staff, pull in any CCTV footage you can get hold of. Marcel, get your make-up on. We need to go and talk to our friend Barrington.'

'Yes, boss. Stilettos or flats?'

Hannah turned and headed back to her office, a big daft smile on her face. She wanted to jump and click her heels in the air.

Things had suddenly picked up.

Out in the corridor, she flipped a finger towards Devereux's office.

16

A gang of youths was milling about in the foyer of Erskine Court. Some were smoking, some supping from cans. As Hannah and Marcel headed for the lift, they heard calls of 'Nee-naw, nee-naw' and 'Five-O!' and 'All right, darlin'?'

Hannah smiled at them and said, 'Calm down, lads. You've got too much Red Bull in those lager cans. One day you might be ready for a proper drink.'

The youths threw ribald comments back at her, but she laughed them off and stepped into the lift.

'You think they're worth questioning?' Marcel asked.

'You think they'd tell us anything worthwhile?' she replied.

The lift took an age to reach the eighth floor. When it did, 801 was directly in front of them. Marcel rapped on the door. It was answered immediately, as if the occupant had been standing on the other side in anticipation.

Hannah wasn't sure what she was seeing at first. The door chain was on, and through the gap she could make out what seemed to be a yeti with sunken eyes. She held up her ID.

'Open up, Barrington. We've got questions.'

Some hesitation, and then, 'Shiiit.'

The chain was taken off and the door pulled wide. Hannah now realised that Barrington was wearing a fur-lined parka that was several sizes too big, as if his mother had given it to him along with the promise that he would grow into it. He had the hood up, the whites of his eyes shining out from its depths, like an animal in its burrow.

'On your way out, Barrington?' Marcel asked as he and Hannah stepped into the flat.

'Nah, man. Why'd you ask?'

Marcel simply waved his hand up and down, indicating the coat.

'Oh, this! Nah, man. Place gets cold, you know? This is just me keeping toasty. Saves on the heating bills, you get me? Some people, they like dressing gowns and shit. Me, this is how I do it.'

'It's only October. What do you do when the ice and snow get here?'

The glow within the hood brightened as Barrington grinned. 'See, that's when I find me a nice woman to keep me warm at night.'

'So you didn't just get a phone call from downstairs telling you that the police were on the way up, and you thought it might be a good time to go for a walk?'

There was a rustle from within the hood, suggesting that Barrington was shaking his head.

'Uh-uh. I don't do walks. I don't hardly go out. I like it here. This is my Batcave, my Fortress of Solitude.'

Hannah sighed. 'But instead of a cape or a mask, you have a parka – that right, Barrington? At the risk of revealing your true identity, can you at least lose the hood for a few minutes? I like to see who I'm talking to.'

'You wouldn't be saying that if this was, like, a Bercow. That shit would be racist, man.'

'The word is burka. Bercow was the Speaker of the House of Commons. And when the parka becomes a recognised item of religious attire, you can take me to court. The hood, Barrington. Now.'

Barrington pushed back his hood and displayed a piano keyboard grin: white teeth separated by dark gaps that were almost as wide.

'Doesn't that feel better, being able to breathe again?' She looked around the living area. Saw untidiness and stains and dust. 'What've you been up to lately?' she asked.

Barrington straightened his arm to point to a frozen image on his television. His hand was barely visible beyond the end of his sleeve. 'Playing on the Xbox, mostly. That zombie fucker is fierce, man. He always smokes me at this point in the game. Always.'

'And this is how you make a living?'

Barrington laughed and stuffed his forearms into pockets that looked capacious enough to hold a week's shopping.

'Nah. This is how I chill. How I wind down.'

'Wind down after what? A hard day's work? What do you actually *do*?'

'This and that. Wheeling and dealing. You know how it is.'

'Funny you should mention dealing . . .' Marcel said.

'Uh-uh. That's just an expression, man. Don't go putting no extra meaning on it.'

'So you're not dealing? That's not how you make your money?'

Barrington put a hand to his heart. 'I am a reformed character. I am rehabilitated, you know what I'm saying?'

'So if we bring in dogs to search the place?'

'Be my guest. I am clean. My crib is clean. I am, like, a polygon of virtue.'

Hannah didn't bother to correct him this time. She knew they had no grounds to search the apartment, so there was little point in pursuing that line of questioning.

'Seen anyone lately, Barrington?' she asked.

'Like who?'

'Anyone. Friends, acquaintances. Even a superhero like Parkaman must have friends, right?'

He shrugged. 'Maybe.'

'Specifically, I'm thinking of Joseph Cobb.'

'Who?'

'Joseph Cobb. And don't tell me you don't know him, because your nose will grow so long it'll be sticking out of your hood.'

'Oh, you mean Joey.'

'Yeah, Joey. Seen him recently?'

Barrington pursed his lips and searched the ceiling for answers. 'Nah. Must be, oh, at least several months since we last hooked up.'

'But I guess you must have spoken to him on the phone at least?'

'Hmm, let me think. Nah. Nothing there, man.'

'Really?'

Another shrug. 'What you want me to say? It's been a while. That's it.'

'Okay.' She paused, watching him. Waiting for him to say something. Barrington's eyes darted around the room.

She said, 'Don't you want to know why I'm asking about him?'

Barrington considered this, then nodded. 'Sure. He in trouble?'

Hannah narrowed her eyes. The question seemed genuine enough, but then Barrington was well-versed in lying to the police.

'Let's just say we're looking for him.'

'Then you came to the wrong place. Like I told you, I haven't seen—'

He was interrupted by a muffled ringtone. Some sexist anti-police rap.

'You want to get that?'

'Nah. It can wait.'

'No, seriously, Barrington. Answer your phone. We've got all day.'

Barrington unzipped a pocket on his coat and reached in. Pulled out a mobile phone. Glanced at the screen before killing the call.

'Who was it?' Hannah asked.

'Unrecognized number. Probably some bitch in India telling me how I got in an accident that wasn't my fault, you know what I mean?'

'No, I don't think it was a sales call.' She turned towards Marcel. 'You trying to sell him something?'

Marcel pulled his own mobile from his pocket. 'Not me. Just trying to have a friendly chat.'

Barrington looked confused. 'What's going on, man? What the fuck is this?'

'Don't panic, Barrington. It's not magic. Detective Constable Lang here just rang your phone. Want to know how he got your number?'

Barrington said nothing. He had enough sense and experience to know when it was time to clam up.

'It was on Joey Cobb's mobile.'

'Okay. So?'

'So, it wasn't just in his contacts. He called you. Saturday, in fact. Several times.'

Barrington's eyes danced again. 'Oh! Yeah! Yeah, I forgot. That's right. We did talk.'

'We know you did. Funny how you forgot, seeing as it was only two days ago.'

'I get a lot of calls. I forget most of them. Life is too short to keep shit in your head for long, you know what I mean?'

'But now that it's all come flooding back to you, what were these conversations with Joey about?'

'Music.'

'Music?'

'Yeah, man. See, he wants to put a band together, and he was asking if I might be interested.'

Hannah noted Barrington's use of the present tense. If he knew about Cobb's demise, he was doing well at thinking on his feet.

'A band? He was asking about forming a band?'

'Yeah. See, he knows I can rap. Joey, he plays the drums, and he knows a couple of other guys who—'

'Cut the crap, Barrington. What time did he come here?'

'What?'

'After the phone calls, what time did he visit you?'

'Wait, did I say he came here? I do not think I said that.'

'We know he was here, Barrington.'

She knew nothing of the sort. Joey was definitely in this building, but so far there was nothing to indicate he visited his prospective band member.

Barrington searched their faces. 'He tell you that?'

'What?'

'Joey. He saying he was here Saturday?'

Hannah flicked her eyes towards Marcel. He arched his eyebrows in return. Barrington's demeanour was very convincing. He seemed anxious to know if Joey had dropped him in it or was looking for an alibi. Either way, he appeared genuine.

'Just answer the question,' Marcel said.

'Yeah. Okay, man, he was here.'

Hannah was glad to get to the truth, but its face was shown too easily. Barrington could have simply kept on denying it.

'What time?'

'Afternoon. Maybe three, round there.'

This chimed with what they knew about the taxi drop-off, which was logged in at ten past three.

'What did he come here for?'

'Nothing. We talked, we drank, we smoked, we played on the Xbox. That's it.'

'That's it.'

'Yeah.'

'Just two friends getting together for a catch-up.'

'Yeah. That so hard to believe? Why don't you ask Joey? He will say exactly the same thing.'

'Then why did you lie to us about seeing him? If this was all so above board, why the secrecy?'

'Because … because I know how it is. I know how you work, man. You hear about two people like us meeting up and you turn it into some kind of a conspiracy, like we're a terrorist cell or something. Like we're Obama bin Laden. That's what you do. That's what you always do.'

Hannah tried not to smile at the name corruption. She didn't want to put Marcel off while he was in full flow.

'You've got form, Barrington,' Marcel said. 'You've both got form.'

'Yeah, and you ain't never gonna let us forget that, right? Well, fuck you too, man.'

'He called you from an unregistered phone. A burner phone. Just like yours. You don't think we should be suspicious about that?'

'Nah, man, I don't. We got a right to talk without The Man listening to everything we say, don't we? Why should you know where we go and what we do every damn minute of every day? Just because we took a few wrong steps in the past, that doesn't mean we lose all our rights, does it? You know what I'm saying?'

'Tell me more about Saturday. You hung out. What then?'

'Nothing. He left. Simple as.'

'What time did he leave?'

'I don't know. Five. Six. Something like that.'

'That's a pretty big timespan. Which was it – five or six?'

'I can't be more pacific, man. We were drinking and smoking. I lost track of time.'

The taxi had been booked to collect Cobb at six o'clock. Given Barrington's hazy recollection, it was possible that Cobb left at just before that time, intending to jump straight into his taxi, but it was equally possible that he departed at closer to five, and perhaps visited someone else in the building or left it entirely. He might have forgotten he'd booked a taxi, or been unable to get back because of what befell him.

The uncertainty of it all was maddening.

'Did he say where he was going after he left you? What his plans were?'

'Not that I remember. Why don't you go and ask Joey?'

Hannah looked at Marcel, and then back at Barrington.

'What?' Barrington asked.

'Joey Cobb is dead, Barrington.'

Barrington stared at her as though expecting a follow-up – perhaps some kind of punchline.

'What?'

'He's dead. He was murdered this weekend.'

Barrington let out a long, drawn-out 'Shiiiiit.' And then: 'Wait. Do you think I got something to do with it? Is that why you're here?'

'He was here, Barrington. You said so yourself. He was here in this flat just before he was killed. And not long after he was killed, he was cut into tiny little pieces and transported to the local tip. I hope now you can see why we need to ask you some questions.'

Barrington became suddenly agitated. 'Wait. Hold on a sec. This is bullshit, man. I haven't got nothing to do with no murder. When he left my place, he was fine. He was walking and talking and in one piece. I don't know nothing about what happened after that. Holy shit. Holy fucking shit.'

'You know what I think, Barrington? I think you're full of it. You're trying to play us. Joey came here for a drug deal. No music, no band, no playing video games. He was doing a deal with you. And maybe that deal went wrong. He tried to rip you off, or you tried the same with him. Either way—'

'No. Stop right there. You can't do this to me, man. This is not fucking right. I am innocent. I got nothing to do with no murder. I haven't been out of this place since Friday, 'cept maybe to go to the corner shop on Saturday morning. Ask my neighbours. Ask them about the music I've been playing really loud, and the computer games. Go ahead, ask them.'

Hannah stood up. 'We will. And then maybe we'll come back and search your flat. One drop of blood, Barrington – that's all it would take. We find one drop of Joey's blood in here and you will be straight back in prison.'

'Then search. Like I said before, I got nothing to hide. I did not kill Joey. Shit, man.'

At the door, Hannah turned back to Barrington one last time.

'Have you got a car?'

'Yeah. Hardly ever use it, though.'

'What's the make and model?'

'Nothing flashy. It's a Vauxhall Corsa. Why?'

'We'll be looking out for it on CCTV.'

'Do that. Go ahead. What I said was the truth. I've been here all weekend. Whoever killed Joey, it wasn't me.'

17

'What do you think?'

They were in a grimy café around the corner from the block of flats. When they first sat down, Hannah had asked for the table to be cleaned. The woman serving them had simply used her arm to brush all the crumbs onto the floor. The tea now in front of Hannah tasted like it had been brewing for a week. Marcel's doughnut looked as though it could act as a serviceable doorstop. Didn't stop him tucking into it, though.

'Not how I thought it would go,' he answered, licking his lips as thick, dark jam oozed down his chin.

'No. Me neither. Lying about talking to Cobb – I expected that. Birds of a feather, et cetera. But then why not keep up the pretence? Why not simply keep insisting that he hadn't actually seen Joey on Saturday? You know how their kind usually operate: they deny everything until we present incontrovertible evidence to the contrary, and then they come up with a new story. Barrington didn't do that. He collapsed way too soon.'

'He seemed worried that Joey might've already given us the information that he was there.'

'But that suggests he believed Cobb was still alive.'

'Could've been a bluff.'

Hannah shook her head. 'I don't think Barrington is that quick on his feet. You saw and heard exactly what I did. Did you ever get the impression he knew Cobb was dead?'

'No. In fact, when we told him about it, his reaction seemed totally genuine.'

'It did. And did you notice how he didn't seem the least bit concerned about us searching his flat or tracking his car? Why would he be like that if he'd just hacked up a body and driven it to the tip?'

Marcel slurped his tea and returned to his doughnut. Hannah took a sip of her own tea, grimaced, then opened a sachet of sugar and poured it in. She never took sugar as a rule, but this called for desperate measures.

'Don't get me wrong,' she said. 'I think that the pair of them were up to no good in that flat. Barrington is a piece of shit, and so was Joey Cobb. They were doing a deal of some kind. But in a way, that's just another fly in the ointment.'

'You mean the money and the drugs we found.'

'Exactly. There is no way on this earth that Barrington Daley would have thrown that away. Some of it probably went through his hands in the first place. But even if we assume it didn't, even if we also make the unlikely assumption that Barrington didn't know Joey had it on him at the flat, I cannot believe that Barrington wouldn't have searched Cobb and his belongings after killing him. He would have found the money and the drugs, and he would have kept them.'

'So where does that leave us?'

Hannah stared out of the window. She could see the upper floors of Erskine Court, a bleak column supporting even bleaker clouds.

'If we give Barrington the benefit of the doubt – and I'm not suggesting for one minute that he's totally innocent in all this – then something happened to Cobb *after* he left the flat. The mobile data tells us he didn't move out of the range of the phone mast that serves Erskine Court. Admittedly, that's a fairly big area, but one thing we do know is that he definitely didn't go home. And yet, someone told the taxi driver that Cobb had arranged a lift with a friend.'

'You think it could have been the killer who spoke to the taxi driver?'

'I think it's likely. I don't think we're at all far away from Joey's murderer.'

'So what's our next step, boss?'

'We start at the place Joey was last seen alive and work our way out. We try to follow in Cobb's footsteps. Somebody somewhere must have seen him.'

'You want me to arrange a door-to-door?'

She pushed her mug to one side. 'No time like the present. Let's make a start.'

She asked the café owner for the bill. While they were waiting, Hannah's phone rang. She answered, listened, hung up.

'Well, that was interesting,' she said.

'What?'

'The lab has found Cobb's prints on the bags of drugs.

They've also found some other prints on them, and on the bin liners.'

'Barrington's?'

'Nope. They're not in the system.' She looked up at the flats again. 'So whose are they?'

18

When Hannah and Marcel returned to the building – now armed with clipboards and writing pads – the youths were still in the foyer. Despite what she had said earlier, Hannah decided they had nothing to lose by asking them a few questions.

As soon as she approached, the lads all stood in a line and put their wrists together, as if waiting to be handcuffed.

'Very funny,' Hannah said. 'Do you lot live here?'

'Depends what you mean by "live"', a ginger-haired lad said. He got the prize for being shorter and uglier than the rest, and was therefore probably the leader.

'All right, Socrates. I wasn't trying to start a philosophical debate.'

'My name's not Socrates. Do I look Brazilian?'

Hannah went to explain that she wasn't referring to the footballer, then decided it wasn't worth the effort.

'So what *is* your name?'

'Phil.'

'Phil what?'

'Phil McCavity.'

This got a laugh from his colleagues, and he puffed out his chest.

'Are you sure it isn't Oscar Wilde?'

'No, I've just told you it's—'

'Never mind. Okay, Philip. Do you live here or not? And before you get all existential on me again, what I mean by that is: is your home address in this building?'

'What does eggs essential mean?'

'Forget the eggs, Philip. Focus your brainpower on the question.'

'Not exactly.'

'So no, then.' She scanned the other faces. 'What about the rest of you?'

No response.

'All right,' she said. 'I'll keep this brief. You clearly spend a lot of time here, although God knows why. Not exactly the Ritz, is it? Have you ever seen this guy here?'

She nodded to Marcel, who began to open up an envelope he was carrying.

'He was here earlier,' the youth said. 'With you.'

'Not my detective, Philip. Try to keep your premature ejaculations in check, if you can.'

This got an even bigger laugh from the gang. But now it was at their leader's expense, and he didn't appreciate it.

Marcel slipped a photograph from the envelope, handed it to Hannah. She held it up for them all to see.

'This man is Joey Cobb. Anyone recognise him?'

She studied the gang as she passed the mugshot in front of their eyes. They remained stone-faced. The leader didn't even focus on the image, but looked past it at Hannah.

'What about you, Philip? Do you know him? Ever seen him in this building?'

The redhead was clearly still smarting from her put-down, and she wished now she hadn't humiliated him.

'Fuck this shit,' he said, and went to push past her.

She grabbed him by the arm. 'Hold on, son.'

He tore his arm from her grasp. 'I'm not your fucking son. I bet you can't even have kids, can you? Any kid of yours would take one look at you and drop dead.'

That was the trigger point.

Until that moment, Hannah had been calm and collected. She'd had control, and everyone had known it.

Now she lost it.

She dropped her clipboard and photograph, then grabbed the lad by his hoodie and spun him around before slamming his back into a nearby wall. Anger surged through her body. Thoughts of violence. A need to inflict damage.

'Boss! Boss!'

She realised that Marcel had his hands on her arms, tugging her gently away from her wide-eyed victim.

She released her hold on the lad. He seemed suddenly very young and very frightened – not of her, or the police, but of life, and what it had done to him. It saddened her that she had just added one more item to his long list of reasons to hate the world.

The gang leader pushed himself off the wall and walked away, flipping his hood up to hide his face. His mates trailed silently after him.

'You okay, boss?' Marcel asked.

Hannah looked at the backs of the figures leaving the building. She thought, What did I do? I had them in the palm of my hand. I had them smiling. And then I had to go and piss it all away.

She slapped the wall. 'Fuck!'

Another mistake. Another stupid mistake. How many more would there be?

Marcel gathered up the photo and her papers from the floor. 'We can go back to the station if you like. I can get a team together for the house-to-house.'

She thought about it, and was tempted. Maybe the office was the safest place for her. Kept away from the minor crises she seemed no longer capable of handling. Prevented from making a fool of herself in public.

'No,' she said. 'I want to get this moving now. I'm convinced there's vital information locked up in this building. Let's go.'

Marcel looked doubtful, but he kept his counsel. 'Okay. How do you want to do this?'

'I'll start at the top and come down. You start at the bottom and go up.'

'Going upstairs is harder.'

'Privilege of rank, Marcel.'

As she said this, she realised that a descent from the summit was probably an ideal metaphor for her career right now.

'Right. See you soon, then. I hope you've been on a first aid course for when you find me having a heart attack on the stairs.'

Hannah pointed along the corridor. 'Go!'

He went. She smiled as she heard him singing, 'You take the high road and I'll take the low road . . .'

After he had disappeared through the double doors, Hannah paused for a moment in the now-deserted foyer. Half the ceiling lights didn't work, casting a gloom over the whole area. Knowing that just above her head were dozens of people carrying on with their daily lives made the silence down here even more eerie.

What were they doing, those people? Watching television? Having sex? Reading the newspaper? Arguing? Crying?

And what about Barrington Daley? Was he panicking? Perhaps wondering if a net was closing in on him?

And, she thought, is there someone up there who knows what really happened to Joey Cobb? Someone who holds a key piece of information that could crack this case wide open?

Has to be. Even if they don't know it themselves.

She steeled herself. Straightened her jacket. Stay professional, she told herself. Do the job the way you were doing it for years before . . . well, just before. Some won't talk to the police. Some will be downright hostile. Don't let it get to you. You've heard it all before, countless times. Water off a duck's back.

She pressed the button for the lift. Heard something mechanical within the shaft getting off its arse and begin lumbering towards her, groaning with age and tiredness.

She glanced back at the double doors to the corridor. Marcel would doubtless be inside one of the flats now, charming some lonely widow into offering him tea and biscuits. Which was fine, provided she could also tell him how she witnessed one of her neighbours hefting bin bags into their car in the middle of the night.

Marcel, you can take a whole Victoria sponge cake from the woman if you can also come back with that information.

The lift was taking ages. At this rate, Marcel would have covered the whole ground floor by the time she knocked on her first door.

She checked her phone while she waited. Lots of emails and messages. She typed out a couple of quick responses.

She heard a ping. In front of her, the lift door squealed open. She looked up from her phone.

Tilly.

There, in the lift. In her school uniform. Almost within touching distance.

A sound jumped from Hannah's lips. A cross between a sob and a yelp of joy.

Tilly. My Tilly. You're here.

And then there was the crack of something slamming into the back of Hannah's head, and she fell forwards and butted the wall, and then came another wallop, this time across the shoulders, and she dropped everything she was carrying and brought her arms up behind her and tried to scuttle away, but blow after blow rained down, and she thought she could hear a voice, somebody calling her a fucking bitch.

And then the onslaught became too much, and the waiting blackness stepped in to claim its prize.

19

She awoke with a start. Blinked. Saw soft brown material and wondered where the hell she was.

A noise behind her.

She rolled over, her hands out to ward off further attacks.

In front of her, a large shape jumped away, as though startled by her sudden movement.

He'll come right back, she thought. If I don't move now, he'll have me again.

She tried to get up. Waves of pain and nausea washed through her body. She let out a groan. Tried again to rise.

'No,' said the figure. 'You should stay there. Have a rest.'

A man's voice. Deep, yet surprisingly gentle.

She blinked some more. The image of the figure came into focus. A big man. Huge. She realised she was lying on a sofa.

I'm his prisoner, she thought. He's brought me here, and nobody else knows where I am. What does he want?

She tried once more to sit up. Something moved on her forehead. She brought a hand to it and felt cold dampness. Blood, she thought, but then she looked at her fingers and saw no redness. She reached up again and pulled a rough layer away from her head. She hoped it wasn't her skin.

'It's a wet flannel,' the man said. 'For the bump. My mum does it for me when I have a bad headache.'

'Who are you?' she asked.

'D-Daniel. Daniel Timpson. I live here. It's my birthday soon.'

Oh, Jesus, she thought. A crazy guy. I'm his birthday present.

'Where am I? What are you going to do with me?'

The man seemed confused. 'I'm . . . I'm not going to do anything with you. Unless you want to. Do you want to play?'

Do you want to play? Something only a serial killer would ask, surely? What kind of perverted games did he have in mind?

'Where am I?' she asked again.

'1204 Erskine Court. I live here.'

'1204 . . . The flats? I'm still in the flats?'

'Yes. 1204. That's on the twelfth floor. If you look out of the window you can see all the way to the comic-book shop. I go there a lot.'

'Why did you bring me up here?'

'I . . . You were hurt. The man was hitting you with a stick.'

Daniel appeared suddenly upset at the recollection. He kept interlacing his fingers and undoing them again.

'So it wasn't you? You didn't attack me?'

Daniel looked appalled. 'No! I would never do that. I don't touch people. It's The Rule. Although . . . although I suppose I did touch you.'

Alarm bells sounded in Hannah's head again.

'You touched me?'

'I had to, so I could pick you up. I'm sorry.'

'No. No, it's okay. The man, Daniel. Who was the man?'

'I don't know. He was wearing a hoodie, and the light isn't very good by the lifts. I came home from the day centre and I saw him hitting you with a stick, and I shouted at him because you're not supposed to hit people, and then he ran away. I didn't see his face.'

One of the gang of lads, she thought. Most probably the one who called himself Phil, proving his manhood to his pals by showing how he wasn't going to stand for being humiliated by a police officer, especially a female one.

'Then I need to thank you, Daniel. You saved me.'

He looked at the floor, embarrassed. 'It's okay.'

'No, really. You did a wonderful thing. Was it difficult getting me into the lift?'

He furrowed his eyebrows. 'I didn't use the lift. I don't trust it.'

'I don't understand. How did you get me up here?'

'I carried you.'

She stared at him. 'What? You carried me? Up twelve floors?'

He nodded, as if it was no big thing.

'Wow,' she said. 'That's impressive.'

'Thanks,' he said. And then, 'What does impressive mean?'

'It means I wish there were more people in the world like you, Daniel. You're one of the good guys.'

He dropped his gaze to the floor again.

Hannah touched the lump on her forehead and winced,

then the bigger lump on the back of her head and winced even more. She tried again to sit up, and cried out as pain fanned out across her upper body.

'You should rest,' Daniel advised again. 'You can sleep there if you want. I can get a blanket and cover you up. My dad did that the other day, and it really helped.'

'No, that's okay. I can't stay here.' She looked around. 'My things. I had a bag and some other stuff.'

Daniel held up a finger. 'Oh. Wait. Here.' He went to the dining table and brought back her bag and clipboard. She marvelled even more at the thought that he had somehow managed to carry both her and her belongings.

'Thank you.' She opened the bag and rummaged around inside for her phone, but then remembered that she'd had it in her hand when she was attacked.

'My phone. Did you pick up a phone downstairs?'

'No. I'm sorry. I didn't see it. It was a bit dark.'

'That's okay.' An easy thing to miss, she thought. It might have ended up in the lift or in a shadowy corner. Either that or her mugger had run off with it.

'Do you have a phone?' she asked.

Daniel frowned and turned on the spot. 'Somewhere,' he said. He scratched his head. 'Wait.' He went out to the hall, then returned, brandishing his mobile. He handed it to her.

It was a primitive device, designed for simplicity of use. Huge buttons rather than a touchscreen. The display was spider-webbed with cracks, and when Hannah tried depressing keys, nothing happened.

'This is broken, Daniel.'

He looked crestfallen. 'I know. My mum says I'm too rough with it. The answer button still works, so she can call me, but I can't call her.' He suddenly brightened. 'But I think I might be getting a new one next week for my birthday. I heard my mum and dad talking about it.'

'Do you have a landline?'

'What's a landline?'

'A separate phone for the flat.'

'No. We don't have one of those. I've seen them on telly, but Mum says we don't need one because we've got mobiles.'

Hannah thought about Marcel, presumably still working his way through the flats below, oblivious to his superior officer's predicament.

'You couldn't do me a favour, could you? My colleague is downstairs somewhere. Probably still on the ground floor. Do you think you'd be able to go and find him for me?'

It was clear from the way Daniel began rubbing his face that he was agonising over the request.

'I'm not supposed to do that,' he said. 'I'm not supposed to leave the flat after I get home. And Mum and Dad don't like me talking to strangers.'

'I'm a stranger.'

'I know. But you needed help. It's a good thing to help people. That's what I think, anyway.'

She smiled at him and nodded. 'Yes. Yes it is a good thing. Perhaps your next-door neighbour has a phone?'

'They don't talk to us. My dad fell out with them when they said I was an idiot. I got the flats mixed up when we first moved here, and I broke my key in their lock when I tried to get in.'

No other choice, Hannah thought. She took a deep breath, hauled herself to her feet. Crashed back onto the sofa again when her balance went out of kilter and nausea hit her.

'Oh, God,' she moaned. 'I think I'm going to be sick.'

This alarmed Daniel. 'Do you need a bucket? We've got a bucket. A black plastic one from B&Q. Should I get it for you?'

Hannah waved a hand. 'No. I'll be okay. I just need to sit here for a while. Could I have some water?'

'Yes. Of course. We have lots of that.'

Daniel walked over to the kitchen area, filled a glass with tap water, then brought it back.

'Thank you. That helps. Where are your parents, Daniel?'

'They should be home soon. My mum went shopping, but then she's meeting my dad at work and he's bringing her home. We're having pizza tonight. Would you like to stay for tea?'

'No. I'd better not. Thank you for the offer, though.'

'You're welcome.'

Impeccable manners, she thought. The parents have brought him up well.

'What's your name?' Daniel asked.

'It's Hannah.'

'Hannah. That's a nice name.'

'Thank you. I like Daniel, too.'

'Thank you. And what do you do, Hannah?'

'I work for the police. I'm a detective.'

Daniel's eyes widened. 'Oh, wow! A detective? Like Columbo?'

'Well, I like to think I'm a bit better dressed than that. Maybe more like Inspector Morse.'

'He's good too. He's very clever. Do you always have to be clever to be a detective?'

'Well, it helps.'

'I couldn't be a detective. I'm a sandwich short of a picnic.'

Hannah spluttered while sipping her water. 'Who told you that?'

'Laurence. At the day centre. He's funny.'

'Well, you can tell Laurence that I think you'd make an excellent police officer. You're brave and you're strong and you do what's right.'

Daniel drew himself up to his full height. Which was considerable.

'Do you stop criminals?' he asked.

'I try to.'

'Adam-9 stops criminals. Do you know Adam-9?'

Something pinged in Hannah's chest. Adam-9. The comics. The television programmes. Tilly had loved them. Hannah was never sure why, but it was one of the few things that had really been capable of holding her daughter's attention, and was therefore in her armoury of rewards for good behaviour.

And then it came back to her. Tilly. In the lift earlier.

Why?

What had she been doing there? And why then? Had she appeared as a warning, to let her mother know that she was about to be attacked?

Stop that, Hannah told herself. Tilly was never there. It was a figment of your imagination.

And yet she had seemed so real, so solid. Not a vague, fuzzy image built from corruptible memory, but there in every

144

wonderful tiny detail, living and breathing and staring deep into her mother's eyes.

Hannah cleared her throat. 'I'm sorry, Daniel. What was that?'

'I was talking about Adam-9. He's my favourite. Do you like him?'

'He's . . . My daughter really likes him.'

She caught herself using the present tense, but she didn't care. After seeing Tilly up close like that, it didn't feel wrong.

'What's your daughter's name?'

'Tilly. Her name's Tilly.'

'That's also a nice name. Did you know there was a Tilly on *Adam-9* once?'

'No, I didn't know that.'

'She was a little girl. Adam helped her. A nasty man took her away from her family, but Adam rescued her.'

This was a revelation to Hannah. She wondered if it was the reason Tilly had been so fascinated by the stories. She wanted to tell Daniel that her own Tilly had been snatched away too, and that she wished Adam-9 could bring her back to her family, but then she decided it would be too much for him to handle.

'Adam's a hero, all right.'

'He is. I've got lots of his comics, and we record all the programmes. Would you like to watch one?'

'I—' She was going to make an excuse, and then she thought, What the hell? This young man has just saved me. Why not indulge him?

'I'd love to,' she said.

And so Daniel put the programme on, and then he sat in his chair, his elbows on his knees and his chin in his cupped hands, staring transfixed at the screen and apparently oblivious to everything else around him.

Just as Tilly had once done.

20

A normal day.

Scott hadn't dared to think it would happen. Following the events of the weekend, he'd found himself constantly worrying about seismic aftershocks, or at least ripples of disturbance.

But no. A mundane working day. A grey Monday just like any other. From start to finish, business as usual. And now here he was, nearly home, Gemma at his side. About to see his amazing son again. They would have a meal together, watch some television. He might open a couple of bottles of beer.

It would get easier, day by day. The images, the horrors – they would fade. Eventually he would find himself wondering if they had even taken place. The mind is good at self-repair like that. It protects itself, just as Scott had protected his son.

But then he unlocked the door and wandered in and saw the smartly dressed woman sitting on the sofa, exactly where he'd put Joseph Cobb, and he saw the lumps and discoloration on her head and forearms, saw Daniel looming over her, and he thought, No, no, please God, no, not again, what has my son done, what in God's name has he done now? And then he heard the intake of breath from Gemma as she followed him into the room, but nothing more, as if she was equally as stunned.

'Hello,' he said, because he didn't know what else to say, didn't know how to make sense of this.

'Mr Timpson,' the woman said, and she put out her hand, and Scott could see that she was wincing as she did so. He took it very gently, for fear of breaking her.

'I'm sorry,' Scott said. 'I don't—'

'Dad! Dad! I rescued her. I saved her. A man attacked her, and I saved her.'

Scott stared at Daniel, and then back at the woman. Could this be true? Or had something gone wrong again? Had Daniel caused this somehow? Could they be that unlucky?

'You have a wonderful son,' the woman said. 'If he hadn't turned up when he did, I could be dead by now.'

'Who . . . who did it? Who attacked you?'

'I don't know. There was a gang of lads down there earlier . . .'

Scott nodded. 'They're a menace. Always hanging about the building. I've told the police about them lots of times.'

The woman went to say something, but was interrupted by stifled giggles from Daniel.

'She *is* the police, Dad! Her name's Hannah, and she's a real detective!'

Scott felt suddenly faint, as though his brain was squeezing the blood out of itself in preparation for flight. The police? This couldn't be coincidence, surely. They know something, he thought. What has Daniel told them?

Behind him, Gemma said, 'I'll put the shopping away,' and he knew she needed to avoid showing her fear. As she sped away with her carrier bags, Scott forced an approximation of cheerfulness onto his features.

'A detective, eh? We like detectives, don't we, Daniel?'

'We do. She's not like Columbo, though. More like Inspector Morse.'

Scott forced out a laugh. 'Are you okay? I mean, do you need an ambulance or anything?'

'No. I'm starting to feel much better. Daniel has been taking good care of me.'

Scott looked at his son again. Daniel was beaming, but Scott still wondered if he'd said something he shouldn't.

'Are you here on official business, or . . .'

'Actually, yes. I was just about to start canvassing the building before I was attacked.'

'Canvassing?'

'Yes. We're hoping that somebody here will be able to supply us with some information.'

Scott watched as Hannah picked up a clipboard from the cushion next to her. He licked his lips, his mouth dry. He had a good idea of what was coming.

Hannah unclipped an envelope. Went to open the flap.

She's going to pull out a photo, he thought. She's going to show us a picture of Joseph Cobb and tell us that he's been murdered. And then Daniel, our honest Daniel, will confess everything.

'Er . . .' Scott said. 'If you don't mind . . .'

Hannah stopped what she was doing. Looked inquiringly at him.

'If this is about a crime, we try to keep Daniel out of things like that. *Columbo* and *Morse* are one thing, but when it's real ...'

Hannah smiled. 'Yes. Yes, of course.'

Scott turned to his son. 'Daniel, would you mind going to your room, please?'

Daniel looked devastated. 'Oh, but, Dad!'

'No buts. We need to talk about something.'

'But it's not fair. I'm the one who—'

'Daniel! Please.'

Daniel lowered his chin to his chest. Sloped off to his bedroom with heavy feet.

'Sorry about that,' Scott said. 'He may not look it, but he's quite sensitive.'

'That's all right. I understand. Now if I could just ask you to take a look at a photograph for me?'

Scott shrugged. 'Sure.'

I don't want to see this, he thought. I don't want to look at that man's face again. How has he come back to haunt me so quickly? How did the police find us?

Hannah slipped out the photograph and handed it over. Scott took it and tried to look without seeing. Tried to regard the image in front of him as a collection of printed dots that collectively meant nothing.

'Have you ever seen that man?' Hannah asked.

Scott shook his head, but the eyes on the sheet of paper were starting to make their presence felt, starting to burn into his skull. He looked away, focused on Hannah instead.

'No,' he said. 'Can't say I have. Who is he?'

'His name's Joseph Cobb. He's a murder victim.'

'Murder? God. Did he live in this building?'

'No, but he visited someone here on Saturday afternoon, not long before he was killed. Are you sure you didn't see him?'

'Certain. I took Daniel to the cinema on Saturday afternoon, and when we got back we came straight up here and didn't go out again. I don't remember seeing anyone else in the building that day, not even the lads you saw earlier.'

He handed the photograph back. That was okay, he thought. I was convincing. I know I was.

But then Hannah looked past him towards the kitchen area.

'Mrs Timpson? Would you mind taking a look at this, please?'

Scott watched Gemma's unsteady progress across the room. She looked pale, on the verge of vomiting.

Keep it together, Gem. Don't go to pieces on me now.

When his wife took the photograph, Scott noticed that her hand was shaking.

'Does he look familiar to you at all?' Hannah asked.

She pulled a face, shook her head. 'Never seen him in my life.'

'And neither of you were aware of any commotion in the building over the weekend? Nobody acting suspicious?'

Scott forced out a laugh. 'This place is full of suspicious-looking people. Sorry we can't help you, though.'

Hannah put the photograph away. 'No problem. I can't expect to strike lucky with the first people I ask.' She winced again. 'Probably the last ones I ask today as well, the way I'm feeling. You mind if I borrow your phone? I need to call my colleague.'

'Of course not.' Scott dug his mobile out of his pocket, unlocked it and handed it over. As the detective typed in a number, he exchanged glances with his wife. Gemma looked terrified.

'Hi, Marcel,' Hannah was saying. 'You mind coming up to get me when you're done there? There's been a bit of an incident . . . I was assaulted. Feeling a bit worse for wear . . . No, I'll be fine. Stop worrying . . . I'll tell you all about it when I see you, okay? Get up here when you can. I'm being well looked after in flat . . .' Forgetting the number Daniel had given her earlier, she looked to Scott, who told her. '. . . Flat 1204. Okay, see you in a few minutes.'

She ended the call and returned the phone to Scott. 'Thank you. I'll be out of your hair soon.'

Scott was desperate for her to leave, but at the same time he had a million unanswered questions.

'That man,' he ventured, 'the one in the photograph. You said he didn't live here. But was he killed here, in the building? I don't feel very safe here at the best of times, but if I thought—'

'We don't know yet. We know he visited someone, but it's quite possible he left the building before he was murdered. Please don't get too worked up about it. I know that a death on one's doorstep can be alarming, but don't be afraid to carry on with your normal lives. I'm convinced we'll catch whoever did this.'

'That's . . . that's good to hear. Thank you for the reassurance.'

Hannah looked out towards the hall. 'You can let your son out now. He's probably desperate to rejoin the party.'

Scott waved the suggestion away. It was the last thing he wanted. 'He'll be fine. He's got a short attention span. He'll have his head buried in a comic or something.'

'Adam-9?'

Scott remembered that Daniel had been watching it when he came through the door. 'You noticed.'

'Big fan of it, apparently.'

Scott was glad to get off the topic of Joseph Cobb. 'Massive. He carries a briefcase everywhere, acting like he's Adam-9. It's his birthday next week. He doesn't know it, but we've got him a proper Adam-9 briefcase, buttons on it and everything, plus an ID wallet and a rubber mask. The mask is a bit freaky, but in the show Adam wears masks that make him look like other people. We never actually see what the real Adam-9 looks like.'

Hannah smiled. 'I know. I've seen it umpteen times myself.'

'You have?'

'Yeah. Courtesy of my daughter. It was ... it's one of her favourite programmes.'

Scott noticed the sudden change of tense, but didn't query it.

Come on, Marcel. Get us out of this. I've run out of things to say.

He was saved by the bell. Gemma answered it, admitting a younger copper who looked like he'd just run upstairs. Scott stood aside as Hannah relayed the barest of information to her junior.

'Next stop the hospital,' Marcel said as he escorted her to the door.

'I don't need the hospital,' Hannah answered. 'I'm fine.'

'You blacked out. That's a mandatory hospital trip. Look at you. You can hardly walk.'

'Stop going on at me like we're a married couple, Marcel.' She turned to Scott and Gemma. 'No offence intended. By the way . . .' She dug a card out from her jacket pocket and proffered it to Scott. 'If you think of anything, or hear something from your neighbours you think we should know, give me a call.'

'We will.'

He watched them leave, still bickering as their voices faded down the corridor. Then he closed the front door and pressed his forehead against it.

'Oh my God!' Gemma said behind him. 'They know!'

'They don't know,' Scott muttered.

'They do. They're on to us. What are we going to do?'

Scott whirled on her. 'They're not on to us. They don't suspect anything.'

'Then why did they come here? You said you'd dealt with it. You told me we were safe.'

'We *are* safe.' He went up to her, lowering his voice to stop this developing into a slanging match that would frighten Daniel. 'You heard what they said. They know Cobb has been murdered, but that's all they know. They're not even sure whether he was killed in this building. They came here first because Cobb visited someone here, and that detective only ended up in our flat because she was attacked. None of that has anything to do with us.'

'But how do they know he was murdered? It's only Monday, Scott. How did they get to us so quickly?'

'I . . . I don't know. They must have found the body.' He avoided saying 'body parts'.

'How?'

'I don't know, all right? I didn't think they would, but they must have.'

'Then it's only a matter of time, isn't it? They'll do tests. Forensics. They'll trace it back to us, Scott.'

He took hold of her upper arms. 'They won't. There's nothing to trace. And even if there was, we're not on their system. They've asked their questions and moved on. We'll never see them again.'

'But what if they *do* come back? What's our story going to be?'

'We don't need a story. We have no motive. We have no past connection with Cobb. There's no reason to suspect us. If they ever come back – which they won't – then we just act dumb. We tell them we know nothing. Okay?'

He could see the fury in her eyes, her utter disappointment after having trusted him to brush this mess out of their lives.

She tore her gaze away and nodded towards the hallway.

'And what about Daniel? What if they ask him what *he* knows?'

21

Ben's mouth dropped open. 'What the . . .?'

Hannah shrugged. 'You should see the one on the back of my head. Puts that one to shame.'

'What the hell happened?'

She brushed past him as she entered the hallway. 'I need a drink. Only I can't have one because I'm pumped full of painkillers.'

'You're avoiding my question.'

She kept going. Into the living room, where she kicked off her shoes and sat down on the sofa. Ben followed her.

'I was attacked,' she said.

'How's the other guy? In a hospital bed, I hope.'

The comment surprised her. 'I think you need to tear up your pacifist credentials. I didn't see the other guy. Bastard whacked me with a stick from behind and then ran away.'

'Where did this happen?'

'Ground floor of a block of flats. We'd just split up to do a door-to-door.'

'And nobody saw anything?'

'One guy came to my rescue. By that time, I was already out of it.'

'What do you mean, out of it?'

She hesitated. 'I mean I'd lost consciousness.'

'You'd lost— Jesus, Hannah. You need to see a doctor.'

'I've seen a doctor. Marcel Lang insisted on it. I've just come back from A&E.'

'You've just— Oh my God. Why am I only just hearing about this?'

'Because I knew exactly how you'd react, and it's what you're doing now, fussing over me like a grandmother.'

'I'm your husband. I'm allowed to fuss. What did they say?'

'That I'll live to fight another day. That I've still got a brain. Technical stuff like that.'

Ben leaned in and began ferreting around in her hair until she slapped him away.

He said, 'Good job you've got such a thick head. Why the hell were you searching buildings anyway?'

'In case you'd forgotten, I'm a detective. I investigate things and look for clues.'

'You're also an inspector and the lead on the case. You should be sitting in an office where it's nice and safe, and sending your minions out to do the dirty work.'

'Yeah, well, I don't trust my minions.'

'You don't trust your own officers?'

'Okay, that's not entirely true. I do trust them. But I need to make sure this one is done right. There's a lot riding on this case.'

'Your control freakery isn't worth getting killed for.'

'I won't get killed. The attack had nothing to do with the investigation. I was just in the wrong place at the wrong time.'

Ben frowned. 'Any ideas who did it?'

'Not sure. We had a slight run-in with some lads who hang around the building. Could have been one of them, but I've got no proof.'

'Well, I hope you've got police swarming all over that place. You need to get the bastard who did this to you.'

'It's fine.'

'It's not fine at all. Assaulting a police officer is not something to be dismissed so lightly, especially when the officer concerned is my wife. I'd go looking for him myself if I wasn't so opposed to confrontation and violence and getting my arse kicked.'

'I don't want to make a big thing of it.'

'Why not? That bump on your head is a big thing. Massive, in fact.'

'Stop making me out to be the Elephant Man. The reason I don't want to make a fuss is because I want to spare my Good Samaritan.'

Ben gave her a knowing look. 'Oh yeah? Tall and dark, is he?'

'Yup.'

'Bravery and strength of a dozen men?'

'Oh yes.'

'Younger than me?'

'Early twenties.'

'I hate him already. What's the deal with this white knight? Think carefully before you answer.'

'For one thing, he didn't really see anything. For another, he's got learning difficulties.'

Ben blinked. 'Oh.'

'Yeah. He took me up to his flat and looked after me until his parents got home. Heart of gold, but not so talented in the intellect department. I really don't want to bother him any further with this. It wouldn't be fair.'

'I don't think it's fair that your attacker gets away with it either, but if that's the way you want to play it . . .'

'It is.'

It occurred to her to tell Ben about the reason why she hadn't heard her assailant sneaking up on her. About seeing Tilly again, so close and so . . . so *alive*. But then she remembered how he'd reacted last time.

'Have you eaten?'

'I had a bag of crisps from the hospital vending machine.'

'And that's it? Christ, are you determined to end up on a slab? Right, give me ten minutes.'

She thanked him as he dashed off to the kitchen. Sometimes she wondered if he minded doing all the cooking and housework, although he never complained about it.

She picked up the remote control from the coffee table and switched on the television. She flicked through the channels, but could find nothing of interest.

Ben brought in a cup of tea. 'Drink that while you're waiting. Leftover curry and rice okay?'

'Wonderful.'

When he disappeared again, she sipped her tea, but was unable to relax. She put down her cup and stood up.

'Just going to get changed,' she called, then went upstairs.

She stood in front of her bedroom door, but didn't open it.

She moved along the landing. Opened the next door instead. The door to Tilly's room.

When she entered and put the light on, it was as if all the sights and smells rushed into her, overwhelming her senses. A shudder passed through her body, and she had to bring her hand to her mouth to stifle a cry. For some reason, the effect on her seemed more potent now than it had ever been.

They had left the room undisturbed since Tilly's death. The bed was made, the cuddly toys lined up on it, awaiting her return. Her hairbrush was on the dressing table, still clinging desperately to her strands. A colouring book was on the windowsill, a green crayon resting on the section she needed to fill in next.

The room was ready for her to come back, and would remain so until Hannah and Ben told it to abandon its vigil.

Hannah went to the large wicker hamper by the window and opened it. She reached in and pulled out an Adam-9 action figure. Beneath that was a stack of Adam-9 comics they had brought back from a trip to Japan. The text was in Japanese, but it hadn't mattered to Tilly, because these stories weren't available in western countries.

She thought back to her vision of Tilly in the lift, then meeting Daniel, and it seemed to her almost as if the latter was simply a continuation of the former: that her little girl had merely changed her outward appearance. Inside that large hulking frame of a man was an eight-year-old. Still simple and pure and kind.

It was probably a ridiculous notion.

But she clutched it to her aching heart nonetheless.

22

When Ronan Cobb turned up at his mother's house on Tuesday afternoon, it was with a sense of satisfaction. By now, word had got around that Joey slept with the fishes, or at least with the rotting bones of fishes and other garbage, and that put people in Joey's line of work on edge. It suggested that reprisals might be coming, that they might be next in the firing line. Experience told them that it was wise to clam up.

But what had begun as a tedious chore for Ronan had been turned by the death of his brother into a calling, and so he'd put the work in. He'd posed a lot of questions, called in a slew of favours, issued a number of threats. And now Ronan, ace private detective that he was (even though this was more an instance of sheer luck rather than investigative prowess), felt he was finally on to something. His mother would be proud.

Myra Cobb looked at him like he was a piece of shit.

'Where the hell have you been?' she demanded.

No 'Hello, how are you?' No 'Would you like a cup of tea or coffee?' No hug or kiss.

Not that he wanted to go anywhere near his mother at the moment. She looked worse than ever. Drunker, and dirtier.

Her hair was lank and shiny with grease, the ends coated in chunks of what looked like vomit. She was still wearing the black armband; it had slipped down to her forearm and was stained with glistening wet trails. Ronan guessed she had been wiping her nose on it.

'Where do you think?' he answered. 'Been trying to find out what happened to Joey, haven't I?'

She appeared suddenly and melodramatically mournful. 'Joey. My beautiful son. They murdered him.'

Ronan wondered if she would put on such an act if he told her he was about to drop dead of terminal cancer or something. He suspected she would order him to pull himself together and get on with the bloody search. Funny how you can have identical twins and still prefer one over the other.

'I'm getting there now, Mam. I've been asking around, and—'

'Useless twat. The rate you're going, the police will have them first, and then what will we do, eh? How will we get even if they're locked up in a cell? Useless bloody imbecile.'

Ronan took a tight grip on the seat of his chair, forcing himself to stay put. He so wanted to walk out and never come back again. His mother seemed to be forgetting that he was also related to Joey, that he might want to get his hands on the murderer every bit as much as she did.

'Anyway, as I was saying, I've been asking around. Ended up talking to Biggo.'

'Who the fuck's Biggo?'

'James O'Rourke. He got the name at school because the teacher kept spelling his name with a lower-case o, and one

162

day he lost it and shouted out, "It's big O, you plank! Big O!" Funny, really, because he's actually pretty small.'

Myra stared at him and downed a swig of her gin. 'Fascinating. What's your point?'

Ronan took a deep breath. 'The point is that Biggo told me he often hangs out with his mates at a block of flats called Erskine Court.'

'Doing what?'

'Nothing much. Just chilling out. But that's not what—'

'Waste of space, all of them. Youth of today. Should be shot, the whole lot of 'em.'

'Yes, Mam. So what Biggo tells me is that he was there yesterday, and the cops turned up. And not just any cops, but that detective who came to see us. He described her down to a tee. She was asking about Joey, about whether Biggo and his mates had seen him there over the weekend.'

Myra finally showed some interest. 'Joey was there? Why?'

'That's what I wanted to know. Turns out Barrington Daley lives in that building.'

'Barrington Daley? That piece of shit? He'd sell his own grandmother if he thought she was worth anything.'

'My thoughts exactly. I wouldn't put it past him to be involved in Joey's death.'

Myra mulled it over, and then something ugly crept into her expression. 'Wait a minute. Why has it taken you this long to get to Barrington? He'd have been top of my list.'

'It didn't. I phoned him yesterday. He denied all knowledge. Said he hadn't seen Joey for ages.'

'You think he was lying?'

'Either that or it's one big fucking coincidence that the police are swarming all over his arse.'

'Don't fucking swear in this house, Ronan. I brought you up better than that.' She glared at him suspiciously. 'When did you hear all this from your friend Biggo?'

'This morning.'

'This morning! Then what the hell are you doing here? Why aren't you at Barrington's place, putting thumbscrews on him?'

'I just told you, Mam. The police are there. They've been knocking on every door since last night.'

'Since last night? Well, they've got to be done by now. Get your lazy arse over there and talk to that motherf— that scumbag. I want to know why the police suddenly find him so interesting. And before you go . . .'

She put down her glass. Pushed her chair back. Ronan raised his eyebrows as he watched his mother actually get up from her seat and turn towards the sideboard behind her. It was the most active he'd seen her in ages. As she bent to open one of the doors, Ronan noticed a dark patch on her grey trousers. She'd pissed herself at some point and failed to notice.

She came back to the table with a shortbread tin. Slid it across to Ronan.

Ronan was moved by the simple gesture. 'Thanks, Mam. Could we have some tea with them? I'm gasping here.'

'Open it, you prick,' she said.

He reached across and lifted the lid. Inside, something was wrapped in an oily rag. He unfolded it.

It was a semi-automatic handgun. A Colt .45. Huge and heavy and lethal.

'Mam. What's this?'

'What's it look like? Take it. You'll need it with a snake like Barrington.'

'Mam, I can't wander into a building full of coppers with a cannon like this on me. That's just asking to be locked up.'

Myra leaned forward. 'Did you hear what they said about Joey? He was murdered and then chopped into tiny little pieces. Whoever did that to him were psychopaths. They won't hesitate to do the same to you. Take the gun, Ronan. You'll be glad you did.'

With reluctance, he picked up the Colt, hefted its weight in his hand.

'It's fully loaded,' Myra said, 'so be careful with it.'

Ronan stared at the weapon. He wasn't going to ask how his mother had acquired such a thing, but he was willing to bet it wasn't the shopping channel.

23

Despite his mother's edict to get his lazy arse straight over to Erskine Court, Ronan gave it another couple of hours for the area to be clear of cops before he ventured through its doors. The lobby was empty when he arrived, and he went straight to the lift. His adrenaline was running high. No telling what Barrington Daley might do when he saw who was at his door. Ronan didn't have much of a plan. What if Barrington confessed to killing Joey? What then? Waste him? Cripple him? What was the appropriate penalty?

He came out of the lift, stood in front of 801 for a moment. He checked the .45 pushed into the back of his waistband, then rapped on the door. When it opened a crack, he shouted 'Boo!' and Barrington screamed.

'Open the door, you pussy,' Ronan ordered.

Barrington took off the chain and allowed him in.

'And take off that fucking hood,' Ronan continued. 'What are you, a fucking Eskimo?'

Barrington pulled back the hood of his parka. Ronan noticed how shaken up he looked, his eyes wide with fear.

'Jesus, man. It's Ronan, yeah? I mean, like, you ain't no ghost, are you?'

'You heard, then? About Joey?'

'Yeah, man. The saddest news. I feel for you, man.'

'How'd you find out?'

Barrington's shrug was barely perceptible within his massive coat. 'Word is everywhere, man. Everyone's talking about it.'

'Plus there have been cops all over the show, asking their questions.'

Barrington's eyes darted, as though he was trying to do a quick assessment of how much he should say. 'Yeah, like they do. They've been knocking on *every* door in this building, man.'

Every door. Meaning, *I'm just one of many.*

'Why?'

'What's that?'

'Why were they here?'

'Search me. I'm guessing someone must have seen him around.'

'They didn't come here because you and Joey used to be tight?'

'Nah, man. Nothing to do with me pacifically. They was rousting everyone.'

'So what happened when they got to you?'

'Usual shit. Routine inquiries is what they said.'

'What'd you tell them?'

'Nothing. Didn't even tell them I knew him. That's for them to figure out.'

'But they showed you photos, asked if you'd ever seen his face?'

'Yeah. I told them I'd never seen the guy in my life.'

'And they were fine with that?'

'Totally, man. I put on a good act, you know what I'm saying?'

'Right.'

The punch from Ronan took Barrington completely by surprise. It split open his lip and sent him sprawling back onto the sofa. As he tried to get up again, blood gushing from his mouth, Ronan pulled out his gun and aimed it at Barrington's face.

'Stay down! Stay the fuck down!'

Barrington cowered, his quivering hands an ineffective shield. 'What are you doing, man? What's going on?'

'Why are you lying to me?'

'What do you mean? What about?'

'The police. They came here *before* the door-to-door started. Two detectives, a man and a woman. They came to this building and they took the lift up to the eighth floor. *Your* floor.'

'All right, all right. They did, yeah.'

'Why?'

'Because they knew about me and Joey. Knew we used to hang out.'

'So what did they ask you?'

'Just if I'd seen him recently.'

'And you said what?'

'That I hadn't. Not for months.'

'Right. Because that was the truth. It's the same thing you said to me on the phone yesterday, so it must have been.'

'Yeah, yeah. Exactly.'

Ronan hit him with the gun, opening up his cheek. Barrington yelped.

'You're lying to me again.'

'I'm not, I'm not.'

'You are. Joey was here. He was out doing deals. The only reason he'd come to this shithole would be to see you. Now tell the fucking truth, or so help me . . .'

Ronan cocked the trigger of his Colt, put it to Barrington's temple.

'All right, Ronan. Cool it, okay? He was here. I bought some gear off him.'

'Did you tell the cops that?'

'I told them he was here, but not about the deal. I'm not stupid.'

'Matter of opinion. What happened then? Deal go south? Did you kill him? DID YOU?'

Muzzle hard to the temple now. Ronan's index finger squeezing against the trigger.

'No! No! Swear to God. He was fine when he left here. Sound as a pound.'

'Then why'd you lie to me? Why even bother making up all this shit if that's all that happened?'

'Because he told me not to tell anyone.'

'I'm his fucking twin brother.'

'I know, but that makes it worse. Joey said he definitely didn't want you or your mum to know.'

'Why? What are you talking about?'

'Your mum hates me. She doesn't trust me an inch.'

'Right now I feel the same way. What's that got to do with anything?'

'Because he was doing deals for her. Your mother. She got him the drugs. He was doing it all for her.'

24

When Ronan left Barrington's flat, he didn't know what to believe. His twin brother was dead, and yet everyone but Ronan seemed to know more of the truth than he did. Barrington, the police, even his own mother were able to see different parts of the picture, while he was completely blind. What angered him most was his mother. She had used him, and that was something he could never forgive.

He wandered aimlessly along the corridor, and then pushed through the fire doors leading to the stairwell. He sat down on the cold, hard steps, took out his phone and made a call.

'Ronan? Where are you? Why haven't you rung me?'

'I'm talking to you now, Mam.'

'Don't get cheeky with me, lad, or you'll feel the back of my hand. I'm still your mother, you know.'

'Yeah. Lucky me.'

'What was that?'

'Nothing. Doesn't matter.'

'Where are you? Have you seen that shitbag yet?'

Ronan couldn't be bothered relating the encounter in detail. 'He doesn't know anything, Mam. I've just spoken to him.'

'What do you mean, he doesn't know anything? You told me the police have been crawling all over his place. Why would they be doing that if they didn't suspect him? Who else lives there that Joey would know?'

Ronan sighed. 'Nobody, Mam.'

'Precisely. You did show him you mean business, didn't you?'

Ronan raised his voice. 'Mam, will you listen to me for once? He doesn't know anything. They got together, did some business, and then Joey left.'

'Business? What do you mean, business?'

'What do you think I mean?' He wasn't going to be any more explicit on the phone.

'For Mental?'

Still sticking to the lie, he thought. One of her sons is dead, and she's lying through her teeth to the other one.

'No, Mam, not for Mental. For you.'

There was a detectable pause before she answered. 'What?'

'You lied to me, Mam. Why?'

'What are you going on about?'

'Barrington told me. Joey was doing business for you.'

'And you believe that grubby little toe-rag rather than your own mother? What kind of son are you?'

'The kind who doesn't like being treated like an idiot.'

'I haven't done any such thing. You've let that sneaky bastard pull the wool over your eyes. You were too soft with him. I've sent a boy to do a man's job. Bloody hell, I could do better myself. That conniving prick probably killed Joey himself. You do know that, don't you?'

'ENOUGH!' Ronan's shout echoed up and down the stair-well. 'Enough, Mam. Stop it. Please. Tell me truth.'

A much longer pause now.

'I needed the money, lad. I'm skint. Joey was doing me a favour. Helping out his old mum.'

Here we go, Ronan thought. Trying to grab the sympathy vote.

'What do you mean, skint? Since when? I thought you were loaded.'

A bark of laughter. 'Loaded? What gave you that idea? Everything I had I spent on you and Joey.'

And now the guilt trip, Ronan thought. Make it my fault.

'You should have told me, Mam. Should've been straight with me.'

'I . . . I knew you wouldn't approve.'

She was right: he wouldn't have approved. Not because he was any better – God knows, he'd done some bad things in his time – but he'd believed that his mother was out of the game, that there was no longer any danger of her going to prison or ending up like Joey.

'Shit, Mam. What were you thinking? Why didn't you just come to me for help?'

'You know me, lad. I stand on my own two feet. Always have and always will.'

So that's it, he thought. Stubborn pride. A dead son because of her inability to deal with the shame of asking for money.

He knew Joey wouldn't have had the same qualms. They might have looked alike, but they never thought alike. Joey would always have done precisely what his mother desired, no questions asked. She had banked on that.

'Come over, Ronan,' she said. 'We can't talk about this on the phone. Come over and we'll have a proper chat.'

'I'll think about it,' he said, and terminated the call.

He sat there for two full minutes, just thinking. This whole thing had turned to shit, and a big share of the blame rested squarely with his own mother. She was the one who'd sent Joey out to do drug deals. She'd lied from the beginning. Had even tried to continue with the lie over the phone.

It made him wonder how much of her grief was real.

Sure, she had wailed enough. Yelled the house down for hours after the police had delivered the news. The gin bottles were in for a battering after that performance.

But was it genuine?

He'd done most of his own crying in private. Was embarrassed to admit it even now. It was how he'd been brought up. A real man doesn't cry, and especially not in front of others.

But this was his brother, for Christ's sake. And not just any brother, but an identical twin. In their younger days they'd done everything together. And although he hadn't spent as much time with Joey since their dad had died, there had still been a connection there that was stronger than any other he had ever experienced.

And now it was over – all because Joey had been sent on an errand by a mother who didn't even seem to know where it had taken him.

It was only when Ronan heard noises coming from further down the stairwell that he hauled himself to his feet and started plodding downwards.

Two flights below, he met the source of the noise. A big bastard. Hardly dressed for office work – hardly keeping with any kind of fashion either – and yet carrying a briefcase. What was that all about?

The guy looked up the stairs at Ronan. Did a double-take. Came to a full stop, staring.

Ronan gave him his best *What the fuck are you looking at?* glare, but the man just stood there open-mouthed.

Freak, thought Ronan.

He continued to descend. The freak remained frozen on the turning.

'Something to say, lad?' Ronan asked.

'H-hello,' the big man said.

'Hello? That it?'

The man searched for words, and suddenly found a whole avalanche of them. 'Are you well? Have you just come from my flat, from 1204? Did my mum or dad tell you my name? It's Daniel. Daniel Timpson. Did you want to sleep on our sofa? It's comfy, isn't it?'

It was then that Ronan realised the guy had been severely short-changed. After the stress of recent events, this light relief made Ronan smile.

'I'm good, thanks.'

Daniel Timpson broke out a massive grin. 'Would you like to be my friend now? We could watch *Adam-9* together.'

'Another time, maybe.'

Ronan squeezed past Daniel's bulk and started down the next flight of stairs. He could feel the man's eyes on his back. At several points he looked up the central tunnel of the stairwell and caught sight of Daniel way above. He was leaning over the metal bannister, just watching and grinning happily. Like a big soft kid.

25

Daniel practically fell up the stairs. He wasn't built for speed, but he made it to his flat in record time. Too excited to find his key, he banged repeatedly on the door and called for his mother.

When she opened the door, consternation written all over her face, he wanted to dance with her.

'Mum! You and Dad were right. I saw him. He's all fine again.'

He entered the hallway, dropping his briefcase and shucking off his coat.

'What are you talking about? Who did you see?'

'Did he come here again, Mum? I saw him coming down the stairs. He smiled at me. I think we're going to be friends now. He's not upset with me.'

Daniel clomped into the living area. He needed a drink of water after his dash upstairs. In a pint glass. He always drank his water in pints. His dad preferred beer, but Daniel thought it was horrible stuff.

'Daniel, what's going on? Who did you see on the stairs? Who's not upset with you?'

Daniel filled his glass and downed it in one long draught.

'Daniel!' his mother repeated. She sounded a bit annoyed now, and he wasn't sure why, because this was such a good thing.

'What?' he asked.

'Calm down and tell me who you're talking about.'

'The man. The one who was here on our sofa. Joseph Cobb.'

His mother flinched. She seemed strangely alarmed.

'I don't think it was him, Daniel.'

Daniel nodded vigorously. 'It was! You made him all better. He had his sleep on the sofa, and now he's good again. That means I didn't hurt him. Not really.'

'I know you didn't really hurt him, but I'm sure this couldn't have been the same man.'

'It was. He walked right past me on the stairs. He smiled at me and spoke to me.'

'What did he say?'

'Well . . . I asked him if he wanted to watch *Adam-9* with me, and he said he would another time.'

'You shouldn't be inviting people to do that, Daniel. What have we told you about talking to strangers?'

'But he's not a stranger. He's the man we looked after, with the money and the gun. Joseph Cobb.'

'STOP IT, DANIEL! STOP IT!'

Daniel blinked. Why was his mother so angry? What had he done wrong?

'I don't want to hear that name again, okay? I don't care who you saw or who you spoke to, just never talk to me about that man again.'

Daniel could feel himself welling up. Everything was too confusing. He had thought his mother would be delighted by the news, and she was completely the opposite.

'Sorry, Mum,' he said.

She stared at him, then nodded. The doorbell rang.

'That'll be your father. I don't want you to say anything about this to him, all right? You'll only upset him.'

Daniel lowered his head. 'Fine.'

His mother went out into the hallway. Daniel knew he would struggle to keep his amazing news to himself. He was no good with secrets. They always jumped out of his mouth even when he tried as hard as he could to keep them locked up inside.

Don't tell Dad about the man, he commanded himself. Say nothing about Joseph Cobb. Nothing.

And then he heard his mother's scream.

26

It was obvious from her reaction that she knew something.

Ronan didn't think he had a particularly scary face. A bit rough around the edges, maybe, but not piss-your-pants terrifying. Plus, he'd put on his best smile when she'd opened the door. He'd had a good success rate with women when showing them that smile.

And yet here she was, screaming the place down.

She knew something.

He barged into the flat. The woman back-pedalled, her hands to her mouth. Ronan pushed the door closed behind him. Through a doorway on the right of the hall, the big bastard appeared. He began steaming towards Ronan and making a weird ape-like rumble in his throat. Ronan decided to take no chances. The guy might have the IQ of a pea, but he was the size of an ox and could do some serious damage.

Ronan pulled out his gun and pointed it at the man-mountain.

'DANIEL, NO!' the woman shrieked. She grabbed Daniel by the arm and did her best to hold him back. 'NO!'

'Listen to her, Daniel. Stay right there, or I'll blow your fucking brains out.' He switched his aim to the woman. 'And if that makes no difference to you, I'll blow your mum's brains out too. How about that, Daniel? You want me to kill your mum?'

Daniel stood there, panting in indecision.

'Move,' Ronan ordered. 'Back inside. Both of you.'

The woman took the initiative, leading Daniel back through the door he had just exited. Ronan followed them into a large living space. This room looked similar to Barrington's, with an open-plan dining and kitchen area, but Barrington didn't get the hallway or the additional bedroom.

That realisation triggered another thought.

'Who else is here?'

'Nobody,' the woman said.

'The bedrooms. Who's in the bedrooms?'

'Nobody. I swear.'

'You'd better be telling the truth, because if I hear the slightest noise that doesn't come from one of you two, I'm going to start blasting. Do you understand what I'm saying?'

'I understand. I promise you, there's nobody else here.'

'Your husband. Where's he?'

'At . . . at work.'

'When will he be home?'

'Any minute now. I thought it was him at the door.'

'Anyone else live here?'

'No. No, it's just the three of us. Look—'

'Shut up. Sit down.' He used the gun to indicate the sofa. They obeyed. Ronan grabbed one of the wooden chairs from the dining table and sat facing them.

'You,' he said to the woman. 'What's your name?'

'Gemma. Gemma Timpson.'

'Okay, Gemma. I don't have to introduce myself. You already know me.'

'No. I—'

'Don't fucking lie. I saw how you reacted out there. I'm guessing you don't scream every time you open the front door. Your son here knows me, too. I wasn't sure at first, him being a bit slow and everything, but he recognised me on the stairs. Isn't that right, Danny boy? Who am I, Danny? Go on, tell your lying bitch of a mother here who I am.'

'You're ... you're Joseph Cobb. And you shouldn't swear. It's not nice.'

'No, you're right. It's not nice to swear. And you know what else isn't nice? Killing people.'

He turned to the mother again. 'See, Gemma? Even your brain-dead son knows who I am. So why don't you? Why are you so sure that a man called Joey Cobb couldn't possibly be sitting here in your crappy little flat, fit as a fiddle? Why would that be so un-fucking-believable?'

'The police.'

'What?'

'The police. They showed us a photograph of a man called Joey Cobb and said he'd been killed.'

Ronan smiled and shook his head. 'Nice try, Gemma. What about you, Danny? Did you only see a photo too, or was I here in the flesh?'

'You were here.'

'That's right. I was, wasn't I? Only your mum seems to have forgotten all about it. Why's that, Gemma? Why are you lying?'

There was no time for a reply. Ronan heard a key turning in the front door.

'Quiet. Not a peep, or your husband dies.'

Ronan got up from the chair and moved behind the living-room door. He heard a 'Hello' from the hallway, and then saw the back of a male figure come into view.

'Hey, you two! Why the silent treatment?'

Ronan pushed the door away. The figure turned. Ronan aimed the gun at the man's face, saw the immense expression of shock.

'Yeah, that's right. You know me too, you fucking piece of shit. Sit over there with the rest of your shitty family. Do it!'

He watched as the man squeezed onto the sofa.

'What's your name?'

'Scott.'

'Surprised to see me, Scott?'

'I . . . I don't know who you are.'

'You don't? You're as thick as your missus, then. Only Danny here seems to know anything, and he's not exactly working with a full deck, is he?'

Ronan resumed his seat on the wooden chair.

'Right. This is how it's going to work. You tell me everything. No making shit up. Just tell me the truth. Right?'

Scott raised a finger, requesting permission to speak.

'What?'

'I'd like to ask if we can send Daniel to his room. He doesn't understand any of this. It frightens him.'

'He didn't seem that frightened when he was coming at me in your hallway. Besides, he's the only one who's told me anything so far. So the answer is no. Danny stays here, with the rest of his retard family.'

'He's not a retard.'

'No? What about you, though, Scott? Can you string a few sentences together for me?'

Scott stared down at the floor. Licked his lips. Rubbed his hands along his thighs.

'I'm not asking you for a fucking wedding speech here. Just start talking. Let it all out.'

Scott finally looked up at him. 'I'm assuming . . . Joey Cobb. You must be his twin brother, right?'

'Give that man a coconut. So what about Joey?'

'You're not Joey?' Daniel said.

'No, lad. I'm not Joey. Joey's dead. But you knew that already, didn't you?'

'My dad said—'

'Daniel!' Scott interrupted.

'No,' said Ronan. 'Let him speak. Go on, Danny. What did your dad say?'

'He said you – I mean Joey – he said you were going to be okay. He said you – Joey – just needed a nice long rest.'

'A rest? Why?'

Scott took over again. 'What you have to understand is that we didn't intend any of this to happen. It was an accident, okay?'

Ronan stared. An accident? What was he talking about? Did he mean he didn't just *see* what happened? That he might be *responsible* in some way?

'An accident.'

'Yes. He got in the lift with me. He became aggressive. We got into an argument.'

'What about?'

'Nothing. I mean, I think he just didn't like the way I looked at him, or something. I don't really know.'

Ronan considered this. It sounded like Joey. He'd been capable of tearing someone's limbs off just for breathing too heavily.

But then Daniel spoke again. 'It was about the stuff in his bag.'

'Shit,' Scott said.

'Wait,' Ronan said. 'You were there? In the lift?'

'Yes. With my dad. We went to the cinema and then we came home. I don't like the lift, but Dad said—'

'You forgot to mention this little piece of information, Scott. I swear to God, one more lie from you ...' He looked at Daniel again. 'What stuff, Danny? What was in the bag?'

'A gun and some money and some bags of powder. He dropped the bag in the lift.'

'I see. And Joey wasn't happy about you seeing it, is that right?'

Daniel seemed to struggle with putting himself in Joey's shoes. 'I think so. He kept asking us what we saw in his bag.'

'So you told him?'

'Yes. I told the truth, like I always do, but it just made him more and more angry.'

'And then what?'

Scott said, 'I told him to leave my son alone, and he turned on me. It started to get physical. I hit him, and he went down, and ... and he didn't get up again.'

Ronan was on his feet, bringing his Colt to the man's head. 'You . . . you killed my brother? Is that what you're telling me here, Scott? You killed my fucking brother?'

'Dad,' Daniel said. 'That's not right. It was Adam-9, remember? He—'

'Daniel!'

'He came to our rescue. He—'

'*Daniel!*'

'He stopped the bad guy like he always does. Like when those boys were attacking me, and I pressed the button on my Adam-9 briefcase and—'

'DANIEL! STOP!'

The silence was astonishing. It was as though it cleared the room for the truth to make its way in. And there the truth was. In front of Ronan in all its bright, shining glory.

'It was you?' Ronan asked. 'You did it?'

'N-no. It was Adam-9.'

'How? How did he do it?'

'He can use a metal robot arm. It can shoot out a long way. He used the arm to grab Joey's neck and pick him up.'

'You picked him up by the neck?'

'No. Not me. Adam—'

And then Ronan was moving the gun across to Daniel, and he was cocking the hammer and pressing the weapon into the young man's skull, screaming at him while ignoring the pleas of his parents, demanding to know why the fuck he had killed Joey, why did he have to go and do that instead of just telling him what he wanted to hear? And then Scott made a move, tried to grab the gun, and Ronan swiped it across his head, and there was more yelling, Scott being held back by his wife and Ronan putting pressure on the trigger, asking this whole fucking dysfunctional family if they were ready to die, right here and now.

It descended into sobbing and panting and whimpering. Ronan stood over them, a searing rage in his head.

'What then?' he demanded. 'After you killed him? What then?'

'We . . . we brought him into the flat,' Scott said. 'We didn't know what else to do.'

'You didn't think to call an ambulance, maybe? Take him to hospital?'

'There was no point. He was definitely dead.'

'All right, Doctor fucking Timpson, so what did you do next?'

'I . . . I'd rather not say.'

'You'd rather not say? Oh, I'm really sorry about that. I'd hate to ruin your day.'

'My family . . . they don't know the details. I told them I'd take care of it. There was no reason to tell them what I did.'

'So these two don't know? They have no idea?'

'No.'

Ronan looked at Gemma, then at Daniel. 'Here's a nice bedtime story for you, Danny boy. You know what your nice kind daddy did to my brother?'

'Please,' Scott said. 'You don't have to do this.'

Ronan ignored him. 'What Daddy did was to cut up my brother into tiny little pieces and then throw him in the rubbish, along with all the banana peels and rotting vegetables and snotty tissues. That's how he looked after Joey. That's how he made him better.'

A stifled cry from Gemma.

'Yeah. Nasty, huh? This is the man you married. What do you think of him now?'

'I didn't know what else to do,' Scott protested. 'He was dead. It was an accident, but I didn't know if anyone would believe it. I was just trying to protect my son.'

Ronan rounded on him with the gun again. 'Protect him? What kind of sicko are you? My brother is dead because of you. You didn't even have the guts to own up to it. Give me one good reason why I shouldn't shoot you all right now. One good fucking reason.'

He took up a two-handed stance with the gun, training it on each of them. Watched as the parents tried to shrink into the couch.

'You want to protect your son? Then protect him now.'

He moved closer to Daniel. Put the gun to his head once more. The pleading resumed.

But not from Daniel. He just sat there, staring straight up at Ronan. His face was impassive. No fear, no anger, no sorrow. Nothing. And what Ronan realised in that moment was that the target of his wrath didn't understand death, and that it didn't frighten him. He hadn't understood Joey's death either. He had truly believed that his parents had somehow managed to mend him. If Ronan told him that he was actually Joey, and that this had all been one big practical joke, Daniel would believe it.

That's how crazy this situation was.

And Ronan didn't know how to process it.

In his head, it would have been Barrington Daley or some other low-life who had murdered Joey. That was the world he and Joey had lived in. Live by the sword and die by the sword. And Ronan would have found that piece of shit and executed him, and everything would have been right again. Balance would have been restored.

But this?

This family weren't even in the game. They hadn't killed Joey to rip him off or for revenge. All that had happened was that they accidentally stepped on the toes of a man who objected to it. It was hard to despise them for that. Even harder to justify ending their days, despite what they had done to cover up their actions.

'Don't move,' Ronan told them. 'Not one inch.'

He moved to the farthest point in the room, on the other side of the dining table, where he could still see the family. He took out his phone and made a call.

'It's me,' he said in a subdued voice. 'I've found them. I know who killed Joey.'

27

'Who? Who did it? Barrington Daley? I want that bastard's head on a plate.'

'It wasn't Barrington.'

'Then who?'

'It was . . . it was a family.'

'A f— What do you mean, a family? Do you mean like the mafia?'

'No. An ordinary family. They've got this kid. He's not all there.'

'You mean a retard?'

'Yeah. It was an accident.'

'Ronan, lad, what the fuck are you talking about? Joey was accidentally killed by some window-licker?'

'Yeah. That's about it.'

'Really? Then how come my son ended up in a dozen pieces on a landfill site? Are you going to tell me that was an accident too?'

'No. They tried to cover it up. They didn't want the lad to get into trouble.'

'Yeah, well that worked well, didn't it? Because now he's neck-deep in shit. What did you do to them?'

'What do you mean?'

'These people who murdered your twin brother. What did you do to them?'

'Nothing yet. I'm looking at them now. I'm in their flat.'

'I see. So you're having tea and cake with them, is that it?'

'Mam, don't be like that. I'm trying—'

'Like what? How should I be? You've found the people who murdered Joey and they're just sitting there? What's the plan here, Ronan?'

'That's why I'm ringing you.' He lowered his voice even further. 'I don't know what to do with them.'

She sighed. 'Do I have to state the bleeding obvious, Ronan?'

He wondered how bad it would be. Broken bones? A long stay in hospital? And who? All of them? Or just make an example of the son?

He really didn't feel comfortable with beating the shit out of a disabled lad, even one built like a shed.

'They owe me,' his mother said.

'What?'

'You heard. Joey started out with twenty-five grand's worth of product on him. I want it back. Ask them what they did with it. Go on, ask them!'

Ronan lowered the phone as he walked over to the sofa. He pointed the gun at Scott again.

'The stuff that was in Joey's bag. The money and the bags of powder. What did you do with it?'

'We . . . I threw it away, along with . . . along with everything else.'

'Liar! All that money, and you just threw it away? I don't fucking believe you.'

'Please! It's the truth. We thought it might be traceable. Plus, we didn't think we should make money out of what happened. It wouldn't be right.'

Wouldn't be right, Ronan thought. Listen to him. Wouldn't be right. Like anyone else would give a shit about right or wrong when they're holding that much cash in their hands. It just shows how screwed-up this whole situation is.

Ronan returned to his corner of the room. 'Did you hear that? They tossed it.'

'Doesn't change anything.'

'What do you mean? They haven't got—'

'I'm not interested! I want it back. I don't care how they get it, but I want my money. They owe me.'

Ronan wanted to puke. This was no longer about Joey. It was about money. That was the only thing concerning her. Maybe it always had been.

He hung up. Went back to the family. The family that looked as though they hardly had two pennies to rub together.

'You owe me.'

They looked at him blankly.

'The cash and the drugs. Twenty-five grand's worth. I want it back.'

'We can't,' Scott said. 'I just told you. We got rid of it.'

'That's your problem. I want my twenty-five thousand back. How you get it is up to you.'

'That's crazy!'

Ronan thrust the gun towards him, and he backed down.

'Look around you,' Scott said. 'We don't have anywhere near that amount of money.'

'You should have thought of that before you killed my brother.'

'Look, I'm sorry, okay? I'm sorry for what happened to your brother. But what's done is done, and—'

'No! It's not done. Not until you pay for what you did. Now, either you get me my money or I tell the police exactly what you and your son did. Your choice.'

'Please! We haven't got money like that.'

'Take out a loan. Remortgage. Sell your car. Rob a bank. I don't give a shit what you do as long as you pay up.'

'We can't get a loan for that amount. And the flat is rented. My car isn't—'

'Shut up. What's your phone number?'

'What?'

'Your phone number. What is it?'

Scott told him, and he typed it into his contacts.

'You've got twenty-four hours,' Ronan said. 'I'll call you tomorrow, and I'll tell you where to meet me with the money. If you don't show up, I'm tipping off the cops.'

'No. Please. I—'

'Twenty-four hours. Don't let me down. If you really want to protect your lad, you'll do what I say. And if the name Joey Cobb still sends shivers up your spine, then wait till you see what Ronan Cobb can do.'

And then Ronan left, a sour taste in his mouth.

28

Scott sat in numb disbelief. It was as though a hurricane had just torn through their home, devastating their lives.

Gemma stood and wandered over to the window, her back to her family. Scott stood up too.

'Gem . . .'

'You said it was over.'

'I know. I know what I said. But—'

She whirled on him. 'YOU SAID YOU'D SORT IT ALL OUT!'

He was conscious of Daniel still on the sofa, and he turned to him.

'Go to your room, Daniel.'

Daniel rose. The expression on his face was hard to read. He seemed to be wrestling with his emotions.

'You lied to me,' Daniel said.

'What? No. I didn't—'

'You did! You told me you made the man better, but you didn't make him better. He's dead, and now his brother is really upset with me.'

'All right, Daniel. Let's talk about this later, okay? I'll explain everything.'

But Daniel was already storming out of the room. 'You lied to me,' he said again. Seconds later, his bedroom door was slammed shut.

Shit, Scott thought. Now everyone hates me.

He tried again with his wife. 'Gem . . .'

'You were wrong, Scott.'

'Wrong? What about?'

'We should have gone to the police straight away. We should have told them exactly what had happened.'

'We discussed all this. We made a decision. We agreed.'

'I don't care what we agreed. I didn't expect this to happen. You promised me it wouldn't. And now we've got both the police and criminals breathing down our neck. We have to tell the truth.'

'No. No we don't.'

'Scott—'

'No, Gemma. It's too late for that. We have to see it out.'

'See what out? You heard the brother. They want money. Money we haven't got. Why didn't you listen to me about hanging on to the money?'

Scott stepped towards her, but she backed away. 'We're not criminals, Gem. It wouldn't have been right to keep the money. You know that.'

'But if you'd kept it—'

'I know. But I didn't, and there's no changing that. We have to make the best of a bad situation.'

She stared at him in disbelief. 'A bad situation? It's an *impossible* situation. You heard that scumbag. When we don't pay him, he'll go to the police. We need to own up before he drops us in it. It'll go in our favour.'

'Gemma. Listen to me. It won't come to that. I'll pay him what I can, and I'll make him understand that it's all we have.'

Her face became suddenly grave. 'Wait a minute. Pay him what you can? What exactly do you mean?'

'Well, we've a bit put by, and—'

'Hold on. You're talking about our savings? You want to give away all of our savings?'

'I don't think we have a choice.'

'No. We worked our fingers to the bone for that money, Scott. Daniel's benefits are in there. Some of that money belongs to him.'

'I know. But this will be *for* him. It'll be for all of us.'

'It's our holiday fund. Our Christmas money.'

'Then we'll have a smaller Christmas this year, and a holiday at home next year.'

'And when the car breaks down? Or something else goes wrong?'

'We'll manage. I'll ask Gavin if he can throw more work my way, or I'll get a weekend job. I'll build up our savings again.'

She looked at him long and hard, and then she shook her head.

'What?' he asked.

'You know what really upsets me about all this? It's not about what you did to protect Daniel. It's not even about how you got rid of the body. What's really pissing me off now is that you're still trying to make all the decisions by yourself. This is *our* money you're talking about, Scott. *Ours*. That makes this a joint decision.'

He knew she was right. With primeval emotions running high, he'd reverted to primeval behaviour.

'Okay,' he said. 'I'm sorry. I was just—'

'I know what you were trying to do. But just try to bear in mind that this affects all of us.'

He showed her a smile of surrender. 'All right. So what's *our* decision?'

She looked down at the floor, then raised her head again. 'I think it's not going to work. I think that Ronan Cobb is evil, and that he's not going to rest until he gets his twenty-five grand.' She paused. 'That said, I don't know what else we can do.'

'So, do I pay him what we've got?'

'Yes. On one condition.'

'Which is?'

'That you don't let him take your life in part-payment.'

Scott couldn't find another smile. The thought had already occurred to him.

'Done,' he said.

She nodded. 'And just remember we're all in this together. Speaking of which, there's another member of the family you need to make it up with.'

Scott hugged and kissed her, then went out to Daniel's bedroom. He knocked and entered. Daniel was sitting on his bed. Scott approached cautiously and sat next to him, exactly as he had done the other day after Daniel had been attacked by the gang of schoolboys.

'You okay?' he asked.

'Not really. I'm a bit upset.'

'I can see that. And I can understand why.'

'You lied to me.'

'Yes, I did. And I'm sorry. I was just trying to help you.'

'I don't feel helped.'

'No, but that's what I was doing. That man. Joey Cobb. He was dead. I didn't want you to know that. If I'd told you the truth, you would have felt terrible, wouldn't you?'

Daniel nodded. 'I suppose so. But . . .'

'But what, Daniel?'

'It was Adam-9. He had to help you. He can shoot out a long arm from his briefcase. Remember? Remember when he used it on the Quark Monster? He was tied up, but he managed to reach the button on his briefcase—'

'Yes, Daniel. I remember that one.'

'And that's what happened. Adam-9 saved you.'

'Yes. Yes, you— he did. And I'm really grateful.'

'But I didn't know the man got killed.'

'No. I know you didn't.'

'It makes me sad.'

'Yes.'

'And his brother, too. Ronan? Is that his name?'

'Yes.'

'He's sad. And very angry.'

'He is. But he'll get over it.'

'Are you sure?'

'Yes. I've just discussed it with your mother, and—'

'You were shouting. Arguing.'

'Yes, we were. But we've sorted it out now. We're fine again. I'm going to get some money tomorrow and give it to Ronan, and he'll be happy again.'

'He won't come back here, will he? He scares me.'

'No, he won't come back. I'll make sure of it.'

They sat in silence for a while, each lost in their own, very different thoughts.

'Can I ask you a favour?' Scott said.

Daniel nodded. 'Of course you can.'

'Can I ask you not to talk to anyone about this?'

'About Ronan?'

'Yes. And also about his brother, and what happened to him when we got out of the lift.'

'I'm not supposed to tell lies.'

'I'm not asking you to lie. I just want you not to talk about it to anyone. That's not the same as a lie, is it? If you're not talking about it, you can't be lying.'

Daniel thought some more. 'Okay. I'll try.'

'Thank you, Daniel.'

'You're welcome.'

Scott went to place his hand on Daniel's back, but paused. He sensed that his son didn't want human contact right now.

He stood up and walked towards the door.

'Dad?'

'Yes?'

'Is it true what the man said? Did you really chop his brother up into tiny little pieces?'

Scott stared into his son's eyes. He would have preferred not to give an answer, because that would be better than lying. Practise what you preach.

'No. Of course not. I think he must have got broken up in the bin lorry.'

Daniel said nothing more, but Scott felt less than worthless.

29

Wednesday morning in the briefing room. Seated around the long table, an array of detectives who didn't seem to have a clue what was going on. Hannah could feel herself sinking into despondency.

'Are you seriously telling me,' she said, 'that not a single person in the whole of that block of flats caught even the merest glimpse of Joey Cobb entering or leaving the building?'

The DC who had broken the news seemed to shrivel in his chair. 'Well, not exactly. It's more accurate to say that nobody is owning up to seeing him.'

'Amounts to the same bloody thing, Simon. Unless you've got some foolproof way of telling us who might be lying, we may as well not have spent all of our time interviewing the occupants of Erskine Court, for all the good it's done us.' She paused while she allowed her blood pressure to return to normal. 'What about the taxi driver?'

Somewhat tentatively, another detective spoke up. 'I spoke to him again. He remembers very little about the conversation he had with Joey. Most of what he does remember was about football.'

'Great. So where does that leave us?'

'We've widened the search,' said Marcel. 'It's perfectly possible that no one we spoke to in Erskine Court was lying. Maybe they really didn't see him. We know he went in there, but maybe he came out again, just like Barrington Daley said. That cell mast signal covers a pretty wide radius. Cobb could have been killed in any of a number of buildings near the flats.'

Hannah knew he was right, of course, but it did nothing to lighten her mood. A larger search area was bad news. It meant more buildings to visit, more people to interview. With zero chance of gaining additional resources to work on the murder of a victim that many saw as unworthy of their attention, it seemed to her that any hopes of solving this case were fading fast.

She wished now that she'd taken more painkillers before the meeting. Her whole body seemed to be throbbing to a steady beat. She had noticed how the eyes of her fellow officers were constantly drawn to the swelling on her forehead.

'What about Cobb's associates?' she asked.

'We're talking to them again, but it's not looking good. Some refuse to cooperate. Those who do speak to us are probably lying through their teeth. Others have gone into hiding.'

'Why? Guilty consciences? You think we should put more effort into finding them?'

Marcel looked doubtful. 'I think they're just scared. The word going around is that this is a gang thing. Someone is out to upset a very big apple cart. People don't want to be around when it all comes crashing down.'

'But what they don't know is that we've got Cobb's money and drugs. That tells me it's probably not gang related.'

'Unless that's exactly what they want us to believe.'

Hannah raised her eyebrows. 'You think they're that clever? Most of the pushers I've met think IQ is a quiz show.'

'True, but there are exceptions.'

'I don't buy it. These are greedy bastards. I don't care how smart they are, put twenty-five grand in front of them and it's like showing the ring to Gollum. And even if one of them does have an IQ in triple figures, why would he think that tossing away all that cash was the most obvious way of throwing us off his scent? What kind of imaginary perpetrator was he hoping to plant in our minds? Someone who quite happily murders and dismembers his victims but has qualms about taking their money? Who the hell fits a profile like that?'

'But you still want us to follow up on Cobb's associates?'

'Absolutely. They were a part of his life. They knew his routine, where he went, who he spoke to. Stay on their backs.' She surveyed the team. 'Anything else? Give me something positive, guys, because this is starting to look bleaker than Marcel's love life.'

She got a laugh, but also hesitation in volunteering information. Eventually, Trisha Lacey raised a finger.

'CCTV,' she said. 'We've pulled in footage from the waste tip, and also from cameras lining the route indicated by the cell mast data.'

'Good. And?'

'We're analysing it as quickly as we can.' Trisha tapped the keys on the computer in front of her, and some grainy images appeared on a large wall monitor. It showed a long line of cars. 'This is the view at the entrance to the tip. Sunday is one of their busiest days, so we've got a lot of vehicles to check.'

'What about inside the premises? Can we see people getting out of their cars?'

'Afraid not. This is all we have.'

Hannah sighed. 'Okay, keep at it. I want you to talk to the owners of every single vehicle that visited that site. One of them has to be our killer.'

30

£4,327.52.

That's how much they had in their savings account.

Scott had checked. First thing he did after arriving at the garage that Wednesday morning.

It came as a shock. He'd thought they had more. Not a lot more, admittedly, but a rounder, fuller figure. Something a little less undernourished.

Ronan wasn't going to like it. There was no way to dress up four thousand pounds to look like twenty-five.

Shit.

But facts were facts. What more could he do? They owned nothing of any real worth. Their biggest possession was the car, but that was an old rust-bucket, and an essential one at that. He wasn't about to risk asking Gemma to sell off her jewellery. Given her current state of mind, she'd probably castrate him.

He worried about it all morning. Throwing himself into his work didn't help. He saw every tyre pressure as 4327.52. Every car had travelled 4327.52 miles. Every invoice he prepared was for £4,327.52.

Shit and arseholes.

If only he had listened to Gemma and hung on to the money. Maybe the drugs too. Just for a while, until the dust had settled. It would have made life so much easier. He should have known that someone would come looking for it. Hauls like that don't get written off. Gangsters aren't known for their devil-may-care attitude. They always want what they see as theirs.

If he'd kept the backpack, he could have simply handed it over to Ronan, and all would be well now. He wouldn't be fretting over the paltry contents of his savings account.

But there was no use crying over spilt milk.

Spilt blood was another matter.

He had put his family in danger. Perhaps they still were, despite all his reassurances to them.

But no, he thought. It doesn't do to think like that. Be positive. Talk to Ronan, man to man. Make him see that you're on your uppers, that you have nothing left to give. Appeal to his humanity. He'll understand.

No, he won't. He'll take one look at your measly four grand and then he'll kill you. And after that he'll go after your family. This isn't going to work.

Shit and arseholes and bollocks.

Scott continued to work. Continued to suffer.

When it came to his lunch break, he told Gavin that he had to dash to the bank. He tried to make it sound like a casual errand, but he felt as though he was establishing an alibi. Gavin munched on his sandwich, apparently oblivious.

When he arrived at the bank, Scott stood outside for a while. This felt so wrong. He was in his oil-stained overalls, but he thought he might as well be wearing a black-and-white striped shirt and a mask.

He took a deep breath and went in. At this time of day, there was a lengthy queue. As he waited his turn, he had to fight to keep his eyes from straying to the security cameras.

Stop it, he told himself. You're doing nothing wrong. Nothing to feel guilty about.

The cashier was young and smiley, her blonde hair tied up in a ponytail. When he told her he wanted to withdraw all the money from his account, he expected her to drop the affability and begin setting off alarms. But she didn't. She simply packaged up the money in an envelope, handed it over and wished him a pleasant afternoon.

Just like that. His life savings, and she couldn't even be bothered to question it.

Which said it all about the magnitude of the sum involved. Water off a duck's back to them.

Ronan's going to feel the same way, he thought. The man probably has more than this in his back pocket.

Be positive. Beg for mercy if you have to, but don't give up before you've even tried.

He left the bank and went back to work, the envelope tucked into a pocket beneath his overalls. Throughout the afternoon he kept pressing his hand to the bulge to make sure it was still there, that virtually every penny he had worked for hadn't simply vanished.

To the bank it might be nothing. To Ronan it might be nothing.

To Scott and his family it was everything.

31

Because Daniel had never seen this bus driver before, he tried to make a good impression. He held up his pass right in front of him and said, 'Hello, Mr Bus Driver. My name's Daniel Timpson and I need to get off this bus when we get to Askew Drive, opposite Asda.' His mum had told him to introduce himself that way, because drivers were usually helpful. This one wasn't. This one just shook his head and scowled, making Daniel wonder if he'd said the wrong thing.

He craned his neck in search of a seat. He liked to sit at the front, but those benches were occupied. It was pretty full downstairs, but he never ventured upstairs – not since that time he was teased by some girls.

He moved along the aisle. Only one unoccupied seat. Well, actually it was occupied by a woman's bag, but he knew that bags don't get their own seats because they don't buy tickets.

'Excuse me,' Daniel said. 'Do you mind if I sit here?'

He put it as politely as he could, but the woman glared at him as if he'd just spat on her.

She picked up the bag, placed it on her lap, sighed heavily.

Daniel lowered himself onto the now-vacant seat. He tried

as hard as he could to obey The Rule, but he was large and it was a tight space, and when he did accidentally brush against her, she tutted loudly and shuffled closer to the window.

Daniel didn't get his Adam-9 comic out. He was too worried about knocking against the woman again. Instead, he sat in silence for the whole journey and thought about what his life was like now.

It made him miserable.

For one thing, it hurt that his father had lied. And it wasn't just a little lie, not like that time he had an injection and his dad said it wouldn't hurt and it did. This lie was about saying a man was alive when he wasn't. Joseph Cobb was dead all along, and his dad had known it.

And if he could lie about that, then maybe he'd also lied about cutting Joseph Cobb into tiny pieces. He'd told Daniel he hadn't done it, but that's not what he'd said when Ronan Cobb had asked him.

He didn't want to believe that his dad could do something like that.

And then there was the money.

His dad had said he was going to give Ronan money so that he'd never come back and frighten them again.

But what money? Daniel's parents were always complaining that they didn't have any. His dad had said the same thing to Ronan (unless he was lying again). So where would they get it from?

Ronan had talked about twenty-five grand. Daniel didn't know how much that was, exactly, but he was convinced it was a lot.

There was also the bad feeling at home.

Mum and Dad snapping at each other. Both of them snapping at him. He couldn't recall a time when it had been as bad as this. Everyone angry and upset.

He just wanted it all to go back to the way it was.

Why hadn't he walked up the stairs of Erskine Court like he always did, instead of listening to his dad? And why did Joseph Cobb have to get into their lift?

When Daniel rose to leave the bus, the woman next to him slammed her bag back onto his seat. He felt awful for making her so annoyed.

As the bus squealed to a halt and the doors opened, Daniel turned to issue his customary thanks, but the driver stared straight ahead, not acknowledging his presence. Daniel closed his mouth without a word, then stepped down onto the pavement. Behind him, the doors slapped shut so quickly they almost trapped his briefcase.

On the busy main road, he felt the eyes of other pedestrians on him. As though they were thinking he'd committed a terrible crime.

Like killing a man.

Anxious to escape the crowds, he hurried onto Marlborough Road. It was quieter here, and he was able to think, but actually he didn't like the thoughts that were racing through his mind. They frightened him.

He was so preoccupied, he forgot to cross over before he reached Dirty Man's house. The man's dog – a small, scruffy amalgam of fur and teeth – ran straight out at Daniel, yapping and snarling, and Daniel had to hop out onto the road to avoid it, even though he knew it was a dangerous thing to do, but probably not as dangerous as the dog. Dirty Man was in his doorway, leaning against the jamb, a cigarette in his hand. He was grinning, and Daniel could see the glint of one gold tooth.

As he marched more quickly down the street, his heart pounding furiously, all he could think about was Perry – the dog that had frightened him that other time, the dog he had killed – and that made him even more upset.

He turned right onto Pickford Avenue. Mrs Romford was out again today, cleaning her car. She was bent over, her head inside the vehicle as she ran a hand-held vacuum cleaner over the driver's seat. Daniel decided to walk straight past. He wasn't sure why, but he didn't want to get into a conversation with her today.

He was only a couple of metres ahead of the car when the vacuum cleaner was turned off and Mrs Romford called out to him.

'Yoo-hoo! Daniel!'

Daniel halted. He knew he couldn't keep walking because that would be rude and it might upset Mrs Romford and it would be just another bad thing for him to think about.

He turned and said, 'Hello, Mrs Romford. How are you today?' And he said it in the brightest, breeziest way he could muster because he knew that it usually made people happy, even though it hadn't worked on the bus earlier.

'I'm fine, thank you, Daniel. And how's your dad?'

Daniel opened and closed his mouth a couple of times as he considered and rejected replies. His immediate urge was to say something like, *Well, my dad's not very happy because he had to get rid of a dead body and I think he might have chopped him into pieces and now the dead man's brother wants money from my dad, and he hasn't got any.* He didn't say any of that because his parents had made it clear that they didn't want him to tell people, but at the same time he didn't want to lie to Mrs Romford, and so he said simply, and after a long delay, 'He's very busy.'

'I'll bet he is. And what about you? You must be very excited.'

'Why?'

'Because a little bird told me that it's someone's birthday soon.'

This puzzled Daniel for two reasons. First, he didn't understand how a bird could tell her anything, and second, he'd already told her that it was his birthday very soon. He distinctly remembered doing so when she was polishing her letterbox.

'Yes,' he said. 'We'll be having chippy chips.' He'd already told her that too, but her memory didn't seem to be working very well.

Not that he was particularly looking forward to chippy chips at the moment. Or even his birthday, for that matter.

'How old will you be?'

'I'll be twenty-three.'

'Twenty-three? My, you're in your prime, Daniel. You'll have all the girls after you soon.'

'I hope not. They teased me on the bus.'

'That's probably because they liked you. Girls do that kind of thing.'

'No, I think it's because I had a sticker on my back that said "I'm Stupid". Laurence put it there.'

She laughed. 'Well, I'm sure they'll come calling for other reasons soon. Wouldn't you like to have a girlfriend?'

He gave it some thought. It wasn't something he'd really considered before. He quite liked the idea of having someone to share his problems with. Someone to walk with and hold hands with and maybe hug and kiss and play games with and . . .

And then he remembered The Rule, and knew it was impossible. He would never have what everyone else took for granted.

'No,' he said. 'I don't want a girlfriend.'

'Hmm,' Mrs Romford said. 'We'll see. You'll change your mind one day.'

No, he thought. I won't change my mind.

'I have to go home now,' he said. 'My mum will be waiting.'

'Okay, then. You do that. Tell your dad I said hello.'

He turned and continued on his journey home, but his legs seemed heavier, and everything inside him felt tight.

Erskine Court loomed into view. Probably for the first time ever, he wasn't sure he wanted to go home. But then he remembered all the things that went wrong whenever he was out in the world, having to deal with other people.

He had a sudden premonition that the schoolboys would appear again, and that they would throw their football at him and call him names, and he wondered whether he could stop himself from hurting them, because that's what he seemed to do now, and even if he could rely on Adam-9 to intervene he wasn't certain that would be any better.

He wanted to swear, but he didn't because he knew that swearing was a really bad thing. Instead he ran. Despite his heavy legs and the tightness in his chest and the fact that he didn't want to be around parents that argued or lied to him or chopped people up, he ran home, craving the safety of his bedroom, where he wouldn't have to worry about The Rule and how he was possibly going to get through the rest of his life without breaking it again.

32

To Scott, the flat seemed filled with tension, as though everything and everyone in it were connected in a web of taut elastic, one wrong move having the potential to cause it all to snap and fly around in a maelstrom. Gemma was standing in the centre of it, as if afraid to set it off.

'You okay?' he asked.

'I'm surviving. About all I can do until this is over.'

'Where's Daniel?'

'In his room. Again.'

It was said with regret rather than accusation, but Scott couldn't stop the feeling of responsibility rearing inside him.

'Is he okay?'

'Not really. He has his problems, Scott, but he's not an idiot. He knows when something's going on.'

He sighed. 'It's going to be okay. Seriously. It'll all work out.'

'Hmm,' she said. Non-committal. Scared.

He pulled the envelope from his backpack and placed it on the dining table.

Gemma stared at it. 'What's that?'

'The money.'

'In there? How much?'

'Just over four thousand, three hundred.'

She sat down and opened the envelope. Pulled out the bundles of cash.

'It doesn't look a lot, does it?'

'I suppose not. But it's all relative, isn't it? To us, that's a hell of a lot of money. I'm hoping I can get Ronan Cobb to see it that way.'

'And if he doesn't?'

Scott had no answer.

'If he doesn't, Scott? What then?'

Scott's phone rang. He took it from his pocket and looked at the screen. An unrecognised number. He knew who it would be.

'Hello.'

'It's me. You get the money?'

Scott stared down at the pitifully inadequate sum on the table. 'I got it.'

'Good. Then we need to meet.'

'Okay. Where?'

'Get a pen.'

'Wait.' Scott went to the sideboard and pulled out a pen and notepad. 'Go ahead.'

He listened and wrote down the directions. The route took him out of town, at least a twenty-five-minute drive.

'When you get to Shiverton Lane, call me back. I'll tell you the last bit then.'

'Why not tell me now?'

'I'm making sure you don't try to do anything stupid. I'll be able to see everything you do from there.'

'I'm not planning to set any traps if that's what you mean. I just want to get this over with.'

'Fine. Let's do that. You clear about where you're going?'

'I think so. What time are we meeting?'

'Midnight. On the dot.'

'Midnight?' He saw the alarm on Gemma's face. 'Why so late?'

'Because I say so. Be there, alone.'

He hung up. Scott lowered his phone and stared at Gemma. She turned the notepad towards her.

'Where the hell is he sending you?'

'Miles away. Middle of nowhere.'

'And you're going? In the middle of the night?'

'What choice do I have? He's calling all the shots.'

'Not if you don't let him. Call him back. Tell him he needs to come here for the money.'

'He won't agree to that. He'll think it's a trap.'

'Then tell him you want to meet somewhere more public.'

'I can't do that either. It'll piss him off. Just ... let me do this, okay? Let me pay him what we can afford, and then we can get on with our lives.'

'Well, then I'm coming with you. That little shit doesn't scare me.'

He looked at her, and knew that she was definitely scared, just as he was.

'I wish you could, Gem. I'd like nothing better than to watch you kick the crap out of the little bastard. But you know we can't do that. He said to come alone. Besides, you need to be with Daniel.'

She hesitated for a few seconds. 'You said something before. About a trap.'

'What do you mean?'

'Why can't we do that? Set a trap. We go to the police and we tell them everything. We get them to follow you, and then they catch him red-handed.'

'It won't work, Gem. He said he'll be watching me when I get to – what's it called? – Shiverton Lane. He'll be able to see everything I do. Do you really trust the police enough not to fuck everything up? And what if they *do* catch him? What then? You think we'll be safe? You think his family or one of his druggie friends won't come after us? And, to be honest, getting to us probably won't be all that difficult when we're sitting in a prison cell for the things we did to Ronan's brother.'

He stopped when he realised how loud he was getting. He leaned towards Gemma and lowered his voice. 'This is our only option. You know that. Let me try.'

She turned shimmering eyes to his. 'I know it's our only option. Deep down, I know that. I just thought … I was hoping one of us might come up with another way out.'

'Me too. I've been thinking about it all day, and I don't have any other answers.'

'It's not fair, is it? We do everything by the book. We work our fingers to the bone. We do what we can for Daniel. Why do these horrible things happen to us? Why can't they happen to someone evil?'

'I don't know. Some people always have it harder than others. It's just the way it is. Maybe it'll make us better people.'

'I don't want you to go, Scott. I don't want you to meet that man.'

'I know. I don't want to go, either. But I have to.'

She jumped into his arms then. Straight out of her chair and into a fierce embrace. Held him like she never intended to release him again.

'Is everything all right?'

This from Daniel, standing in the doorway.

Gemma turned away, both to hide her upset and to scoop the money furtively back into the envelope. Scott forced a smile onto his lips.

'Hey, bud! How were things at the centre today?'

'Okay. I didn't do much. Just some drawing.'

His spirit was clearly low, his frame sagging. It tightened a noose around Scott's heart.

'Hey, suppose we have bacon and eggs and beans for tea? Fancy that?'

'With waffles?'

'We can have waffles. Are you up for that?'

Daniel nodded. 'That would be nice. Can I put the telly on?'

'Sure. Go ahead.'

He watched his son lumber to the sofa and fiddle with the remote, then he turned to Gemma again.

'Go and sit with Daniel,' he said. 'I'll get the tea on.'

He watched her drift away. There was nothing left to discuss.

The evening came and went, but the tension only increased. Untasted mouthfuls of a meal were separated by perfunctory snippets of conversation. When Scott packed Daniel off to bed, he broke The Rule and hugged him, knowing that he might never get a chance to do so again, but at the same time telling himself not to be so melodramatic, that it would all work out. Daniel seemed confused, panicked by the cocktail of emotions in himself and his parents.

After that came empty hours in front of the television, Scott and Gemma together but separate, each cocooned in their own solemn thoughts. He kept checking his watch, and was aware that Gemma side-eyed him each time.

When it seemed she could bear it no longer, she said, 'I'm going to bed.'

'It's only ten o'clock.'

'I don't want to see you leave. I want you to go out quietly, and then come back to me and climb into bed and tell me everything has been sorted out.'

'Gemma, don't worry. It'll be okay.'

'I *do* worry. I haven't stopped worrying since you brought Joey Cobb into our home. I need it to stop now.'

She leaned in to kiss Scott long and hard, then stood up. 'You stay safe. No heroics. No stupidity. I don't care about the money. I just want us all to be together again.'

He watched her disappear, and felt lonelier than he ever had in his life, the weight of what was to happen sitting heavily on his shoulders.

33

Rather than trust the directions he had hastily scribbled down earlier, Scott used a navigation app on his phone to direct him to Shiverton Lane. He was truly out in the sticks now. The occasional cottage or farmhouse, but mostly fields of cows and sheep, ghostly statues in the silver moonlight.

He slowed the car and pulled onto a grass verge, then took out his phone and called Ronan. He answered immediately.

'Yeah?'

'It's me. Scott. I'm on Shiverton Lane, like you said.'

'Okay, good. Have you seen a sign for Hamley Mill yet?'

'I don't think so. I've pulled over.'

'Start driving again. Put your phone on speaker and keep the line open. Look out for a brown sign.'

Scott did as he was told. He drove slowly, his eyes peeled. A Mercedes zoomed up behind him and then overtook, disappearing within seconds. After that, there was no traffic.

'You're getting close,' Ronan said. 'Slow down.'

Braking to a crawl, Scott wondered how it was possible for Ronan to see him. Where the hell was he hiding?

'I see it now,' he said. 'You want me to take the turn-off?'

'No. Drive about another hundred yards, then pull in and turn off your engine.'

Scott took a wild guess at the hundred-yard distance, then found the most level piece of verge he could before stopping the car.

'Perfect,' Ronan said.

'What now?'

'Get out of the car.'

Scott picked up his backpack and phone from the passenger seat, then climbed out. He turned off his phone's speaker and put the device to his ear.

'What now?'

'You should see an entrance to a pathway on the other side of the road.'

'I see it.'

'Then start walking. I'll be waiting for you. Don't forget the money.'

Scott locked up the car and slipped his arms through the straps of the backpack. It was overkill for all it contained, but he didn't want Ronan suspecting the truth before he'd had a chance to talk things over with him.

He crossed the lane and started up the path. To his right were tall hedgerows. On his left, barbed wire bordered a huge field. In the far distance he could just make out the lighted windows of a house – the nearest signs of civilisation and a possible sanctuary if he needed it.

The path became ever steeper. After a few minutes, he paused and looked back the way he had come. He saw now that anyone up here would have an excellent view of car headlights on the lane. It would have been impossible to bring along a posse of police officers without being spotted. Ronan had done his homework.

A heavy snort made Scott leap away. He landed in a ditch, dropping his phone.

'Shit.'

He looked up and saw a horse staring at him over the hedgerow, a glint of amusement in its eyes. He wondered if the nag made a habit of alarming people like that.

He found his phone, but it was only after dusting himself off that he became aware of a tinny voice emanating from it. He brought it to his ear again.

'Scott! Are you there?'

'I'm here.'

'Where the hell did you go? All you've got to do is follow a fucking path.'

'It's okay. I'm here.'

'All right, then. Have you seen a stile on your left yet?'

'A what?'

'A stile. A set of wooden steps.'

'No . . . Wait. Yes. I see it.'

'Climb over it, into the field.'

'Okay. Done.'

'You see the hill? With the big tree on top of it? Look in that direction.'

Scott looked. He saw several brief flashes of a torch.

'I see you.'

'Walk towards me.'

Scott began walking again. The ground itself was fairly dry

and firm, but he grimaced every time one of his feet sank into what was presumably a huge cowpat. He wished he'd worn wellington boots.

The hill was much steeper than the path, and his breathing became heavier as he ascended. Ahead, he thought he could see a figure stepping out from beneath the canopy of the ancient tree. He started going over the lines of dialogue in his head – the words he'd been shaping and rehearsing all day. The words that might just save his life, and the lives of his family.

His legs became heavier. The pack on his back became heavier. He didn't want to be here. He didn't know if he would ever leave.

The torch came on again, shining directly into Scott's eyes. He halted. He could hear himself panting.

'Hello, Scott.'

Ronan came down the slope towards him. When he was just feet away, he flicked off the torch. The light of the moon was enough for Scott to pick out the features that belonged simultaneously to one who had died and one who would kill. Either apparition was terrifying.

'You got something for me?' Ronan asked.

Scott slipped one of the straps of the backpack from his shoulder, but kept the other in place. He tried to act as though his load was much more of a burden than it was.

'Before we do this, I want you to know that you're taking everything from us. This is all we have in the world. I hope you'll understand that we're not trying to—'

'Cut the crap, Scott.'

'W-what?' He hadn't anticipated an interruption. Heartfelt

speeches weren't supposed to be interrupted, especially when they involved appeals to humanity.

'Just give me the fucking money.'

Apparently, humanity wasn't Ronan Cobb's strong point.

Scott kneeled on the ground while he opened the backpack. He withdrew the thick envelope, then stood again and held it out towards Ronan.

Ronan put his torch back on, as if he needed the additional light to convince his disbelieving eyes.

'Is that it? What else is in the bag?'

'My flask. And my sandwich box.'

'A flask and— Fucking hell, did you think we were going to have a picnic? Give me that fucking envelope.'

He came over to Scott, snatched the package, walked back to his spot. He tore into the envelope and started pulling out its contents.

'How much is here?'

'Four thousand, three hundred and twenty-seven pounds and 52p.'

'Four thousand, three hundred and twenty-seven pounds? Are you—?'

'And 52p.'

'Oh, 52p! Well, that makes all the difference, doesn't it? I can do a lot with fifty-two fucking pence. For a minute there, I thought you were trying to take the piss. But now I know you're serious, we can close the deal.'

'I . . . Like I said, it's all we have. I can show you my bank statement.' He started to reach into the backpack again.

'No, I don't want to read your fucking bank statement,

Scott. What do you think I am – the fucking taxman? What sort of game is this?'

'No game. I've done my best. I have no more money.'

'Four grand is chickenfeed. You owe me twenty-five. Where's the rest of it?'

'I . . . I don't know what you want me to say. I don't have it. I work in a garage. My wife works part-time at a supermarket. We don't own property or any valuables. We can't get a loan from the bank. My car is only worth its scrap value. Please, I'm not trying to cheat you. I just don't know what else I—'

And then Ronan was tossing the envelope and his torch on the ground, and he was pulling out his massive gun and striding towards Scott.

Scott put his hands up and tried to back away, convinced he was going to slip and that the sudden move would look like an attempt to escape, provoking Ronan to begin shooting.

'Not good enough, Scott! Not anywhere near good enough.'

'Please, I . . . Look, maybe I could pay you off more slowly. A chunk of my wages every month. How does that sound?'

Ronan rubbed his chin like a theatre villain. 'A monthly instalment plan? Interesting.'

'Yes! And even if you wanted to charge a small amount of interest . . .'

'Well, yes, of course there'd have to be interest, but I'm sure we could agree on a fair percentage rate.'

He paused.

And then suddenly dropped back into his normal persona.

'Don't be fucking stupid. Doesn't work like that. How long do you think it would take you to pay back twenty-five grand with interest? I'd be an old man by then. I want my money now.'

'And I told you I don't have it. Please, you're asking me to do something that's not possible.'

Ronan advanced again, his gun raised. 'Everything is possible. You just need to try harder.'

'I *have* tried. Please. Look at my bank statement. It's—'

'Which knee, Scott?'

'W-what?'

'I'm going to shoot you in one of your knees. I'm allowing you to pick which one.'

Scott backed away again. He felt himself beginning to slide down the hill. He glanced quickly behind him, taking in the vast, empty space. Nobody to help. Nobody even to hear the shots.

'Don't even think of running, Scott. You run, and I'll shoot you in the back.' He cocked the gun, lowered it to point at Scott's right knee.

'Wait! Wait! Maybe ... maybe I could get some more. I could try. Let me try.'

'Oh, so you're willing to give it a proper try now? Actually put some effort in?'

'Yes. I'm sure I could get some more. A lot more, probably.'

They stood silently on the hill for what seemed an age. Scott could hear the pounding in his chest.

Ronan lowered the gun. 'Do it. Don't say I never did anything for you. And remember why you're in this mess in the first place. Your son murdered my brother, and then, *then*, you threw away his body and our money. Don't you forget that.'

'I won't. Thank you. Just give me a few days, and—'

'Twenty-four hours.'

'What?'

'You've got until tomorrow night. I'm not waiting any longer for my money.'

'One day? I can't possibly—'

'No more negotiations, Scott. I'm being more than generous as it is, and you're getting on my nerves. I'll call you tomorrow to arrange a meet. Now get out of my face.'

'Please, I—'

But Ronan was already turning and walking away, picking up the envelope and torch, disappearing into the black shadows beneath the tree.

When Scott got home, he moved as silently as he could. He wanted to shower, to remove the odours of sweat and cow dung that were clinging to him, but he didn't want to wake the others.

His family. His precious wife and son.

He had done this for them.

Done it? This wasn't over. Not yet. Another long fearful day lay ahead.

He doubted he would sleep, but he crept into the bedroom and stripped off his clothes and climbed into bed, if only to be near to his wife.

Tears sprang from his eyes.

'You're home,' Gemma said, her back still to him.

'I'm home.'

'And you're safe? You're not hurt?'

'I'm not hurt.'

'Did he accept the money?'

'He did.'

'And?'

'And what?'

'Is that it? He just took it and went?'

'Yes.'

'And he's not coming back? He doesn't want more?'

'No. I told him we didn't have any more. There was nothing else to discuss.'

She finally turned over in the bed.

'Why are you crying?'

'Relief. It's been a tough day. I'm just glad it's all over.'

'Hold me,' she said. 'Hold me tight.'

34

Thursday morning. Breakfast time, but not like any other.

She knows, Scott thought. Or at least she suspects. She just doesn't want to say. Doesn't want to stress the lie to breaking point.

Because that's what he was living now. A big fat lie. The guilt of it was already ballooning inside him. That big talk he'd had with Gemma about joint decisions, about being in this together – well, he'd thrown all that out of the window. He told himself he was doing it from the best of intentions. If this all went tits-up, then the less Gemma knew about it the better. If she didn't know the truth, there'd be nothing for her to cover up. He was doing this for her, and for Daniel.

So then why did it feel so painful?

Daniel was less reserved than his mother. 'Did you pay that man?' he asked.

'I did.'

'Will he leave us alone now?'

'Yes. He promised he would.'

'Good. I'm glad to hear that.'

'And I'm glad that you're glad. Eat your toast, Daniel. It's nearly time to go.'

He looked across at Gemma, but she had suddenly found her cereal intensely interesting.

His phone was still off. He didn't want to risk a call from Ronan while he was with his family. They'd know.

As he'd predicted, and despite his exhaustion, he hadn't slept. Money was on his mind again. More specifically, how to get hold of some. He knew he couldn't find all twenty-five thousand, but what if he could at least get into five figures? Ten grand is a lot of money in anyone's eyes, right? Ronan would have to be pleased with that. And he'd already made a down payment, so that left only £5,700 to find.

Only £5,700.

Easy to say. Not so easy to do.

But he had a plan.

Marcel intercepted Hannah on her way out of the office.

'Got a minute, boss?'

She tried to read his expression. Tried to figure out whether this was good news or bad. If it was bad, she was going to kick someone in the crotch.

She nodded. Marcel led her over to Trisha Lacey's desk. Hannah decided that kicking her in the crotch wouldn't be quite as effective.

'What have we got?'

'This is the CCTV from the tip,' Trisha said. 'We're making good progress with the vehicles, but I wanted to show you this one.' She moved the image on by a few frames, then pointed to a silver car.

'Okay. What about it?'

'Let me zoom in.' Trisha tapped a key a few times, magnifying the rear section of the car. 'See that plate?'

Hannah squinted. 'I can't make it out. It looks like it's covered in mud or something.'

'Right. A few of the vehicles have had dirty registration plates, but if we can't figure them out on the way in, we can usually get them on the way out.'

'What do you mean?'

'This is from a camera at the entrance to the tip, looking inwards, so it captures vehicles just as they come in through the gates. Now, a few minutes later, we see the car coming out again.'

Trisha worked her magic and found the same car on an image with a timestamp several minutes after the previous one. Now it could be seen from the front. Trisha zoomed in on the registration plate again.

'Still unreadable,' Hannah said.

'Yes. Some of the characters are partly visible, but if they're what we think they are, they don't match anything in the system.'

'You think this was done deliberately? A faked plate?'

'It could be just coincidence. Maybe the car drove through mud and the registration was accidentally obscured. But there's something else.'

Trisha used her mouse to move the viewpoint to a higher position on the car, directly over the driving position.

'The sun visor's down,' Hannah said.

'Yes, ma'am. And I don't know if you remember, but Sunday

was a really cloudy day. There was no reason for anyone to lower their visor. Unless . . .'

'Unless they were trying to hide their face from the camera.' Hannah straightened up. 'Right. Do we know the make and model of that car?'

It was Marcel who answered. 'Thought you'd ask that, boss, so we did our homework. It's a Toyota Avensis saloon.'

'Gold star for both of you. Draw up a list. Silver Toyota Avensis registrations, ranked according to distance of owner's address from the crime scene.'

'There could be a lot of them. And it's possible that the owner doesn't live anywhere near the scene or the tip.'

'There could, Marcel. But unless you've got a better idea . . .'

'No, boss. We're on it.'

'Thank you. Keep me informed. I want to know the minute you find anyone who seems the least bit iffy.'

'Iffy. Right, boss.'

'What the fuck is this?'

Ronan had known this was coming. He'd put up his mental shields in advance.

'It's all he had. Every penny.'

'There are coins in here. Actual coins!'

'I told you. Every penny.'

Myra glared at him. 'And you just accepted it and sent him on his way?'

'Course not.'

'Then what did you do? Put a bullet in him? Break his legs?'

'No. I told him it wasn't enough.'

'I see. And you thought that a verbal warning was adequate, did you?'

'He got the message.'

'Really? When you didn't give him so much as a flick on his ear?'

'Mam. I threatened him with the gun. He understands. But to be honest . . .' He let it fade out. He wasn't sure he should be injecting a note of pessimism into this discussion.

'What?'

'Nothing.'

'No, go on. Make my day even more miserable than it already is.' She tapped the black armband she was still wearing. 'I shouldn't need to remind you that your brother is never coming back to us. Not ever. Those sons of bitches took him away, and now they need to pay.'

'With money?'

Myra slammed her palms on the table. 'With whatever it fucking well takes! With their worthless lives, if necessary. I'm not letting them get away with this, and I hope you're not thinking that way either. So go ahead. Enlighten me. Let me know what's on your mind so that I can set you straight again. Jesus, Ronan, I thought you were better than this.'

Ronan considered staying mute, but anger drove the words from his lips.

'I was about to say that it doesn't matter what we do. That family don't have any more money. I've been to their crummy flat. They don't have a pot to piss in. We can threaten them all we want, hurt them all we want, but there's no way they're going to come up with twenty-five grand. So if you want me to go back there and leave the parents more brain-dead than their moronic son, that's fine. But just accept that they're never going to find the dough.'

He found he was panting after his rant, but he felt so much better for it. Even his mother appeared surprised at how the worm had turned. She picked up her glass and sat back, a curious smile on her blubbery lips.

'I know.'

Ronan frowned. 'Know what?'

'That this Timpson bloke isn't going to come up with the goods. Not without some help. That's why I need him to believe we're people he can't mess with.'

'Mam, what are you talking about?'

She took a slug of gin, started pouring another. 'I know what you think of me,' she said. 'You think I'm past it. That I'm just your old mum, drinking herself gaga and with no idea of what's going on in the real world.'

'Mam, that's not what I—'

'Well, let me tell you something. I've been ducking and diving since well before you were born. Your dad didn't get where he was all by himself, you know. We worked together, and I still know a thing or two. So, while you've been pissing around like an amateur, I've been making some enquiries.'

'What kind of enquiries? What's this got to do with Joey?'

'Everything. I'm not finished with those bastards who murdered him. Not by a long chalk. They don't know what I'm capable of.'

Even Ronan felt a little afraid now.

'And what are you capable of?'
'Plan B.'
'Plan B?'
'Yes, lad. Plan B.'

35

Scott spent most of his morning throwing furtive glances towards Gavin, waiting for the right opportunity. But every time he summoned up the nerve, the phone would ring or a customer would arrive, and the moment was gone.

At just before eleven o'clock, he went over to the sink and filled the kettle.

'Fancy a brew?' he called.

'Always,' Gavin answered. 'Have we got any chocolate digestives left?'

'Well, I didn't finish them off yesterday, so unless you've been rooting...'

He poured water over two bags of Yorkshire tea. Two heaped spoonfuls of sugar in Gavin's mug. Gavin was just finishing off on a Volkswagen. There wouldn't be a better opportunity. It had to be now or never.

Scott's mobile trilled. He looked at the screen. It was Ronan. *Shit.*

He hastened out of the garage as he answered the call. 'Hi,' he said, trying to sound jovial for Gavin's benefit.

'Hello, Scott. How's it going?'

'All right.'

'Well, that sounds positive. Where are you up to with the money?'

'I'm sorting it.'

'You are? How?'

'Just . . . Does it matter? I've still got the rest of the day, haven't I?'

A chuckle from Ronan. 'You have. That's why I'm calling. To set up the meet.'

'All right. Where this time?'

'I thought I'd make it easy for you and go with the same place as last night. Same time, too.'

'You mean midnight?'

'That's exactly what I mean. Is there a problem?'

'It's late.'

'What, is it past your bedtime? Sorry, pal. You'll just have to drink lots of coffee or something.'

'Can we make it earlier?'

'Earlier? You want *less* time to find the money?'

'Yes. Please.'

A pause. 'What the fuck is this, Scott? Have you got something in mind for our meeting? Something I wouldn't like, maybe?'

'No, nothing like that. It's just . . . look, I haven't told my wife about this. She thinks it's all sorted. If I'm out at midnight, she'll know something's wrong.'

'You haven't—' Ronan let out a whoop of laughter. 'Unbelievable. So you really want to meet earlier?'

'Yes, please.'

'All right. Let's make it ten o'clock. That do you?'

'Yes. That would be fine.'

'Good. I'm glad to hear it. I wouldn't want to come between a man and his wife. Not unless he was planning to cross me.'

'I'm not. I swear.'

'Then I'll see you at ten. Have a nice day now.'

The call ended. Scott went back into the garage, his mind still buzzing.

'That tea will be stewed, you know,' Gavin called.

'Oh yeah. Sorry. I'll make a fresh one.'

He prepared tea again, then took the mugs and biscuits across to a worktable where he sat alongside Gavin.

Gavin slurped his tea and took a huge bite from a chocolate biscuit. 'Oh, that's good,' he said, crumbs spilling from his mouth.

'Gav,' Scott began. 'Can I ask you a favour?'

'You're not going to ask me to check out your prostate again, are you? Because, to be honest, it's becoming too much of a regular thing.'

'Very funny. No, it's more serious than that.'

Gavin dropped his grin. 'Why? What's up?'

'I've . . . I've got myself in a bit of trouble.'

'What kind of trouble?'

'Financial trouble.'

'Financial. You mean you've run up some debts?'

'Yes. And I was hoping . . . well, I was wondering if I could ask you for a loan.'

Gavin lifted his mug. 'How much are we talking about, mate?' He took a sip of tea, his eyes inquisitorial over the rim.

'I need . . . I need five thousand, seven hundred pounds.'

The splutter sent a spray of fluid right across Scott's overalls. 'How much?'

'Five thousand, seven hundred.'

'Jesus! I thought you were going to say a couple of hundred or something. How the hell did you end up owing that much?'

Scott shrugged. 'Bad decisions, I suppose. Not being disciplined. Putting my head in the sand, hoping it would go away. That kind of thing. It happens.'

'I know it does, but I never thought . . . well, I just didn't think it would ever happen to you.'

'What can I tell you? You never know what goes on in other people's lives, right? I mean, I can't tell you how embarrassing this is for me. But I can't ignore it any longer. It's only going to get worse. And that's why I'm coming to you. As a good friend.'

Gavin's pained expression wasn't encouraging. 'You know that the banks are a lot more sympathetic than they used to be, don't you? They're usually willing to come to some sort of an arrangement with—'

'It's not my bank that's the problem.'

'Credit cards, then. Same thing applies. They—'

'Not a credit card company, either. I don't have a great credit score, Gav. I had to go . . . elsewhere.'

Gavin stared. 'You mean a loan shark?'

'Not the description they use, but yeah. I thought it'd be okay, but it's the interest. It's crippling me. The debt has just gone up and up. I've already paid them all my savings, but . . .'

Gavin blew out a long stream of air. 'Shit. I don't know what to say, mate.'

'I know. It's my fault. Nobody else to blame. But I can fix it. If I can just pay these guys off, I can get back on track. Look, how long have I worked for you?'

'Well . . . since you left school.'

'Since I left school. Right. That's a long time, isn't it? And have I ever let you down?'

'No.'

'Haven't I always done a good job?'

'No question.'

'And I'll continue to do a good job. You can take the loan out of my wages. Or I can work extra hours to pay it off, whatever you prefer.'

Gavin sat back and pushed his fingers through his hair. 'I don't know, mate. That's a lot of money.'

Scott raised his arms, indicating the expanse of the garage. 'You have a good business here. Lots of customers. I don't know what your books look like, but—'

'Not as good as you might think. You'd be surprised. Parts, rates, taxes, overheads, employee costs – they all take big bites out of a small business like this.'

Scott didn't like the way this was going. He particularly didn't like the way Gavin had put emphasis on *employee costs*, as though he were more of a liability than an asset. As though he'd been doing Scott a favour by keeping him on all these years.

But he didn't know what else to add. He wasn't going to beg. Wasn't about to humiliate himself. All he could do was stare pleadingly at his boss.

Gavin's chair creaked as he shifted on it. He seemed incredibly uncomfortable. 'Look,' he said. 'There's no way I can hand over that much money. But you're a good mate and a great worker and I've known you a long time, so here's what I'll do. I'll lend you three grand.'

'Three?'

'Best I can do, mate. Sorry. If I could come up with more, I would. You know that.'

Scott knew nothing of the kind. He firmly believed that Gavin could easily afford a lot more.

But then why should he? Why would he take the risk with someone who has already confessed to being crap with money?

He let out a long, shuddering sigh of relief. 'Thanks, Gav. That will really help. If I pay that off, I should be able to get the debt under control again.'

Gavin raised his eyebrows. 'You don't sound very sure.'

'No. I'm sure.' He put his hand out. 'Thank you.'

Gavin shook hands. 'No problem. I'm going to make you work for it, though, so be prepared.'

'I am. Fully.' He paused. 'There's . . . there's just one other thing.'

'What's that?'

'The money. I need it today.'

'Today?'

'Yeah. Sorry, Gav. I'm supposed to meet these guys tonight. If I can't give them anything . . .' He put on his best expression of dread.

'Okay. No time like the present, I suppose. I'll go to the bank at lunchtime.'

'Thanks. You don't know how much this means to me. You've just saved me.'

Which wasn't quite true. Three grand wasn't enough. It didn't take him close enough to the ten-grand target, and even that figure was one born from hope.

He needed more. And that meant he'd have to execute the second part of his plan.

The more dangerous part.

36

Daniel needed to talk.

He had tried with his mother at breakfast, after his dad had left for work, but she didn't want to know. She'd almost screamed at him that she didn't want to hear any more about it, and that he shouldn't mention it to anyone, not a soul, do you hear me?

It was sealed tightly inside him, and its pressure was painful. He felt like a bottle of lemonade that had been shaken up, its contents desperate to explode.

He knew he couldn't let it out, but he was hopeless at keeping secrets. Now he was terrified to say anything at all.

It made things difficult at the day centre. When the carers asked him questions, he responded with one-word answers – sometimes not even that, but instead a shrug or a nod or a grunt. Earlier, Mrs Collins had asked him if he wasn't feeling well, and Laurence had said he was a miserable tosser, which he didn't think was very nice. When he didn't join in any of the group activities, they had allowed him to sit in a corner away from the others and do his own thing.

That thing was drawing.

He had spent hours on this picture. Or, rather, a sequence of pictures. A complete comic strip – his biggest project yet. He'd had to use the reverse side of a length of wallpaper to fit it all on.

Mrs Collins came over again, leaving everyone else watching a television programme.

'Hello, Daniel,' she said.

He didn't want to answer, but it felt so rude. It might upset her.

'Hello, Mrs Collins.' There. That's one, two, *three* words. Three whole words.

'Do you feel like coming over and joining us?'

He looked across the room. Saw the transfixed faces bathed in the ghostly glow of the television. All except Laurence, who stared back and flipped up his middle finger.

Daniel returned his attention to his picture. 'No, thank you.'

Three words again. She can't get unhappy about that many words.

'You're very quiet today.'

Oh. She is upset. I don't want to upset Mrs Collins. She's too nice.

'I'm fine,' he said.

He tried to colour in, but he could feel her eyes on him, and it was making his crayon stray over the lines.

'Come on. Come and watch the programme. It's about animals in the snow. You like animals.'

He was sorely tempted. He did like animals. He particularly liked watching Arctic foxes pouncing on things beneath the snow.

'Sometimes I do. But sometimes they bite.'

'That's true, but only when they need to eat. Or when they're afraid.'

As she said this, she reached out her hand and placed it on Daniel's forearm. It was breaking The Rule, but he didn't mind. It felt so nice. It made him want to cry.

She said, 'Has something happened, Daniel?'

Has something happened? He didn't know where to begin. Didn't know where to start with the tale of a man who got killed and chopped into tiny pieces and whose brother got angry and came after his family with a gun and asked for money and—

'I don't want to talk about it,' he said. Which wasn't a lie, because he really didn't want to tell that story. Not in words, anyway.

Pictures were a different matter.

'All right,' Mrs Collins said. 'But if you change your mind, I'm always willing to listen. You know that, don't you?'

He wanted to cry again.

'Yes. Thank you, Mrs Collins.'

She laughed. 'When are you ever going to start calling me Kim, like everyone else?' She rubbed his arm a little, then stood up. 'That's a fantastic drawing, Daniel. Adam-9 again?'

He nodded, and as she walked away he sat back in his chair and looked down at his artwork.

Adam-9, briefcase in hand. A long metal arm protruding from the case and holding up a man in its claws, squeezing his neck.

This was Daniel's release. His way of getting the truth out so he didn't blow up. It was the best he could do. The most accurate he could be. Adam-9 had stopped the man in precisely the same way as he had put an end to the Quark Monster.

One thing bothered Daniel, though. A huge hole in the story.

He wasn't carrying his briefcase when the man called Joey had died.

And if he didn't have the Adam-9 briefcase, then . . .

But he didn't want to think about that.

37

Timing was critical.

After promising Gavin to put in longer hours, he couldn't rush home early. On the other hand, he needed to allow enough time for his scheme to be carried out.

If, in fact, it *was* going to be carried out.

A voice in his head was telling him that this was a ridiculous idea. That it didn't stand a cat in hell's chance of success.

But what choice did he have? It was in for a penny, in for a pound.

Or lots of pounds in this case.

He parked at the rear of the flats, facing the building. From here he couldn't tell if anyone was milling about in the foyer.

Normally, he dreaded encountering the youths. Today they were on his wish list.

He locked the car, then checked the door handle to make certain it was secure. His backpack was in the boot, three grand nestling within it. He didn't like leaving it there, but he had no choice, and it wouldn't be for long. What pricked his conscience more was the look of concern on Gavin's face when he'd handed the cash over. It pained Scott that he was about to betray his friend by taking such a huge gamble with it.

As soon as he entered the building he heard the raised voices, the laughter, and he said a mental thank-you.

There were five of them today. They were drinking, smoking. As always, the one known as Biggo seemed in charge, the others laughing too hard at his jokes.

Scott approached them.

The tallest one spotted him first. 'Oh, here we go,' he said. 'It's him again.'

The others turned. They seemed mildly amused rather than aggressive.

At least for the present.

'All right,' Biggo said. 'I hope you've brought my brick back. I'm missing that brick. It was my favourite.'

'Can we talk?' Scott said.

'Sure. Pick a subject.'

'What about business?'

'Business?' Biggo took a swig of lager. 'What kind of business? Monkey business? Dog's business?'

'Financial business. I want to talk to you about money.'

Biggo looked at his friends. 'Oh, well, we're always interested in money, aren't we, lads? Makes the world go round, doesn't it? Go ahead, mate. Talk to us about money.'

'I want to talk to you. Just you. In private.'

'Ooh,' said one of the gang in a high-pitched voice. 'He fancies you, Biggo. Wants to get you alone.'

Laughter followed, quelled suddenly by a sharp glance from Biggo.

'You're serious, aren't you?'

'I am.'

Biggo drained his can, then crushed it in his hand and tossed it aside.

'Step into my office.'

He moved away from the others, and Scott followed. His 'office' turned out to be a quiet, dark alcove at the far side of the lobby. There was a distinct odour of urine.

'Talk to me,' Biggo said.

Scott looked behind him, checking that the rest of the yobs weren't trying to listen in.

'I know what you get up to here,' he said.

'Oh yeah? And what might that be?'

'I'm not stupid. I've seen what you sell. The little packets.'

Biggo's eyes grew cold. 'Pal, I hope this isn't the start of some kind of shakedown. You're playing with the wrong—'

Scott put up his hands. 'No. Please. That's not what I meant. I meant . . . look, I need to make some money.'

'Don't we all? Have you got a get-rich-quick scheme or something?'

'I was hoping you might have.'

Biggo snorted. 'You've got to be joking. Have you taken a proper look at those lads? Not exactly dripping with Rolex and Gucci are they?'

'No, but I thought . . . well, if I could invest in something . . .'

'An investment? You mean you've already got some money?'

'Yes.' Scott had to force himself not to tilt his head towards his car outside.

'How much are we talking about?'

'Couple of grand.'

Biggo stared at him. After what seemed like a full minute, he suddenly grinned. It made him appear even more ugly than usual.

'That makes a difference.'

'Does it?'

'Course it does. You know the best way to make a shitload of money?'

'No.'

'Start off with a shitload of money. That's how it works. Haven't you noticed how the rich always get richer?'

Scott looked around. He felt awkward, out of his depth. He knew about cars; he didn't know about drug dealing.

'What kind of profit could I make?'

'With a couple of grand? You could double that easy. Maybe more.'

Scott did some quick mental calculations. He didn't want to risk the whole three thousand. But maybe two. Two would be okay. If he could double that – a conservative estimate according to Biggo – then that would be four, plus the thousand he kept back. Adding that to the money he had already paid brought it to a grand total of nine thousand, three hundred. That was pretty damn close to his 10K target. And if Biggo was as confident as he sounded, it might be even closer.

A cloud of suspicion crossed his mind.

'Why don't *you* do this?' he asked. 'I mean, keep doubling your profits?'

Biggo looked irritated. 'I already told you. You need to start big to earn big. Nobody is interested in the loose change I've got in my pockets. The chickenfeed I make goes on weed and beer.'

Scott thought some more. He'd landed in an alien world without the right survival gear. Gut instinct was all he had to go on. That and a dash of desperation.

'All right, let's do it,' he said.

Biggo laughed. 'Let's do what?'

Scott felt even more inept. 'A deal. I want to make a deal. I can put in two grand.'

Biggo looked at him long and hard, then shook his head. 'How do you think this works? You think you can just hand over two grand and then I buy product, sell it on, and give you four back? Name me one business that operates like that.'

Scott was glad of the dim lighting, because he knew his cheeks were burning.

'All right. So how does it work?'

'This is a market. Supply and demand; everyone in the chain takes a cut.'

'That sounds . . . complicated.'

'It's the way it is. Factory workers get paid shit, but we end up paying a fortune for the things they make. I hardly ever went to school and even I know that.'

Scott glanced at his watch. The evening was ticking away. 'Yeah, I know. What I meant was . . . I was hoping it would be simpler. Quicker.'

'How quick, exactly?'

'Today. Now.'

A guffaw of laughter this time. Enough to make Biggo's mates look over, wondering what they might be missing out on.

'Now? Like, right this minute? Jesus, you're a dark horse, aren't you?'

'What do you mean?'

'I mean you. Mr Respectable. Getting all huffy with us because we don't shut the door of your precious building. Looking down your nose at us. And now you want in? You want to be one of us?'

No, Scott thought. I don't want to be one of you. You're scum. I'm nothing like you. I'm using you, that's all.

'I need the money.'

'Why? What's the rush?'

'Does it matter? I just need it. Can you help me or not?'

They stared into each other's eyes. Scott felt as though it was some kind of test of his sincerity, and that to break eye contact would be a mistake.

Say yes, he willed. Don't make me beg.

'Let me make some calls,' Biggo said. He moved away, headed out of the building.

Through the glass doors, Scott saw Biggo pull a mobile phone from his hoodie. He turned to find the other youths looking at him in silence, their eyes glinting. Temporarily leaderless, they seemed to Scott like an anarchic pack of wolves that had scented blood and were tempted to rip him apart.

He checked his watch again. Prayed that Gemma didn't wander down into the foyer. Outside, Biggo had lit up a cigarette and was smiling as he talked into his phone. It all seemed far too casual for what was, to Scott, such a momentous negotiation.

He breathed again when Biggo re-entered the building.

'Okay,' Biggo said.

'Okay what?'

'It's on. The deal you asked for.'

Scott was suddenly at a loss for words. Unbelievably, a mountain had been turned into a hillock. It all seemed too effortless.

'It's on?'

'Yup. Figure I gave them was two grand. You're still going with that, right? I don't want to have to call them again.'

'No. I mean yes. Two grand. But . . .'

'But what? Don't be wasting my time here.'

The question had been burning in Scott's mind for the past few minutes. He knew it was disrespectful, but he had to get it out in the open.

'I just want to know . . . what do you get out of this?'

He expected a storm. What he got was a smile.

'You're starting to think like a businessman. I get a percentage.'

'Does it come out of my profits?'

'You should still double, even after I take my cut.'

Which made Scott wonder exactly how much money was being made in total, and whether he should have pushed for more. It would have been so much sweeter to hit that ten grand.

But that bridge had been crossed. He'd learnt a lesson that he hoped would never come in useful again.

'And we can do it this evening? I need the money by nine o'clock at the latest.'

He had pushed for a ten o'clock meeting with Ronan, and needed to build in travel time plus the possibility of delays.

'You'll have it by nine.'

Scott wanted to say thank you. It was the way he'd been brought up. But he got the feeling that it would be a sign of weakness.

'I'll get the two grand,' he said, and started to move away.

'Whoa! Hold on there, cowboy.'

'What's wrong?'

'First of all, you don't just hand over your money like that. You don't know me from Adam. What are you planning to do – ask for a receipt?'

'I don't know. I thought—'

'Secondly, this isn't *my* deal. It's *your* deal. I just set it up. I ain't gonna get caught by the cops making a deal this big.'

'I don't understand. How do I—?'

'I've arranged a meet, okay? Eight o'clock on Shardlake Street, not far from the big B&Q. You know it?'

'I'll find it.'

'There are some flats opposite the playground. He'll be in number 46 on the fourth floor. Be there with the money. You'll buy a package. Don't worry – the guy handing it over is sound. Bring it straight back here to me, and I'll buy it off you with the four grand.'

'I thought you didn't have that kind of money.'

'I don't. It won't be my money. That's my side of the deal, and you don't have to worry about it. Now, you still want to do this?'

Scott thought for a few seconds. It was as he'd decided earlier: in for a penny, in for a pound.

'Yes. I want to do it.'

'Sweet. Welcome to the club.'

38

He wasn't the most accomplished of actors, and Gemma had known him long enough to see through it, but he went through with the charade anyway.

'Okay if I go out for a couple of hours later on?' he asked.

She turned from her position at the stove, where she was boiling potatoes. He saw the flash of suspicion in her eyes.

'Where to?'

'I asked Gavin about doing some extra hours. You know, so I can build up our savings again. He said we should talk about it over a drink. I couldn't really refuse.'

'Have we got enough money left for you to go out drinking?'

It was a loaded question. Combative because of their financial situation, the emphasis on it being *their* money. In better times she would have thought nothing of his request. But he knew also that she was refusing to challenge him explicitly. She was allowing him the opportunity to tell the truth, while letting him know that it was a limited-time offer.

'I won't be long,' he said, his voice weak. 'I'll just have a couple.'

'Fine,' she said, and buried her face in a cloud of steam,

cutting him off until he decided to become her husband once more.

He pulled the car up in front of the railings alongside the playground, and cut the engine. It was five minutes to eight, but at this time of year it was already dark. Dense clouds had rolled in across the moon, and most of the streetlights here were broken. This was a rough area; he wouldn't have felt safe even in full daylight.

He looked across the street at the characterless slab of flats. Four storeys high. Balconies running the length of each floor. A few windows lit up, but most tightly curtained against passers-by. One man silhouetted in front of his open door, smoking a cigarette.

Scott waited for the man to disappear into his flat before leaving his car. He locked up, then dipped his hand into the inside pocket of his jacket. Two grand. The other thousand was now in his glove compartment.

Let's do this.

He took a deep breath and crossed the street. To the left of the building, a narrow concrete staircase led up to the first floor. He started to ascend, the rusting metal bannister cold and rough against his palm. Sounds of domestic life leaked from windows above: rock music, a child's cry, a drumkit.

A figure stepped out in front of him at the top of the stairs. Scott's first thought was to move to one side to allow him past, but the figure stayed put.

Scott looked more closely. Saw it was a man in a hoodie.

Saw the plastic pig mask over his face. Saw the huge knife glinting in his hand.

Scott turned to go back down. Another hooded male stepped into view at the bottom of the steps. A cow mask this time, but also armed with a knife.

Scott did the only thing he could to get out of there, which was to side-vault over the bannister. He hit the concrete floor hard, and felt something go in his ankle. He wanted to head back to his car, but cow-man had already cut him off. His only escape route was in the opposite direction, along a narrow channel between the building and a brick wall. He ran, spears of pain shooting up his leg, the pounding of footsteps getting ever closer behind him.

And then the way ahead was suddenly blocked. A sheep and an unusually tall goat. They just stood there in his way. Behind, the first two did the same.

And then all the farmyard animals began slowly closing in. They had no need to hurry now.

'Help!' Scott shouted. 'Help me!'

The only answer he got was the distant barking of a dog.

He ran at the brick wall. Jumped. His fingers just managed to find the top edge. He clung on, his feet scrabbling for purchase.

But then they were on him, clutching at him, dragging him back down. He swung wildly with his fists and managed to connect, resulting in a satisfying crumple of plastic. His reward was to be tossed heavily onto the unforgiving floor, and then all he could do was pull himself into as tight a ball as possible, his arms cocooning his head as the men punched and kicked and stamped, launching blow after blow into his ribs, his back, his legs, until he felt his body had been turned to mush and he was just one big bag of pain.

He was barely aware of what came next – of the hands on him, probing and searching, and then the dwindling echoes of leisurely paced footsteps – but when he finally unfurled he knew what had happened. He didn't need to check his pocket to know that his money had been taken. This was no random mugging.

He'd been set up.

Four assailants, one much taller than the others. Undoubtedly Biggo's compatriots. Biggo would be waiting back at Erskine Court. Preparing his speech about how he'd pulled a lot of strings to broker this deal and how it was such a massive disappointment that Scott had fucked it all up by losing the money.

And what made it all so unutterably worse for Scott was that it was entirely his own fault. He had approached *them*. They had acted according to their nature, and he had encouraged it.

God, how easily he had swallowed the lies, the hyperbole. Double my money? Thank you very much, I'll take that. All done and dusted in a couple of hours? Fantastic, where do I sign?

Why hadn't he taken more precautions? Why was he such a fucking idiot?

Why, why, why?

An urge to weep overwhelmed him, and he let it come.

He had a loss of two thousand pounds and a broken body to show for his troubles.

It was what he deserved.

39

The pub wasn't the most salubrious she'd been in, and some of its clientele looked downright leery, but Marcel Lang had been right about the food. She'd opted for the seafood linguine, while Ben had gone for the steak and ale pie. Both were superb.

The wine wasn't bad, either. Hannah had confirmed that several times over.

'So,' Ben said, 'you still haven't told me why we're out on a Thursday night.'

'Do we need an excuse?'

'I don't, but you normally do, especially when you're busy on a big case.'

'Hmm,' Hannah said, and quaffed some more wine.

'Ah, I get it. The case *is* the excuse.'

She sighed heavily. 'It's not looking good, Ben. I feel like we're chasing shadows. The case landed on our laps on Sunday, and we still don't seem to be any further forward.'

'Any suspects?'

'No. Not really. Everyone we've spoken to who might have a possible motive also has an alibi. I think there's someone we're missing. The problem is finding them.'

'Well, what if it's someone who *doesn't* have a motive?'

She stared at him, wondering if it was the wine that stopped her understanding Ben's contribution.

'What do you mean?'

'What is it you detectives always say? Means, motive and opportunity – isn't that right? Do you always need all three? What if the killer had the means and the opportunity, but not the motive? Why couldn't it have been just a spur-of-the-moment thing? Or even an accident?'

'An accident? Ben, if I drove home now after all this wine, I might hit someone and kill them. And, if I were not the virtuous, upstanding individual you see before you, I might flee the scene in panic. What I would almost certainly not do is go back and collect the body, with the aim of chopping it up later and dumping it at a rubbish tip.'

'No, but—'

'Besides, the indications are that someone grabbed him by the throat and broke his neck. That doesn't happen *accidentally*. Cobb lived in a world where violence and death were always around the corner. Someone must have had it in for him.'

Ben raised his pint glass. 'If you say so. I bow to your superior knowledge.'

She clinked glasses, but what he'd said was still on her mind. Dismissive though she'd been, there was something else in his words – something already fading in her alcohol-fogged mind.

'Tell me that again,' she said.

Ben frowned. 'Okay. I bow to your—'

'No, not that. The earlier stuff about means, motive and opportunity.'

Ben looked to the ceiling as he tried to recall his thoughts. It was clear to Hannah that she wasn't the only one affected by the drink.

Ben ruffled up his hair and put on his best Stan Laurel voice. 'Well, the killer ... he has an accident and he loses his motivation. And then the other guy has the opportunity to find it again, and ...'

Hannah roared with laughter. 'See, this is the only excuse I need to come out for a meal with my husband. I need to have some fun. Enough about my job. Tell me what you got up to today.'

So he told her – about the sculpture he had worked on, and the music he had listened to, and the funny story he had heard on the radio, and the woman he had bumped into in Tesco who'd had the biggest nose he'd ever seen – and to most people it would probably be the most mundane stuff ever, but to Hannah it was everything she wanted to hear. It was normality. It was a million miles away from death and misery and the stress of not being able to address the world's imbalances, and it made things sane again.

After a dessert and some more wine, and then coffee and some more wine, Ben signalled for the bill. While he tried to pay with a card that seemed reluctant to surrender his money, Hannah taxed her eyeballs with the problem of focusing on her surroundings.

And then she saw her.

Tilly.

Standing in the doorway between the lounge and the bar area.

She was as blurry as everything else, but it was definitely her. School uniform and shiny shoes and that curl of hair across her forehead.

And then she was gone again. A couple of steps to her left was all it took to open up that wound in Hannah's heart.

'I just need to pay a visit,' Hannah said.

Ben didn't even glance her way. 'Yeah, I'll go myself as soon as this is sorted.'

She left him and the waiter struggling with the credit-card machine, then walked unsteadily through the doorway. She looked in the direction Tilly had gone, expecting nothing because that's what Tilly did: she came and she went in a flash, leaving devastation in her wake.

But Tilly was waiting at the top of the stairs.

Hannah followed. As she got about halfway up, Tilly turned and walked away again.

Hannah reached the top. A wood-panelled corridor led to the toilets. Tilly was standing outside the door to the ladies. Hannah stood still, fearful that any further approach might cause Tilly to move away again.

The door was opened, and the sound of a hand dryer rushed out, closely followed by a woman who was still rubbing her hands together. The woman smiled at Hannah as she passed by. Behind her, the door began to close slowly. Tilly slipped into the bathroom before it shut.

Hannah ran to the door, shoved it fully open again.

The room looked empty.

There were three stalls. Two of the doors were open; the middle one was half-closed.

'Tilly?' she said. 'Are you in there?'

She went to it and opened it wide.

Nobody.

She sighed.

The blow to the back of her neck was merciless. She pitched forward into the cubicle. Unseen hands grabbed her by the hair, landed another couple of punches on the side of her head, and then her face was being forced into the toilet bowl and she could see grey water and foul stains beneath, could feel the fumes forcing their way into her nostrils, and her arms flailed for something, anything, that could help her. She tried to yell for help, but her attacker must have pressed the flush button, and she had to take a deep breath and hold on to it for dear life as the water covered her face, and all sight and sound left her as she focused on staying alive. She put her hands on the sides of the bowl and desperately tried to push herself up, but he was too strong for her, and the water wasn't retreating and she thought she would die there.

But then sound returned, air returned, and she breathed again – a huge rasping inhalation as she filled her lungs. She could hear the cistern filling all too rapidly, and she knew he would try again to make her drown, and she really didn't want to suffer such an ignominious death, or any death for that matter, and she opened her mouth to call out once more, but this time it was choked off by something rough and sharp and bristly, and she realised that he had grabbed the toilet brush, the shit-covered, bleach-soaked toilet brush, and he was forcing it into her mouth, across her teeth, jabbing at her, into her eyes and her ears. She kicked out wildly, hoping to catch him in the groin or the thigh, to inflict enough pain to make him stop, even for a second. But then the water cascaded in again, covering her head, cutting off her senses, and she knew that this was it, this time it was surely the end.

And then he was gone, the weight of him disappearing as if he had never existed. She pushed herself out of the water and sucked in huge lungfuls of oxygen and tried to squeeze the foul water out of her eyes with her fingers, and she coughed and spluttered and spat as she crawled on her hands and knees out of the cubicle, not caring about the whereabouts of her attacker, but so, so grateful to be alive.

He was still there.

He was on his back on the floor. Straddling him was a man who was landing punch after savage punch, extracting blood and teeth and screams of pain as he roared his fury.

And that man, her saviour, was Ben. Mild-mannered, violence-hating, love-thy-neighbour Ben.

She had to stop him. Had to place her hands on his wrists and tell him softly that it was enough, it was over.

It was her first opportunity to get a proper look at the coward who had attacked her from behind not once, but twice.

And although his features were caked in blood, she recognised him immediately.

40

Ronan Cobb stood beneath the oak tree and watched the distant car headlights slow to a crawl and then stop. A minute later he caught glimpses of torchlight as Scott Timpson made his way up the lane towards him.

He genuinely hoped that Scott had somehow managed to get the money together.

But he doubted it.

His expectation was that his mother's so-called Plan B would have to be put into action, and he really didn't want that to happen.

She had surprised him with that one, all right. He hadn't realised how well connected she still was, how she had maintained a finger on the pulse. How dangerous she was. Behind the alcohol was a woman who still commanded respect.

He wished that her recent actions could have been driven by love rather than ruthlessness. Joey was dead. She didn't seem to realise that they would never share jokes and meals with him again. The only hole in her life was one that needed filling with money. Ronan found that disappointing and sad. He would do exactly what she told him

to do – of course he would – but something about this ran-
kled. It felt wrong.

He decided it was better not to think about it too much.
There was a job to be done.

He watched the light from Scott's torch as it arced over
the stile and then glided towards him. Ronan switched on his
own torch. What he saw shocked him.

Scott was practically dragging himself up the hill. He was
having trouble putting weight on one of his legs, and he
was clutching his side as though in agony. He looked like a
wounded animal.

Jesus.

'Okay, Scott. You can stop there.' Ronan closed the gap
himself. He shone his torch into Scott's face and watched him
recoil from the brightness. 'What the fuck happened to you?'

'Long story. I won't bore you with the details.'

'That's fine. I can manage without the foreplay. Have you
got the money?'

Scott hesitated, and Ronan knew instantly that the news
would be grim. He watched as Scott withdrew an envelope
from his jacket.

'Toss it over.'

Scott did so, but grimaced with the pain of it.

Ronan turned his torch on the envelope. It was smaller than
the previous one. He picked it up, hefted it in his hand. It was
far too light.

'How much, Scott?'

'A thousand.'

Shit. One thousand. One measly thousand.

'Why'd you even bother? This is an insult.'

'It was the best I could do. It was this or nothing. I brought it to you because . . .'

'Because what, Scott?'

'Because I wanted to show good faith. Because we had an agreement.'

'Our agreement was for you to get the rest of the twenty-five thousand. This is pitiful.'

Scott raised a finger in dispute. 'No. What I said was that I thought I could get more money. I kept my word.'

'Fuck's sake, Scott. What do you think this is? You think this is some kind of game? What you've given me here is a fucking slap in the face.'

'It's not meant to be. I swear. I nearly got killed getting you that money.'

Ronan looked at the sorrowful wretch and felt a pang of sympathy.

Stop it, he told himself. Remember what he did.

'I don't give a shit. What's really getting me fucking annoyed, though, is you treating me like I'm some kind of joke.'

'I'm not. I did my best. You have to believe me.'

'I don't have to believe nothing. This is it, Scott. You had your chance and you screwed up.'

'What . . . what are you going to do?'

Ronan reached to his waist and pulled out the Colt .45. He jacked a round into the chamber, saw how Scott flinched at the noise.

'Don't worry, Scott. I'm not going to kill you. Remember what I said last night about shooting you in the kneecap?'

Scott backed away. 'Please. Don't.'

'I won't. Not one kneecap, anyway. This time it's both of them. You know what a gun like this can do to someone's knees, Scott? It's not a pretty sight. You might never walk again.'

'Please. I—'

'So you don't have to pick a kneecap. Your choice is different now.'

'What do you mean?'

'After I shoot you, I'm going to take your phone. You're going to have to drag yourself out of here. Even if you make it back to your car, you won't be able to drive it with those crippled legs of yours. You'll probably have to flag someone down, if anyone comes this way, and if they're willing to stop. By then I'll have paid a visit to your flat.'

'My flat? Why? Why my flat?'

'I told you, your choice is different now, Scott. You have to decide between your wife and your son. Which one do I kill?'

Scott looked as though he'd already taken a bullet. 'Kill? No. Why? Why do you have to kill one of them?'

'An eye for an eye, Scott. You and your family are responsible for my brother's death. It's payback time. It was the money or a life, and you've chosen to give up a life.'

'No. I . . . Then I choose me. Not my family. Please, not my family.'

So, Ronan thought, the man's got some balls after all.

'Sorry, Scott. Doesn't work that way. Make your choice.'

'I can't! How can I possibly choose who you should kill?'

'Because if you don't, I'll waste both of them.'

'*Please! I can't.*'

'Then say goodbye to your legs *and* your family. I'm sure you'll miss them all.'

Ronan marched forward, pointed his gun at Scott's right knee.

'NO! PLEASE! I'LL DO ANYTHING!'

The magic words. Plan B – subtitled 'The Pact with the Devil' – was in effect. Ronan almost found a smile.

'Anything?'

'Yes. Anything. Just . . . don't hurt my family.'

Ronan counted to five, to give the impression he was thinking it over.

'There might be a way.'

'Name it. I'll do it. Whatever it is, I'll do it.'

Ronan relaxed his gun hand, dropping his arm back to his side. 'It'll be dangerous, but if you can pull it off, you should be able to pay me back with interest.'

'I don't care how dangerous it is. If it saves my family and gets you your money, I'll do it.'

Ronan nodded. He was getting all the right answers.

'There's a guy. A drug dealer. Tomorrow afternoon, between four and five, he'll take possession of a bag of money – a white Adidas sports bag. Thing is, he'll only have it for a short time. It'll be picked up from him again at seven o'clock. You'll need to get it from him before then.'

'Get it from him? What do you mean?'

Christ, thought Ronan. Why do I have to spell it out?

'I mean take it. Steal it. You do whatever you have to do to get that money from him, and then you bring it here and give it to me.'

'How much money will he have?'

'Hard to say. Depends on how good a day it's been. It'll be a lot, though. Enough to cover my losses so far – the losses *you* caused. And, by the way, don't get tempted to skim from the top. I'll get accurate figures afterwards. I'll know.'

'I don't want the money. I just want to put an end to this.'

'Then you'll do it?'

'I . . . You said it's dangerous. How dangerous?'

'This guy, he's not just going to hand over the money. You'll need to go in hard and fast.'

'And . . . if I fail? If I get killed trying?'

'You can consider your debt paid. I won't go after your family.'

Ronan watched as Scott searched the sky for guidance.

'It's a deal. If you can promise me that my family will be safe, whatever the outcome, it's a deal.'

'I guarantee it. You get me the money or you die trying. Either way, your family will never hear from me again.'

'Okay. Who's the guy? Who am I stealing the money from?'

'That's the beauty of it. He lives in the same building as you. Goes by the name of Barrington Daley.'

41

Hannah desperately wanted in on the interview.

She had been home – brushed her teeth and gargled, had a shower, brushed her teeth and gargled, got dressed, brushed her teeth and gargled – and now she was back at the station. She wanted to look her attacker in the eye as she asked him what had been going through his head. And, in return, she wanted to give him her side of the story.

But it was against regulations. For one thing, she was still under the influence of alcohol. For another, she was the victim, and therefore it would be a conflict of interest for her to take part in the investigation. It wasn't even a case for CID. She would just have to trust the pair of interviewing officers, while she made do with watching it all on a live camera feed.

He had turned down the offer of legal representation. Said he had nothing to hide, that he was proud of what he did. 'Bitch deserved it,' he said. 'What would you do if someone murdered *your* mother?'

It was a one-sided interview. The doctor had inspected his wounds and given him the all-clear, and now he wanted to get it all off his chest. His hate for Hannah was the only fuel he needed to keep talking, the brief interjections from the officers serving only to keep him on track.

'My mother was a good woman,' he told them. 'Okay, maybe she didn't make the best decisions when it came to men, but that didn't make her a criminal. Didn't mean that your detective bitch friend had to make her so scared that she had to run away. Why didn't she just let her go instead of chasing her right into the path of a train? My mum didn't deserve that.'

'That incident was investigated thoroughly, Shane,' one of the officers said. 'DI Washington was—'

'Yeah, yeah, don't even go there, okay? You lot always close ranks. You cover it all up. Maybe if you'd done your jobs properly and punished that woman – fired her or something – then maybe none of this would've happened. But no. She was allowed to carry on as normal. Like my mum didn't even count.'

'And that made you angry enough to go after DI Washington?'

'I hated her. Simple as. I wanted to hurt her. I didn't know how I was going to do it, but I wanted revenge.'

'So how did you go about it?'

'I went back and read all the reports about my mum's case. One of the papers mentioned the police station where Washington worked. I started parking up outside and waiting for her. It took me a while to figure out which car she used, and then I started following her. The first few times, I kept losing her in traffic. And whenever I managed to track her all the way, there'd always be other people there – other coppers. I had no chance to get near her. But then this one time she went into a block of flats.'

'Erskine Court.'

'Yeah.'

'And what happened there?'

'She and another copper talked to a gang of lads, but then the lads came out. When I walked towards the flats, I could see that she'd split up with the other detective and she was alone by the lift door. I had a piece of wood with me, under my coat, and I went inside. She didn't see me, and I knew this was my chance. I started hitting her. She tried to get away, but I just kept hitting her, and then she went down. I . . . I don't know what I was going to do then.'

'Were you trying to kill her?'

'No. Not kill her. I just wanted to hurt her. I needed to punish her. But then this bloke came into the building. He saw me and shouted something, and I ran out the back door. I didn't know how bad her injuries were, but to be honest I didn't really care. I did what I had to do. For my mum.'

'So why wasn't that enough for you?'

'It was. I'd got it out of my system. I didn't feel like I had to do any more to her. I didn't follow her or anything. And then tonight . . .'

'Tell us about tonight, Shane.'

'She turned up again, didn't she? Walked straight into my pub, my local boozer. Bold as brass. Like she was taunting me or something. I was in the bar, but I could see through into the lounge. She sat there with her bloke, eating and drinking and laughing, and I got madder and madder, and the more I drank, the worse it got. She had no right being there. Felt like she was taking the piss.'

'So how did the fight start?'

'She got up and came straight towards me. I thought she'd spotted me, but her eyes were all weird, like she was too bladdered to see straight. I watched her go up the stairs, and I should have gone home then, but I couldn't. I was too angry. I went after her, and I saw that the door to the ladies' toilet was open, and she was just standing there with her back to me, and there was nobody else around. Something snapped. I had to let her know that she couldn't keep turning up on our doorstep and causing us grief. She needed to be taught a lesson.'

Shane sat back in his chair. 'I know you're going to lock me up for this, but I don't care. That bitch took my mother away from me, and there's nothing you can do to me that's worse. I might be going to prison, but she's going to hell for what she did.'

Hannah turned the volume down and stepped away from the monitor. She needed no further reminder of how she had ruined lives.

Scott sat in his car and polished off the second of the two cans of lager he had purchased from a twenty-four-hour supermarket on the way home.

He stared at Erskine Court. No signs of life in the lobby, but he didn't really care. He wasn't going to get into an argument with the youths. He couldn't prove they'd mugged him. One of them probably had a scabby lip or a swollen cheek, but that wasn't proof.

Besides, he had only himself to blame. It had always been a risky gamble. Even if the drugs deal had run as advertised and he'd made some extra cash, Ronan probably wouldn't have let him off. He needed an accomplice, and he'd already decided it would be Scott Timpson.

There was no backing out now. If he didn't try to get the money from Barrington Daley, Ronan would come after him and his family. If he *did* try, there was a good chance he would be killed, but at least Daniel and Gemma would be safe.

That's all that matters, he thought. That's what this has been about all along.

He climbed out of the car, entered the building and took the lift up to the top. Halfway up, he got the sudden impulse to press the button for the eighth floor. When it stopped there and the door opened, he stayed in the lift, staring at flat 801 opposite. Tomorrow, he would cross that threshold, and he might die for doing so.

The lift closed off the view and took him to a safer, more familiar set of numbers. As he entered his own flat, he tried to straighten up and look as though he hadn't been run over by a bus.

Gemma was curled up on the sofa, drinking tea and watching an old film. As soon as she turned to him, he could tell that she saw through his deceit. He bent to kiss her, allowing the escape of alcohol fumes to add weight to his story, even though the simple act sent flashes of pain through his ribs.

'Good time?' she asked.

'Yeah, it made a nice change. Been a while since me and Gavin had a pint.'

He came round to join her on the sofa, and could feel her eyes on him all the way.

'What's up with your leg?' she asked.

'I, er, I fell down some steps. I wasn't even that drunk.'

'You haven't broken it, have you?'

'No. Just a sprain, I think. Bashed my ribs a little, too.'

'Bloody hell, Scott. You've only been gone for a couple of hours and you end up in this state.'

He smiled, shrugged. That hurt too.

'So what did he say?' she asked.

'Who?'

'Gavin.'

'Nothing much. We talked about the footy, mostly.'

'I meant what did he say about the money?'

'Oh. Yeah. He was really good about it. Said he's got plenty of work coming in if I want it. I'm starting tomorrow, in fact.'

'Tomorrow? When tomorrow?'

'I'll stay at the garage a bit longer. Do a couple of extra hours. That's okay, isn't it?'

She stared for an uncomfortably long time. 'Sure,' she said flatly. 'No time like the present, I suppose.'

'That's what I thought.'

She turned back to her film and sipped her tea and left him in a silence that was drowning him. He watched with her for a while, but the black-and-white images felt alien. They were pictures from a long time ago, infused with an innocence and morality that didn't fit into the world he now knew.

After a few minutes he said, 'I think I'll turn in. Long day ahead tomorrow.'

'Okay,' she answered. 'I'll just watch the end of this.'

He smiled, kissed her on the cheek, tried not to show his suffering as he rose from the sofa.

In the bathroom, he decided on a shower rather than a bath. He stripped off slowly, each garment inducing its own particular form of pain. He looked at himself in the mirror, at the array of colours blemishing his body. He touched a particularly dark spot on his chest and winced, wondering if the rib might be broken.

He turned on the shower and climbed in. Stood still while the needles of heat massaged him with simultaneous pain and relief.

When he could take no more, he turned off the water and threw back the curtain. Through the clouds of steam he saw her.

Gemma clamped a hand to her mouth, but a sob still spluttered through her fingers.

'Look at you,' she said quietly. 'Look at you.'

He climbed out of the tub and stood naked before her. There was no point trying to hide it now.

'You should see the other fella,' he said, but she didn't laugh.

She crossed the room. Stroked a finger across his mottled chest.

'I came in here to have it out with you.'

'Catch me when I'm naked and vulnerable, eh?'

'Something like that.'

'And now?'

'What do you mean?'

'You still want to have a go at me?'

'No. I want to hug you. But I'm afraid of breaking you.'

'Just be gentle with me,' he said with a smile.

She put her arms around him, but with no pressure, her

own flesh barely touching his. He felt a droplet run down his shoulder, and he wasn't sure whether it was from the shower or Gemma.

'We can't go on like this,' she whispered in his ear. 'Lying to each other, I mean. Pretending. We've always been honest with each other. Always.'

'I . . . I'm trying to protect you, Gem. You and Daniel.'

'I know, I know. But look what it's doing to you. They've got you now, haven't they? You belong to them.'

'Gem, I—'

'It's okay. You don't have to tell me the details. I just don't want it to change you. I don't want it to come between us.'

He pulled back and looked her in the eye. 'It won't. Here's the truth, Gem. Tomorrow it will be over. When I come home tomorrow night, it'll be done.'

He saw her doubt, and it didn't surprise him. He had developed a history of making unfulfilled promises recently.

'I mean it,' he continued. 'No more lies. It ends tomorrow.'

'But you will come home?' She looked him up and down, waved her hand to indicate his battered form. 'No more of this?'

'No more of this.' Which was the truth, whichever way it went. 'They had to teach me a lesson, that's all. Tomorrow, all I have to do is deliver a package.'

'If it was as simple as that, they'd do it themselves. It'll be dangerous, won't it?'

'Not if I play my cards right.'

She searched his face. 'You're not lucky at cards. This family has never had much luck.'

'Then maybe it's about time things changed,' he said.

42

Hannah was surprised to find that Ben was still up when she got home. For some reason she had expected him to be tucked up in bed, fast asleep after his earlier exertions.

'Well hello, Bruce Wayne,' she said as she entered the living room.

Ben closed his book and got up from the sofa. He pushed his hands into the pockets of his dressing gown and shrugged.

'Well, you know, I don't like to brag . . .'

'Talk about hiding your light under a bushel. Where the hell did that come from?'

He looked suddenly guilty. 'Did I go too far? Are you ashamed of me?'

'Are you kidding? Come here.'

She kissed him long and hard, then hugged him tight until her arms ached. Her head was aching too after the battering it had taken from alcohol, adrenaline and a toilet bowl.

'You know how I hate violence,' he said.

'Yes, I know that.'

'It always has to be a last resort.'

'Yes.'

'But you're my wife, and that little shit was hurting you. I couldn't allow that.'

'No. That's very logical.'

'I think so, too.'

'But you also enjoyed it, right?'

'Hell, yeah. It was a blast. In fact, I'm thinking of joining the police so I can beat up more people.'

Hannah pulled away. 'First of all, that's not exactly a great summary of what we do in the police. In fact, it's downright insulting. And secondly, you'd make a terrible copper.'

'That's also insulting.'

'But true.'

'Well, yeah, probably. I make great tea, though. You want some tea?'

'I'd love one.'

When he went out to the kitchen, Hannah sat down on the seat he had occupied. She glanced at the book he'd been reading. *Harnessing Your Chi: Strategies for Focusing Your Internal Energy.* She smiled. Copper, indeed.

But that was why she loved him. Because he was all the things she wasn't. His yin to her yang. Or vice versa. He'd know the answer to that one.

He came back into the room a few minutes later. 'One cup of builder's brew extra strength and one cup of lapsang souchong. You can take your pick.'

'Hmm, that's a difficult choice. I'll have the one I can spell.'

'You're not making it easy. I've seen your police reports.' He handed her a mug and sat next to her. 'How'd it go at the interview?'

She quickly summarised, her mind already racing ahead to the next topic of conversation.

'Ben,' she said.

'Hannah.'

'I need to talk to you about something.'

'Shit, I knew it. I'm in trouble, aren't I? I *did* go too far, and now you're going to arrest me or put me in a choke hold or something.'

'It's serious, Ben.'

He paused. 'Okay.'

'It's about Tilly.'

'All right.'

'If you don't want to talk about her, then I'll stop right now.'

'No. Go ahead. You obviously need to get it off your chest. You're still seeing her, aren't you?'

She nodded. 'More than ever. Only . . .'

'What?'

'Now it's starting to worry me.'

'Why?'

'It's happening at the weirdest of times.'

'Weird in what way?'

'I told you how I saw her just before the thing with Suzy Carling, right?'

'Yes.'

'What I didn't tell you is that I also saw her just before both attacks by her son.'

'You saw her tonight, in the pub?'

'Yes. She was standing in the doorway when you were paying the bill. I followed her upstairs.'

'You didn't say anything.'

She frowned. 'What was I going to say, especially with the waiter standing there? Excuse me while I just check on my dead daughter that nobody else can see?'

'No, but . . .'

She took his hand. 'Ben, that's not the point I'm trying to make. I'm not saying all this to upset you.'

'I know that. But then what is it that's bothering you?'

'I . . .' She had her words ready, but they seemed so ridiculous in her head. 'Oh, I don't know. Forget it. I'm just tired.'

He squeezed her hand. 'No. Please. You need to talk about it, and I need to know what it's doing to you. What is it, Hannah?'

'It's just . . . Look, I know it's all a figment of my imagination. My subconscious or whatever, playing tricks on me. I know all that. But . . .'

'But what?'

'What if it's something more?'

'Like what?'

'What if she's trying to tell me something?'

A longer pause now. 'Hannah, are you talking about some kind of communication from the afterlife?'

'I know, it sounds stupid. But think about those three events. Suzy Carling. The attacks. Tilly was there each time. I keep wondering whether . . . whether she was trying to hurt me.'

'Hurt you! Why would she do that?'

'I don't know. Because she's upset with me. Because I didn't try hard enough to save her.'

Ben shook his head vigorously. 'You know she wouldn't do that. She loved you. If she really was trying to communicate, it would have been to help you or to warn you that danger was nearby.'

'Is that what you think – that she's trying to help me?'

He sighed heavily. 'No, Hannah. I don't. She's not trying to hurt you and she's not trying to help you. She's not there at all. You know that as well as I do. The last time we spoke about this, you told me you'd seen her quite a few times, isn't that right?'

'Yes. Once at the supermarket. Again in the park . . .'

'And did anything bad happen then? No. This is classic confirmation bias, Hannah. You're focusing on the events that support your wonky hypothesis while conveniently ignoring the ones that don't.'

She considered this, and knew that he was right.

'So what's going on with me?' she asked. 'Should I see a doctor?'

Ben folded her arms around her. 'You don't need a doctor. This is your way of coping with what happened to Tilly, and that's perfectly okay.'

'You think she'll ever stop coming?'

'When you're ready, but I don't think you need to push her away. She'll go in her own good time.'

'I'll never forget her, though.'

'No. I don't think either of us could ever do that. One way or another, she'll always be with us.'

*

Hannah woke with a start, convinced that someone had just prodded her through the duvet.

She raised her head and blinked, but saw only patterns of darkness, black on grey. Next to her, no doubt dreaming about his heroic antics, Ben slept soundly.

She checked the clock and saw that it was twenty past three in the morning. She turned over and closed her eyes again.

Then she heard the footsteps.

Here, in the bedroom.

They were followed by a series of metallic pings, as though somebody was running a hand along the brass rails at the foot of the bed as they went past.

Just as Tilly had always done.

It was a thing of hers. Every time she walked past the foot of bed: slap, slap, slap, ping, ping, ping. The sound had always made Hannah smile.

She sat up, alert now. Heard nothing more except a gentle murmur from Ben.

A dream state, she told herself. You imagined it.

But then her eyes caught movement. A dark shape, slipping through the doorway. A Tilly-sized shape.

More footsteps, along the landing now, and then the creak of another door.

The door to Tilly's bedroom.

Her heart pounding, Hannah slipped out of bed. She moved silently and swiftly out to the landing. It crossed her mind to put a light on, but she didn't want to ruin things. If Tilly was here, she didn't want to do anything that might frighten her away.

She went to Tilly's door. It was partly open, and Hannah couldn't remember if it had been that way when she'd gone to bed.

She opened it wider and stepped inside.

Tilly's curtains had not been drawn, and the streetlamps were casting a weak grey light into the room. Enough to see what was here.

Enough to see Tilly.

She was sitting on her bed, perfectly still. She was in her school uniform again. Shiny shoes pressed tightly together, inches above the floor. Her expression was unreadable. Was she happy to be here, or sad? Or was she simply here to deliver a message of some kind?

'Tilly?' Hannah whispered.

Tilly didn't move.

Hannah started to head towards the bed, but stopped in her tracks when she saw how Tilly tensed.

'I'm sorry,' she said. 'Please don't go.'

It doesn't matter why she's here, Hannah thought. I'm just happy that she is. Look how beautiful she is.

Tears sprang from Hannah's eyes. She wanted desperately to hold her daughter and never let her go. This vision of her wasn't enough.

'What is it, Tilly?' she asked. 'Are you missing me? Because I miss you so much.'

The tears flowed more freely. Hannah wiped them away with the back of her hand to stop them blurring what little she could see of her daughter.

'Talk to me, Tilly. Please, talk to me.'

And then Tilly moved.

She slid off the edge of the bed, but didn't come towards her mother. Instead she walked across to the window and stood looking down at the large toy hamper.

'What is it?' Hannah asked.

Tilly continued to stare at the hamper. Hannah took a few tentative steps towards it, and Tilly didn't move.

'What is it?' she asked again.

She knelt down in front of the hamper. Lifted its lid. The first thing she saw there was one of Tilly's favourite teddy bears. She lifted it out and held it up in front of her.

'This? You want Bramley?'

But Tilly didn't even give it a glance. Hannah looked again. On the top, where she had left them, were all the Adam-9 toys and comics and games that Tilly had once loved so much.

She pulled out an Adam-9 action figure and a comic. 'These?'

And this time, Tilly looked her directly in the eye, and she knew she was right. What she couldn't understand at first was why.

But then it hit her.

She pictured Daniel, her rescuer, sitting in his chair in exactly the same pose that Tilly used to adopt. Transfixed by his favourite television programme the way Tilly used to be.

And she remembered her discussions with Ben.

'You want me to let you go, don't you? You're not here because you want to be, but because I'm keeping you here. I'm stopping you leaving. That's right, isn't it?' She looked into the hamper again and rummaged around. 'All of these things – I keep them to remind me of you, but you're telling me they would make somebody else so happy. You want me to—'

Tilly was gone.

Hannah jumped to her feet and scanned the room. But she knew she was alone again.

Tilly had delivered her message, and Hannah had received and understood it.

Time to move on.

43

Hannah had hoped that Friday morning would be different. After all she'd been through the previous night, she'd assumed that she was owed one to redress the balance, and that all the answers she needed for the Joey Cobb case would fall into her lap.

It wasn't like that.

In fact, it felt as though she was nowhere nearer solving this case than she was at the beginning.

What made it worse was that this wasn't true. She had mountains of evidence and witness statements. She knew approximately where and when Cobb was murdered, where his body parts were deposited, and even the make and model of the car that was probably used to transport his remains. She had Cobb's possessions – notably the drugs and money. She had the fingerprints and DNA found on the bin liners and the drug packets, and she had transcripts of interviews with nearly everyone Cobb had spoken to in the hours leading up to his death. She knew his enemies, and she knew every detail of their alibis.

So why couldn't she make that final step? Why wasn't there enough in that huge mountain of material to establish the identity of the killer?

She couldn't blame her team. They had worked tirelessly. Done everything asked of them.

So it must be me then, she decided. Devereux threw down the gauntlet, and I made the mistake of picking it up. I thought I could win. Was I too arrogant? Or just too lazy? Have I really done everything I could have done?

She got out of her chair and left her office. Wandered into the squad room and went straight across to Marcel's desk.

'How are we doing with that list?' she asked.

'The Toyotas?'

'Yes, the Toyotas.'

Marcel held up a sheaf of printed papers annotated with lots of his scribbles.

'Still working on them.'

'Let me see.'

He handed the list over. She flipped through the pages.

'Not as many out there as I thought. Looks like you've done most of them.'

Marcel picked up another, longer list from his desk. 'We haven't started on this lot yet.'

Hannah blew air out the side of her mouth. 'Shit. All right, give me a few pages.'

'Boss?'

'We need everyone we can get on this. The answer's in there – I know it is. So gimme.'

Marcel handed her a few pages from the top. She went straight back to her office and placed the list in front of her.

'Right,' she said to herself. 'Here we go.'

An hour later, she was starting to regret volunteering.

It seemed that almost everyone she spoke to either didn't understand what was being asked of them, or else led really complicated lives that they felt compelled to bring into the conversation.

One more, she thought, and then I'm breaking for coffee.

She picked up her phone and tapped in the last known number of the next car owner on the list. It rang for ages, and she was on the verge of giving up when it was answered.

'Hello?'

'Hello. Is that Mr Rodney Parkes?'

'Yes.'

'Hello, Mr Parkes. This is Detective Inspector Hannah Washington of Stockford Police. I wonder if I might ask you a few questions?'

'Police? Did you say police?'

'Yes, that's right. Nothing to worry about, but if I could just—'

'Why would the police be calling me?'

'It's just routine, Mr Parkes. It'll only take a couple of minutes of your time, if you don't mind.'

'Well, okay, but I haven't done anything wrong, have I?'

'Not that I'm aware of. Perhaps if you could just let me ask my questions?'

'Okay. Sure. Go ahead.'

'Our records show us that you're the registered owner of a silver Toyota Avensis, is that right?'

'Sheila.'

'I'm sorry? Are you saying you're not the owner?'

'No. I mean yes, I am the owner, but I call my car Sheila. It's my wife's name.'

'You call your car the same name as your wife?'

'Yes. In her memory. She died three years ago, rest her soul. The big C. It's a terrible illness, you know. Terrible.'

'Yes. I'm sorry to hear—'

'Anyway, she loved our car. I often suggested getting something different, something newer, but she wouldn't hear of it. So I've still got it. I look after it in the same way I looked after her. When she gets sick, I get her fixed. I wasn't able to do that with my wife.'

'No. Could I ask if—'

'I never break the speed limit, if that's why you're calling. I don't drink and drive, either. I also don't park on yellow lines or in disabled parking bays. In fact, I've never had a fine or points on my licence.'

Hannah wanted to tell him to shut up. If everyone on the list was like Mr Parkes then no wonder it was taking so long to work through them.

'That's very commendable,' she said. 'But if you don't mind, I'd like to ask you about last weekend.'

'Last weekend? What about last weekend?'

'Specifically Sunday. Did you drive last Sunday?'

'Sunday? Let me think. Sunday. Yes, that's right. I did. I went to the beach.'

'You drove to the beach? Which beach would that be?'

'It's called Playa de El Palo. Do you know it?'

'No, I can't say I do. Where is that?'

'Just outside Málaga.'

'Málaga? Málaga in Spain?'

'Is there another?'

'Wait. Let me get this straight. Last Sunday, you drove all the way to a beach in Málaga?'

'Sure. It's not that far. Couple of miles, maybe.'

Hannah rubbed her forehead. It was beginning to ache.

'So . . . what you're telling me is that you were staying there, in Málaga?'

'Yes. What did you think I meant?'

'You have an apartment there?'

'Yes. A timeshare.'

'When did you go?'

'Thursday. Not yesterday, of course. The previous Thursday.'

'So you went to Málaga last Thursday. In late October.'

'October is a nice month in Málaga. Not too hot, but not cold either. Nothing like it is here. Very pleasant.'

'And when did you come back?'

'Tuesday. I wanted to stay longer, but I had to be back for my sister's birthday party. She was sixty this week. Two years younger than me. I took early retirement, you know. They kept putting the pension age up, and I thought to hell with this, I'm getting out of here before I drop dead on the factory floor. I worked in a biscuit factory, did I tell you that?'

Hannah ignored the question. She didn't want to get into a long discussion about the merits of bourbons versus custard creams.

'So you were away from Thursday to Tuesday, and on the Sunday you drove from your apartment down to the beach?'

'I did.'

'With Sheila?'

'No. I already told you: she died three years ago.'

'No. I mean you drove in Sheila the car? The Toyota?'

'No. I had a hire car. A little Fiat. Sheila would never last a journey like that, all the way from England to the south of Spain. She's getting on a bit. I don't think she'll ever be as old as my wife, but then I've probably not got that many years left either. I have very high blood pressure, you know, and I get angina.'

Hannah was beginning to think Mr Parkes was unlikely to be the killer she sought.

'Mr Parkes, is it possible that anyone could have used your car without your permission while you were abroad, particularly on Sunday?'

'Used Sheila? No. Not possible.'

'You seem very certain.'

'I am. She was locked away.'

'Locked away? Where?'

'In the garage.'

'You have a garage?'

'No. I mean the garage where they fix cars. Like I said, when Sheila gets sick, I get her better, and I always use the same doctor. Been using them for years. Very reliable, and they don't charge the earth, either. They picked it up while I was away, fixed it, and brought it back again on Tuesday.'

'Who might they be?'

'Crossland Garage. Bryant Street. You know it?'

'Can't say I do.'

'Very reliable. Very nice fellas. Gavin Crossland and his mate whose name I can never remember. Like the polar explorer guy.'

Hannah had no idea what he was talking about, and no desire to pursue it.

'Thank you, Mr Parkes,' she said. 'You've been very helpful.'

Helpful in using up a big chunk of day I'll never get back, she thought.

'That's it? You just wanted to ask about my holiday?'

'As I say, this was just a routine call.'

'I took pictures. You want to see them? There's a pool and everything. Okay, I have to share it, but in October it's very quiet, and—'

'Goodbye, Mr Parkes.' And she hung up.

She brought her pen to his name, ready to cross it off her list.

Would you be happy, she asked herself, if one of your team left it at that?

Check out every story. And then double-check.

She googled Crossland Garage and found a phone number. She called it.

'Crossland Garage.'

'Hello. It's Stockford Police here. Detective Inspector Hannah Washington. Is that Mr Crossland?'

'It is.'

'Just a quick question or two, Mr Crossland. We're trying to trace a Toyota Avensis that may have been used in a crime recently, and I believe you fixed one last weekend. Is that correct?'

'Yup.'

Thank God for conciseness, she thought.

'Could you confirm when it was that it was brought in and how long you had it for?'

'Let me think ... We picked it up Friday. Took it back Tuesday.'

'Do you normally keep cars for so long?'

'Not normally, but the owner had gone away on holiday.'

'Is there any possibility that the vehicle could have been used without your knowledge over the weekend? I'm thinking of Sunday in particular.'

'No. We're closed on Sundays, and the car was locked up in the garage. Safe as houses here.'

'You're sure?'

'Absolutely. Wouldn't have mattered anyway.'

'What do you mean?'

'The car's gearbox was knackered. We had to tow it here. Didn't fix it till Monday. Before then there's no way it could be driven.'

'Thank you, Mr Crossland. You've been very helpful.'

'No problem.'

She ended the call. Looked again at her list. Crossed off Mr Parkes.

Better luck next time, she thought.

Scott Timpson couldn't believe his luck.

She hadn't recognised his voice.

But then why would she? They'd had one short conversation at the beginning of the week. She's probably spoken to hundreds of people since then, he thought. Probably doesn't even remember my name or what I look like.

But what if Gavin had answered? He might have dropped me in it by saying the car had already been fixed before Sunday.

Definitely a lucky escape there.

Although . . .

How did they get onto the car? How the hell did they track it to the garage?

How much closer will they get?

What if they decide to search the car? They'll find forensic evidence. They'll come back to the garage and make the connection to me.

'Shit,' he said quietly, his fist tightly clenched. He could hear Gavin on the other side of the garage, putting a wheel back on.

He paced up and down for a few seconds, ignoring the pain that still wracked his body.

Wait, he told himself. Calm down. You heard her on the phone. She doesn't think it's that car. They're probably looking at hundreds of cars, from CCTV or something. If they really thought it was that one, they'd have come here in person. A routine inquiry, that's all it was.

He took several long, deep breaths. He knew he couldn't let this get to him. His nerves were shot already.

He had to keep his wits about him for what he needed to do later.

44

Hannah had her defences up even before she went into DCI Ray Devereux's office. She suspected he wasn't about to offer a pat on the back. More likely a kick in the arse.

He'll ask me to run through our progress on the case, she thought, and he'll question my judgement, and then he'll summarise by telling me how I need to pull my socks up. That's usually how these things go. He'll do it nicely, though. Probably wearing a smile as he points out my deficiencies.

She quickly found out that her suspicions were unfounded.

Things were much, much worse.

'Come in, Hannah,' Devereux said, indicating the chair on the other side of his desk.

No smile. Uh-oh.

'I don't suppose you've seen the local rag today, have you?' he asked.

She glanced at the folded-up newspaper in front of him. 'No. Why?'

'Take a look.' He slid it across to her.

Hannah read the headline:

TRAIN-DEATH DETECTIVE IN SCRAP WITH VICTIM'S SON.

Fucking hell, Hannah thought. She continued to read:

A high-ranking police detective who was investigated for her part in a fatal chase was involved in a fist fight yesterday with the dead woman's grieving son.

Detective Inspector Hannah Washington of Stockford Police had been the focus of an inquiry in September regarding her actions during an investigation into the whereabouts of a known criminal, Mr Tommy Glover. What began as routine questioning of Ms Suzy Carling, who was Glover's partner at the time, quickly degenerated into a foot chase that led to Ms Carling running onto a railway line in front of a high-speed train.

Ms Carling was killed instantly in the collision, but although she had never been arrested, charged or named as a suspect in any crime, the inquiry later cleared Inspector Washington of any wrongdoing in taking up the pursuit. Mr Shane Carling, son of the deceased, denounced the decision at the time, declaring it a 'travesty of justice'.

In a bizarre twist last night, Inspector Washington chose to dine at the King George pub in Stockford, where Mr Carling, a regular at the pub, was already drinking at the bar.

Witnesses report how an intense 'scrap' broke out between Mr Carling and Inspector Washington in the upstairs toilets, with the detective aided in the struggle by her husband Ben. The fight resulted in Mr Carling sustaining injuries that made him look 'like he'd gone ten rounds with Tyson Fury'.

Hannah pushed the paper back towards Devereux. She'd had enough poison.

'Bullshit,' she said.

'What is?' Devereux asked.

'All of it. It's so biased, for one thing. I'm the "Train-Death Detective" and he's the "grieving son"? Give me a break. And then they make it sound like I'd gone to that pub because I knew he'd be there—'

'*Did* you know he drank there?'

'Of course not. Do you think I'd be stupid enough to go there if I had? I went there because Marcel Lang recommended it. Carling can't be that much of a regular, because Marcel has eaten there several times and he's never bumped into him.' She jabbed at the paper. 'And then there's all this shit about a "scrap". It wasn't a fucking scrap. It was an assault. By Carling. If Ben hadn't turned up, I'd have been the first person in history to have been murdered with a fucking bog brush. Who are these so-called witnesses anyway?'

'All right, Hannah. Calm down. I'm just trying to get to the bottom of this.'

'Fine. Watch the interviews with Carling. He puts his hands up to all of it. If anyone's a "victim" here, it's me. Twice, in fact!'

'Yes, about that ... There's nothing in your reports about the first assault.'

'That's because it wasn't worth reporting. I didn't see who it was, and neither did anyone else.'

'But it was serious enough for you to require hospitalisation?'

'That's an exaggeration of the truth. I dropped in to A&E because Marcel Lang insisted on it. It wasn't that bad.'

'I've already spoken to Marcel about it. Apparently you lost consciousness.'

'For a while, yes. I'm fine now.'

Devereux tapped his fingers on the desk, giving Hannah the impression that he was choosing his next words with care. It seemed ominous.

'Is it possible,' he said, 'that you knew more about your attacker than you were willing to admit at the time?'

Hannah stared at him as she tried to process this.

'Wait. Are you asking what I think you're asking?'

Devereux hesitated. 'It is being suggested in some quarters—'

'No, don't mince your words, Ray. You're saying did I know it was Carling who attacked me in the flats? And if so, is that why I went to his boozer, so I could provoke him into having another go, giving me the excuse I needed to beat the crap out of him? That's what you're saying, isn't it?'

'It's . . . a hypothesis that's been put forward.'

'It's bollocks is what it is. And you should be ashamed of yourself for repeating it. You *know* me, Ray. You know I wouldn't do something like that.'

Devereux flushed, but Hannah wasn't sure if it was out of embarrassment or anger.

'Look, I don't for one moment believe there's any substance to this. But you know what it's like when rumours start flying round.'

'Yes, I know what it's like. And what I expect to happen when they do is for my line manager to quash them before they spread. So let me make this as clear as fucking crystal. I had no idea that the man who attacked me in Erskine Court was Shane Carling. The only reason I didn't report it was that the young man who chased him away had learning difficulties, and I didn't see any point in putting him through a legal process that would have gone nowhere. Furthermore, I had no idea that Carling was a regular at the King George. Now, will that do, or do you want me to put it in writing?'

She could see that she had pushed back a bit too hard. Devereux was definitely looking flustered now.

'All right, Hannah. Point taken.' He nodded towards the newspaper. 'But this is still a problem.'

'It's only a problem if we don't ignore it for the trash it is.'

'It's not that simple. It raises your profile, and not in a good way.' He picked up the paper and began reading. '"Washington is currently the senior detective investigating the murder of Joseph Cobb, a prominent gangland figure. These latest events have prompted some to question Washington's suitability for the role, with one close family member of Cobb commenting that they had 'lost all faith in the police'."'

'You know who that'll be, don't you?' Hannah said. 'Myra Cobb. She'll be saying that even when we find her son's killer.'

'Yes,' Devereux said slowly, and there was something in his tone that turned that single word into a hundred more.

Hannah shook her head. 'No, Ray. Don't say what you're about to say. We're making good progress on this case.'

Devereux sighed. 'It's been nearly a week now, Hannah. A week. And I'm not convinced we've got much to show for it.'

'We've got tons to show for it. We're hot on the tail of the car that was used to dump Cobb's body. As soon as we find it, we've got our man.'

'Well, that's good news. But if that's the case, it shouldn't be that difficult for another lead to tie up the loose ends.'

'Another lead? Why do we need another lead?'

Devereux picked up the paper and dropped it again. 'This! It's bad PR, Hannah. We can't simply ignore it. We have to restore public confidence in our ability to investigate serious crimes.'

'What are you talking about? Carling attacked me. Not the other way round. What part of that is so hard to understand? If you want to restore confidence, try standing up for your officers. Try issuing statements about what really happened instead of pandering to media hacks. If you remove me from the investigation, you might as well put a huge question mark against the rest of my career.'

'I'm sorry, Hannah. The decision has already been made. After end of play today, I'll be taking over as SIO on the Cobb case.'

Hannah stared at him open-mouthed. 'No, no, no. This isn't about public confidence. It's not about that shitty little newspaper. It's about me. It's what you wanted all along. This story has just given you the extra ammunition you need to finish the job.'

'Hannah, I think you should stop there, before you say something you regret.'

'You set me up for a fall, Ray. You thought I wasn't up to it anymore, so you threw me in at the deep end, expecting me to drown. But I'm swimming like a fish, Ray, and you don't like it. That shabby article is your excuse to make accusations of impropriety, even though you know I've done everything by the book. I have done everything you've asked of me, and more. Admit it, Ray. You're shafting me.'

Devereux shifted uncomfortably in his chair. 'Hannah, you have to understand that this wasn't a unilateral decision on my part. As I said, I'm getting pressure from above—'

'Fuck you, Ray!' She jumped out of her chair. 'Fuck all those above you, too, but most of all fuck you for not having the balls to defend me.' She stormed away, but paused at the door. 'Good luck with your next promotion,' she said, 'but I hope you remember the people you walked over to get it.'

45

It felt to Scott as though something was gnawing at his insides. Work couldn't distract him. The only thing on his mind was the upcoming encounter with Barrington Daley. He didn't know anything about the man except that he was a drug dealer. He imagined a scarred, tattooed, muscle-bound maniac with a gun in each hand, willing to cut down anyone who came within a hundred metres of his contraband.

He tried telling himself it wouldn't be like that. Barrington would be just an average-looking guy, no bigger than himself. Probably meaner, though. Quicker to resort to violence almost certainly.

Still scary.

Scott had never instigated a fight. He could count on one hand the number of punch-ups in which he'd been involved, and they had always resulted from others making the first move. Like yesterday, for example. And look how that turned out.

Which was another problem. After the beating he'd taken, he was hardly match-fit. He couldn't afford to allow things to get too physical. His body wouldn't cope.

Go in fast and go in hard. Overwhelm the opposition. There was no other way.

He'd considered all the alternatives. He'd thought about taking the family and running away, but where would they go? And how would they manage without money? He'd also thought again about Gemma's advice to go to the police, but he knew he was in far too deep for that now. At best, they'd all end up in prison; at worst, dead.

No, this was his only option. He had to see it through. And he had to come out on top. Then this nightmare would be over.

When he saw it was after four o'clock, the thing inside him began scurrying and chewing again. Ronan had told him that the money drop-off would take place between four and five. It could be sitting there right now in Barrington's flat. A white Adidas bag full of cash, just waiting for Scott to come and get it, thereby solving all his problems.

At five o'clock, Scott visited the toilet for the second time in ten minutes. The rodent in his belly seemed to be using his intestines as a skipping rope.

He drank water from the tap, then washed a couple of handfuls over his face.

He needed Gavin to go home now. Only two hours left until some unknown third party collected the money from Barrington's flat. That couldn't be allowed to happen. To be on the safe side, Scott intended to turn up at six. He didn't want to take the risk of someone else knocking on the door while he was there. One drug dealer at a time was plenty, thank you.

He had preparations to make. But to carry them out, he

needed Gavin to go home. Gavin was usually anxious to make a quick getaway on Friday afternoons, but there was no sign of him packing up yet.

Please don't let this be an exception, Scott thought. Not today of all days.

He left the washroom. Gavin was typing something on the computer.

'Not off to the pub tonight, Gav?'

'Yeah, in a minute. I just need to run off an invoice for the VW job, but I can't get the damn printer to connect.'

'I'll sort it out if you like. You get going. I'll lock up.'

Gavin raised his head and smiled. 'Don't go putting an extra couple of hours on your timesheet. I know you owe me, but this is five minutes' work we're talking about.'

Scott laughed, and hoped it sounded genuine. 'I'm sure you'll get it out of me one way or another.'

Gavin left his chair and started collecting his things. Scott took his place and pretended to look busy. He'd encountered this problem before and knew it was a simple Wi-Fi issue that could be resolved in seconds, but he wasn't going to let his boss know that.

'Right,' Gavin said. 'See you Monday.'

'See you, Gav.'

Scott tapped a few random keys, stopping when Gavin exited the garage. He waited until he heard Gavin's car rev up and zoom away.

He checked the clock again. Quarter past five. Time was being swallowed up.

Quickly restoring the printer connection, he printed the

invoice and placed it on the desk. He left the computer running for now. He was going to need it.

He went to the double doors at the front of the garage, swung them closed and bolted them. Then he locked up the door to the reception area.

He went back to the office, past the computer. Halted in front of the steel filing cabinet – the one that Daniel had moved in here without even emptying it. Kneeling down on the floor, he slid open the bottom drawer. It was full of customer records, but he wasn't interested in those. He reached underneath the drawer, found what he wanted. He stripped the duct tape away and brought out the plastic bag and its contents.

He opened up the bag and took out the single item. Hefted its weight in his hand. Considered its power.

The gun.

Joey Cobb's gun.

He still wasn't entirely sure why he'd held onto it. He'd thrown away all the money, the drugs, but he'd kept the one thing he thought he'd never need.

His memory was that it was a just-in-case impulse. At the time, he'd been ninety-nine per cent certain that his crimes would never be discovered. But there was still that other one per cent. He'd known what Joey Cobb was, and therefore what dark forces his sudden disappearance might attract. The gun was insurance, nothing more. He'd hoped that, when everything died down, he could retrieve it and dispose of it.

But all that had changed. This gun might be the only thing that could enable him to get out of this mess.

There was just one problem. He didn't know how to use it.

He had never in his life handled a real gun, let alone fired one. He believed he could figure out what to do with a revolver, but this wasn't one of those. It had buttons and catches on the side, and he didn't know what any of them did. He had watched plenty of action movies and seen how characters often pulled back the top part of the gun before firing, but he didn't know why they did that. Would he have to do the same with this one, or would that completely mess it up? Was the gun even loaded?

Scott carried the weapon across to the computer, then opened up a private web page so that his search history wouldn't be recorded. He typed in the text inscribed on both sides of the gun and started reading through the results. He discovered that the gun was manufactured by Smith and Wesson, and that the model was a 9mm M&P Shield, the M&P standing for 'Military and Police'.

Delving deeper, he watched various YouTube videos and read the user manual carefully. He found out that the gun was a semi-automatic, meaning that each pull of the trigger would fire a bullet, eject the used cartridge, and load the next round into the chamber. It also had a double-action trigger, meaning that the hammer did not have to be cocked initially to enable firing.

With the manual open on the screen in front of him, he investigated the buttons on the pistol. He worked out how to use the safety catch and operate the magazine release. Removing the magazine revealed to him that it held eight rounds. Operating the slide mechanism like they did in the movies ejected another.

He put it all back together again. Nine rounds in total. Such lethal, destructive force in his hand.

He was almost ready.

He took a key down from the board on the wall and left the office. From a recycling bin in the garage he took out a handful of outdated vehicle manuals, then lined them up face-out on a shelf, like a column of soldiers. He went over to a souped-up Audi hatchback fitted with an after-market sports exhaust that kept backfiring. He climbed in, started it up, and lowered the driver's window.

He cycled his foot on the accelerator, heard the explosions it generated.

He took the gun from his lap, aimed it at the books on the shelf, squeezed the trigger slowly, just like the videos had taught him.

The kick took him by surprise. The roar of the weapon was intense. He watched a book fly into the air, scattering fragments of paper. He sat there for a minute, just staring at the devastation.

When he turned off the car engine, he found himself panting with exhilaration. He understood now why gun owners could become so intoxicated with their prized possessions.

He got out of the car and went to the books. When he finally located the slug, he was amazed at how deep it had burrowed. He dug it out and slipped it into his pocket. Then he found the spent cartridge on the floor and pocketed that too. The books went back into the bin, buried much deeper than before.

Scott stared again at the gun in his hand. He knew what to expect of it now, what it was capable of. Death in an instant.

Yes, an instant. Not even a second of pain.

He sat down in the driver's seat of the Audi again, sideways on, his feet on the garage floor. His eyes were still on the gun. He raised it, pressed the muzzle into the hollow beneath his chin.

A little bit of pressure on the trigger, he thought. That's all it will take, and all my troubles will be over. No more sleepless nights. No more worrying about killing or being killed. I'll be out of it forever.

So do it, then. Go on. Stop thinking about it and do it.

But then other voices intruded. Gemma and Daniel.

What about us? they asked. *Why would you run away and leave us to deal with your mess?*

He lowered the gun again.

Someone else would have to die.

46

Familiarising himself with the gun had taken far too long. By the time Scott had driven home through the rush-hour traffic, it was quarter past six. He was already fifteen minutes behind schedule.

There was no sign of Biggo and his mates, but he had to share the lift with a woman who looked to be about a hundred. He had to keep the doors open for her while she wheeled in her tartan shopping basket at the pace of a snail on tranquilisers.

'Which floor?' he asked when she had finally conveyed her bones across the threshold. He was aware how terse it sounded, but he had no time for pleasantries.

'One, please, dearie.'

One fucking floor.

He jabbed the buttons for the first and the eighth floors.

'I got stuck in this lift last week,' she said as the lift rose.

Scott grimaced. Please don't break down again, he prayed. Not now, of all times.

He willed the doors to open. When they finally consented, he had to wait another age for the woman to get herself out of the lift again. As she shuffled through the doorway, he wanted to launch a foot into her back to speed things up. Finally the doors closed behind her.

Focus now, he told himself. You'll only get one shot at this. No pun intended.

Shit, this isn't funny. It's insane. Who do I think I am? Al Capone? I have a fucking gun in my backpack. How did I let it get to this?

He began to pace in the lift, felt it rock with his movement.

Go ahead, he thought. Drop like a stone. Smash me to bits in the basement. It would be so much easier. Take the decision out of my hands. I don't know if I can do this.

You *can* do it. You *have* to do it. Think about Daniel. Think about Gemma. You can't let them down.

And then the lift slowed and jerked to a halt. The doors opened, and he was looking at that number again.

801.

Scott stepped out of the lift and stood in front of flat 801, just staring at the digits. Behind him, the lift closed itself up and abandoned him, as though it wanted nothing more to do with this.

He moved closer to the door. A part of him hoped there was nobody home, but he could hear the sound of a video game from inside.

Last chance to consider alternatives. Final opportunity to call it a day. But you'll need another plan if you do.

Time's up.

MOVE!

He rang the doorbell.

The computerised noises from within ceased. The inside of

Scott's mouth turned to dry, dusty cement. His heart felt as though it was in spasm.

The door opened, but it was on a chain. Scott could just about see a man on the other side. Looked like . . . looked like he was wearing a parka with the hood up.

'Whassup?' Barrington asked.

Scott cleared his throat. 'Sorry to bother you, mate. I'm a plumber, working in the flat directly below yours. They've got a leak in their bathroom ceiling. I've checked it out, and it looks like it's coming from your place.'

To add weight to his story, Scott shifted his backpack. It jangled with the spanners and wrenches he'd tossed in there.

'My place?' Barrington said. 'I haven't seen no leak. How's it coming from here?'

'You got a bath or a shower?'

'A bath. Shower over it.'

'Yeah, it's common in these flats. The sealant along the edge of the bath shrinks and pulls away after a while. Only takes the tiniest gap for the shower water to run down the side of the bath and into the flat below. You wouldn't even notice it, but it's a big problem for the people downstairs.'

Open the door. Just open the door and let me in.

'I get it, man, but now's not a good time, you understand? I'm expecting company.'

Yeah, company. So you can offload your drugs money.

'All I need to do is replace the line of sealant. It's a two-minute job.'

'Sorry and all that, man, but it's not, like, convenient, you know what I'm saying?'

312

Scott shrugged, the tools clinking again. 'All right, but I'll have to go back down and tell your neighbour, and I can't get back out here again for a couple of days.' He lowered his voice conspiratorially. 'Between you and me, he's a pain in the arse. You're going to have a fight on your hands, so good luck with it.'

Barrington considered it. 'Two minutes?'

'Max.'

Let me in, let me in.

'Okay. Don't want to upset the neighbours, right?'

Barrington took off the chain, opened the door wide. Scott stepped inside.

The first thing that struck him was that the layout of this corner flat was very different from his own. Instead of a hallway, he had walked straight into the living area. Two doors to his left led, presumably, to a bathroom and a bedroom, whereas his own flat also had a second bedroom.

'Your heating okay?' Scott asked.

'Yeah. Why d'you ask?'

'The coat. Plus, it feels pretty chilly in here. You want me to take a look at your boiler some time?'

He wondered if he was going too far with the act, but Barrington didn't seem concerned. As if only just made aware of how he appeared, Barrington pulled back his hood. Scott was relieved to see that he didn't look as menacing as he'd anticipated. In fact, there were marks on his face that suggested he'd taken something of a beating recently.

'Heating costs money,' Barrington said. 'Speaking of which, you're not gonna charge me for this, right? I mean, I'm not the one asking you to do this.'

'No, don't worry. No charge.'

He started moving to his left.

And then he saw it.

The white Adidas bag. Just sitting there on the glass coffee table. Pregnant with cash.

Keep going. Don't stop, don't react.

'Hold up, bro.'

Scott halted, his heart leaping into his mouth.

'That's my bedroom,' Barrington said. 'You want the other door.'

'Right,' Scott said. He adjusted his path, thinking to himself, Don't look at the bag, don't look at the bag.

He entered the bathroom. It looked like it hadn't been cleaned in months. Thick tide marks on the sink and bath. White splashes of what looked like toothpaste on the tiles. A mirror so clouded with dust and grime it was barely usable.

'Excuse the mess,' Barrington said, closing the toilet lid and picking up a pair of boxer shorts from the floor, as if that fixed the problem.

'I've seen worse.' Scott went across to the bath and flicked at the sealant along one edge. It came away easily, as he'd expected it would. He'd had the same problem in his own flat.

'See?' he said. 'This is the problem. It's not blocking the water. Every time you put the shower on, some of the water escapes down here.'

'So, like, what do you need to do?'

'I take this out, put in some new stuff, that's it.'

Barrington moved closer. 'Go for it.'

Scott nodded, but he was thinking, Move back so I can get my gun out.

He smiled. 'I work better with a cup of tea.'

Barrington narrowed his eyes. 'Two minutes, you said.'

Scott shrugged. No tea.

He slipped his backpack from his shoulder, opened it up, felt around inside. Barrington wasn't moving, wasn't giving him any space. Scott found what he wanted. His fingers curled around the handle. He pressed his index finger lightly on the trigger.

Barrington didn't budge.

Scott was left with no choice.

He yanked out the gun.

47

'Wait,' Barrington said. 'That's the same colour, right?'

Scott held up the sealant gun so that Barrington could get a better look. 'Yep. Bright white. With an anti-fungal agent, too.'

Barrington nodded in approval, and Scott reached across the bath to begin pulling away the old sealant. The sudden movement sent what felt like a red-hot poker through his ribcage.

'You okay?' Barrington asked.

'Yeah. Fell off a ladder last week. Bruised my ribs.'

'Right. Only, I saw the way you were walking in here, too. I never knew plumbing could be so, like, dangerous.'

'You'd be surprised. We go into lofts, under floors. It's not all as simple as this.'

'Guess not.'

Scott turned away again and continued stripping out the sealant, but thoughts were burning in his head: *What if Barrington knows the scum downstairs? They're all into drugs, right, so what if they talk to each other? What if the lads told him about a guy from this building who they beat up and robbed recently?*

No. Don't think that way.

He picked up the sealant gun. 'Out with the old, in with the new,' he said cheerily, but got no response from Barrington. The proper way to do this was to clean the area thoroughly, mask off the edges with tape, and put water in the bath to weigh it down, but he was relying on Barrington having little or no knowledge of DIY.

He began squirting the gunk along the edge of the bath. The combination of pain and Barrington's intense scrutiny made it probably the worst job he'd ever done. The line of sealant was wiggly and uneven, bulging in some places and stringy in others, but it suddenly occurred to him that he might be able to use it to his advantage.

'I just need to neaten this up. Have you got a damp cloth I could use?'

He said it as casually as he could, wondering how such an innocent request could be refused.

Just turn your back and start walking. A little bit of space and time – that's all I need.

But Barrington simply reached to a shelf next to him, grabbed a blue cloth and tossed it into the bath.

Scott picked up the cloth. 'It needs to be damp.'

Barrington pointed at the bath taps. 'You're a plumber, right? You know what they do?'

Scott turned on a tap and wet the cloth. He started to run a plastic scraper along the line of silicone, wiping the excess away on the cloth. When he was done, it didn't look half bad.

'That it?' Barrington asked.

'All there is to it,' Scott answered as he dropped his tools back in his bag. 'Told you I wouldn't be long. If you can, give it a few hours to cure before you get water on it again.'

Barrington nodded, but stayed within touching distance.

Jesus. Is he ever going to allow me room to breathe?

He stood up, waited for Barrington to lead the way out.

'Go ahead,' Barrington said.

Scott wanted to sigh in frustration. He started walking, his unfastened backpack still in his hands. In the living area he saw the Adidas bag again – a stark reminder of why he came here.

It's now or never.

He stopped, turned. Started to open up his backpack again.

'You mind if I leave you my card?' he asked. 'You know, in case you need any plumbing work done in the future?'

He started to reach into the bag. Barrington was only a couple of feet away, but it was the best he was going to get.

'Wait,' Barrington said.

Scott froze, his hand partway into the bag.

'The guy below me,' Barrington continued. 'You said the leak was in his ceiling.'

'That's right.'

'His bathroom ceiling.'

'Yes.'

'So how come you didn't know which door to go through to get to *my* bathroom?'

Scott's brain stalled, exhausted by the effort of the charade. He knew he should have an answer ready on his lips, but it wasn't there. Panic mounting, his eyes darted in search of an answer . . .

And alighted on the Adidas sports bag.

He slid his gaze away again as quickly as he could, praying that Barrington hadn't noticed.

'Well, see . . . the flat downstairs . . . I got confused with—'

But it was clear that Barrington had caught wind of something awry. His eyes narrowed.

Do it now!

His fingers dived into the backpack. Barrington dived at him. Scott produced the semi-automatic just as Barrington cannoned into his solar plexus. He back-pedalled, slammed into a glass-fronted cabinet. One of its doors smashed, showering him with a cloud of shards. The pain in his ribs intensified a thousandfold. He shoved back, tried to bring his gun up, but Barrington was gripping his arm with one hand while throwing wild punches at him with the other. Desperate to bring an end to his battering, Scott wrapped his free arm around his opponent, and they waltzed around the room in a deadly embrace, toppling chairs and sending the contents of shelves cascading to the floor. Scott brought his knee up into Barrington's groin, then fired a kick into the man's midriff to tear him away, but Barrington came straight back at him with a head-butt that smacked into his cheek and sent flashes of light across his vision. Scott let out a roar and wrenched himself out of the clinch, but his gun snagged on Barrington's parka and dropped to the floor. Before he could reach down for it, Barrington sailed into him again, and then they were both rolling on the carpet, both aware that the weapon would bestow on its possessor instant superiority.

Barrington managed to get on top for a brief moment.

He threw two punches into Scott's face, then launched himself towards the gun. Scott grabbed Barrington's ankles and dragged him back, an instant before his opponent's fingers touched the butt of the weapon. He clambered over Barrington's spine, digging in heavily with his knees, then threw himself forwards. As his outstretched hand slapped against cold metal, he felt a sudden sharp pain in his leg. He twisted his body, saw that Barrington had sunk his teeth into his calf. Using the gun as a club, he swung it into Barrington's head. Barrington released his grip and tried to spin away, but Scott was already on him, snarling and yelling and swearing, and feeling how good it was, after all the fights he had lost since he was a kid, after the beatings and humiliation he had taken recently, how exhilarating it was to emerge victorious. Bringing the gun to the temple of his snivelling, shrunken opposition, he felt all his pent-up anger and frustration surging down his arm and into his trigger finger, and he emitted a cathartic roar that drowned out all else.

Afterwards, sitting in his car outside the building, he wanted to cry.

He hadn't dared to believe he could get this far. Never thought he had the strength, the guts, to accomplish what he had. Truth be told, he'd been convinced he'd be dead by now.

He turned to look at what sat in the passenger seat. It was all the proof he needed that he had finally stopped being a loser.

The white Adidas bag. He had taken a peek inside. Had

marvelled at the jumble of fat cash bundles. He had no idea how much was in there; it was beyond his imagining.

He was nearly home and dry. One more errand to make.

So hold back those tears, he thought. Just for a short while.

48

'What time is it?' Ronan asked.

The barman pointed emphatically at the clock behind him in a way that suggested he was always being asked this unnecessary question. 'Five to seven.'

'Really? Where does the time go, eh? Is there a match on at seven?'

'Not tonight, far as I know.'

Ronan didn't care if there was a match on or not. His only objective was fixing in the memory of the bartender that he was here in the pub at this time.

Ronan handed his debit card across. 'Can you a print off a receipt, please?'

Card rather than cash. A time-stamped receipt. Further evidence that he was many miles away from Barrington Daley. Whatever had taken place at the flats, it had probably resulted in a dead body, and since there would be obvious connections between that corpse and the killing of Joey Cobb, Ronan wanted to be able to demonstrate that it had nothing to do with him, Your Honour.

He was conveniently ignoring the fact that establishing this alibi wasn't his own idea. It was his mother's, who had surprised him yet again that her knack for criminality was still as sharp as a razor blade.

As he walked back to her with the drinks – a gin and tonic for her and an orange juice for himself as the designated driver – he realised that this was the first time in months that he'd seen her beyond the boundaries of her farmhouse. Come to think of it, it was that long since he'd seen her out of her kitchen.

Not that she'd made much of an effort to mark the occasion. She'd thrown on a clean-looking cardigan, but that was about it. Hadn't even brushed her teeth.

He realised that she had become the butt of the joke among three girls at a nearby table. They kept glancing her way and giggling. She didn't seem to have noticed; or, if she had, she didn't care. It both saddened and angered Ronan, and at any other time he would have said something, but right now he didn't want to embarrass his mother, and he didn't want to kick up a fuss that might result in their being thrown out. At least the girls would remember her presence here if asked.

In the farmhouse earlier, he had pondered on her degeneration since his father had died. Before that, she'd been strong, assertive. Sober, too. If she had ever taken a drink back then, it was either on special occasions or else done out of his sight. He certainly couldn't recall her being so inebriated that she pissed herself where she sat.

And her looks – where had they gone?

Back at the house, his eyes had strayed to the old photographs on the dresser behind his mother. She had never been glamorous, but there had been a charming and fresh-faced quirkiness to her appearance. A hint of dizziness, impulsiveness and hunger for fun.

And now look at her, he thought as he set the drinks down and watched her immediately pick hers up and begin guzzling. Compare and contrast.

'What time is it?' she asked.

'Getting on for seven.'

She nodded. 'Pick-up's about now, and we've heard nothing. Bastard's dead. Good riddance.'

And what difference has it made? Ronan thought. Scott Timpson is dead, but Joey's still dead too. How has this helped anyone?

Ronan's mobile chirruped. He glanced at the screen.

Well, well, well.

He tried not to smile as he answered the call.

'Hello?'

'It's me. Scott Timpson. I did what you asked.'

It took Ronan a while to find words. His mother was staring at him.

'You . . . you did it? You got what you went for?'

'Yes. I'm looking at it now.'

'And what about our mutual friend?'

'He's no longer a problem.'

Shit, Ronan thought. He's talking like someone out of a fucking spy movie. Suddenly he's a professional.

'And you're in one piece?'

'I'll survive. I just need to get this off my hands.'

'So let's meet. Usual place?'

'I'm leaving now.'

The line went dead. Ronan looked at his screen again, his eyebrows still raised in surprise. Scott Timpson was all business now. No time for idle chit-chat.

'What?' his mother asked.

'He did it. He got the money.'

'What? He's having you on.'

'Mam, this isn't something he'd joke about. I think we underestimated him.'

She didn't look convinced, but then her phone pinged. She opened its cover and squinted at its screen.

'Well, fuck me,' she said.

'What is it?'

'Pick-up never happened. Barrington Daley isn't coming to his door or answering his phone.' She looked up again. 'Seems like your boy was telling the truth.'

Ronan allowed his smile to surface. 'You get your money plus interest. Timpson and his family get their lives back. We're in the clear. Happy days.'

He raised his glass, but his mother didn't join in the celebration.

'What's happening about the money?' she asked.

'He's on his way to our meeting point. I'll need to leave in a minute. Want me to take you home first or come back for you?'

She licked her lips. 'You do know what this means, don't you?'

He didn't like the sound of this. 'What? What does it mean?'

'Timpson is the only thing connecting us to the money and to whatever's happened to Barrington.'

'Mam . . .'

'I don't have to spell it out for you, do I?'

'Mam . . .'

'Sometimes I wonder how you get through life, Ronan. You're not very quick off the mark, are you?'

But he knew exactly what she was getting at, and it poked at something deep in his chest.

'He's done everything we asked him to do, Mam. There aren't many people who could take on the likes of Barrington Daley and come out a winner.'

'You sound like you want to give him a medal.'

'Not a medal, no. But I made a deal with him.'

'Well, now you can unmake it.'

'He's got a family.'

His mother slapped her bicep, where her black armband was hiding beneath her cardigan. '*I* had a fucking family until he came along.'

You've still got a family, Ronan thought. Or don't I count?

He lapsed into a morose silence. Words failed him.

'You know there's no alternative,' she said. 'If the police get to Timpson, they get to us. With him out of the picture, we're safe.'

Ronan suspected that she'd had this in her head all along. It was all part of her Plan B. Grand strategist that she was, she left nothing to chance.

'I don't like this, Mam.'

She leaned forward and patted his arm. 'Sometimes we all have to do things we don't like.'

But not you, he thought. You like this. You love it. And you're not the one who has to do the dirty work.

'So you'll do what's right,' she said. 'Won't you, lad?'

Ronan took a final swig of his orange juice. Not exactly the Dutch courage an executioner needed.

49

This was turning into a bit of a routine.

Standing here at the top of the hill, watching the other man trudge towards him. Each time, Scott Timpson looked more weary than before. More broken.

The sky was clear now, but it had rained solidly for hours earlier, and the field was sodden and slippery. Ronan could see that Scott kept stopping to free his feet from the clinging mud. The effort seemed to drain him a little more each time.

Ronan could also see that Scott was carrying a weighty sports bag.

How the hell did he manage that? Ronan wondered.

But, as he'd told his mother, Scott had a family. It was amazing what strength you could find when you needed to protect the ones you love.

He wondered if his own mother would kill to save him. She was certainly capable of killing, but he thought of her as more of a reaction killer – murder committed in revenge. Would she kill to save him if it meant putting herself at risk? Say, for example, she had the choice of taking a million pounds and flying off to Mexico, or killing a man to save the life of her son, knowing that she'd go to prison for it.

He suspected her choice would involve a sombrero and a hammock.

He looked down again at the approaching figure. The poor guy was probably feeling pretty relieved that he'd almost reached the end of his ordeal. Of course, he had no idea what that ending would involve.

Ronan reached around his waist and touched his fingers to the Colt tucked under his belt. It saddened him that he would have to put it to use. It also irritated him that he hadn't seen this coming. Once again, his mother had been one step ahead of him.

Still, he thought, we are where we are.

He stepped out from beneath the canopy of the old tree, switched on his torch. Ahead, Scott halted.

'Come a bit closer,' Ronan commanded.

He watched the man continue his struggle up the hill.

'That's enough. So, you got the money.'

Scott looked at the bag in his hand, then back again. 'I got it.'

'I'm proud of you. To be honest, I didn't think you could do it.'

'Neither did I.'

'How'd you manage to pull it off?'

'A bit of desperation, mixed with some ingenuity.'

Ronan smiled. 'A side order of violence?'

'Some of that, too.'

'How does it feel? Barrington Daley was a tough opponent for a first match.'

Scott shrugged. 'It's always nice when the underdog wins.'

'You cover your tracks?' Ronan asked. The answer didn't matter. What mattered was that Scott believed he'd be going home.

'I think so. I'll take my chances.'

Ronan nodded. 'Toss the bag over.'

Scott heaved the sports bag into the air. It thudded onto the grass just a couple of feet away from Ronan. It was a good throw, but Ronan saw how the effort sent Scott into a spasm of pain. Scott clutched at his sides, then thrust his hands into his coat pockets and shivered against the cold.

This will be like putting down a sick dog, Ronan thought. A mercy killing.

'You looked inside?'

'Yes.'

'Take any out for yourself?'

'No. It's all there.'

'I believe you. How much?'

'I didn't count. A lot. It's all yours. I'm not interested in the money.'

It wasn't often that Ronan heard people say such things. In his world, wealth and power were everything.

He stepped forward and unzipped the bag. Shone his torch inside. Whistled.

'You're right. That's a lot of money.'

'So my debt's paid, right?'

Ronan pulled the gun from his waistband. He heard Scott's sharp intake of breath.

'Almost.'

'Almost? What do you mean, *almost*? We had a deal.'

'And I'm sticking to the deal. I'm a man of my word, Scott.'

'So why the gun?'

'The deal was that if you got the money, I wouldn't hurt your family. I didn't say anything about what would happen to you.'

'That's just playing with words. Why do you need to kill me? I did everything you asked.'

'That's your answer. Only you know the request came from me. Unless, of course, you told your wife what you've been up to.'

'No! She knows nothing about this. Nothing. You promised you wouldn't hurt her.'

'And I'll keep that promise. But as for you, Scott . . .'

Ronan racked a round into the Colt's chamber. He raised the gun.

The explosion split the night. Ronan saw the spear of flame that jumped between them.

And then he felt the pain. He wondered why something had just punched him in the abdomen, and then he realised that the gunshot wasn't his, that the flash of light had torn out of Scott's coat pocket and then jumped across to rip through his guts, and then the pain suddenly increased an order of magnitude and he knew he had to do something to rescue the situation, but even as he brought his own gun up again, he saw Scott advancing on him with new-found energy in his step, and then there was another explosion, another intensely bright spike that found his chest this time, smashing through his breastbone and carving a tunnel through his lung. He dropped to his knees, forgetting about his gun, thinking only about the rapidly increasing possibility of his death right now. He realised that Scott had closed the gap, was standing right over him, and he accepted that yet again he had not planned for all eventualities, and that he must be such a disappointment to his mother.

'We had a deal,' Scott said to him.

Such a disappointment.

He didn't hear the third gunshot – the one that hollowed out his left eye and expelled much of his brain through the back of his skull.

Scott watched as Ronan's head kicked back, and for a second it was a toss-up as to whether the momentum would fold him backwards or the incline of the hill would topple him forwards. Gravity won out, and the body pitched towards Scott and planted its face wetly in the mud. Scott stood over it, his rapid breathing creating a mist that added a surreal aura to this view of a man with a glistening black hole in the back of his head.

He knew he shouldn't have left it so late. He had taken too much of a risk in waiting until Ronan was pointing a gun at him. He should have begun blasting away as soon as he was in range.

But he had wanted to allow Ronan the opportunity to do the right thing. Perhaps if he had just taken the money and told Scott that they were all square . . .

But no. That wouldn't have helped. Scott had already made his assessment. He had come here knowing that Ronan had to die. He couldn't trust the man to leave him and his family alone.

Waiting until he had no choice but to shoot just made it easier.

I've gone from a man who hides dead bodies to one who creates them.

He jumped at the sound of an engine roaring into life. From beneath the huge tree, a pair of dazzling white headlights lit him up. He narrowed his eyes, tried to understand what was happening.

And then the engine was revved even harder, and a huge beast of a vehicle came hurtling out of its lair towards him. Scott fired two shots towards it, but it felt like throwing pebbles at a rhinoceros. He turned and began racing down the hill, but his damaged ankle quickly gave way on the wet ground, and he tumbled head over heels, each bounce sending rockets of pain through his body. He got to his feet again, picked up his pace. To his left, the edge of the field was separated from the path beyond by a barbed wire fence backed up by hedgerow so dense it seemed impassable. Ahead, though, he could see the stile. If only he could get to it . . .

He had no chance. The ancient Land Rover, sure-footed with its four-wheel drive, closed the gap too quickly. He imagined he could almost feel the heat of its engine as it rumbled up behind him.

A split-second before it slammed into his spine, Scott threw himself to the left. He felt a whoosh of air as the Land Rover missed him by millimetres, and then he hit the ground again. He looked up to see the vehicle brake and then twist slowly in the mud, gradually turning to face him again like it was gliding on ice.

They stared at each other for several seconds, man versus machine, each waiting for the other to make a move. Scott saw that his route to the stile was now barred. He'd have to find another way to escape.

He stood up again and started running towards the field's perimeter. Behind him, the Land Rover growled. Its wheels span in the mud, affording him precious seconds to open up a lead. Every muscle and joint in his body was on fire, but he refused to give up. He'd come too far for that.

In the dim light, his eyes searched frantically for an escape. He was willing to take his chances with the barbed wire, but the hedgerow might as well have been a brick wall.

He glanced behind him. Saw the Land Rover lurch forward as it found traction. It thundered towards him.

And then he saw it. A narrow gap in the hedgerow – just wide enough for him to squeeze through. All he had to do was get over the wire fence. Just one last effort.

But then the monster was on him once more. Knowing he wouldn't make it to the fence, Scott jinked to the side again, just before the vehicle crushed him.

This time he left it too late. The Land Rover's wing mirror smacked into his shoulder blade. He heard the bang and the shattering of glass, and his eyes filled with visual static as he went spinning into the barbed wire fence. He felt the stab of its razor-sharp needles, heard it tear his coat to shreds as he rebounded onto the sodden grass.

He lay still, unable to move. His body had given up. He had pushed it beyond its limits.

It took all his effort just to raise his head. The Land Rover had stopped just yards away. He saw the driver's door open. Someone climbed out. The reflected light from the vehicle's headlamps was enough to show him some detail.

It was a woman. Dressed in an oversized waxed jacket and green wellington boots, she cut an imposing figure. Her hair was unkempt – wild, even. There was an expression of fury and contempt on her face that could only belong to someone with death on their mind.

Not what you want to see on a person clutching a twin-barrelled shotgun.

As she plodded towards him, Scott fanned his arms across the ground in search of his own weapon. There was no sign of it. He was defenceless.

'You killed my boys,' she said.

He said nothing, because he had no good response. It was time to die. He was not an especially religious man, but he prayed that this would be enough for her. That she wouldn't go after his wife and son.

She stood just in front of him. Exhausted, he lowered his chin back into the cold mud. He could see only her wellington boots.

'You killed my boys,' she said again.

He closed his eyes and waited for the inevitable.

The shots rang out across the countryside. Animals flinched and ran. Birds scattered.

No human batted an eyelid. To those who heard, it was just another unremarkable sound in the distance.

50

Another death. Another waste of life.

Scott raised his eyes. Saw her wellington boots again. The soles of them this time.

He pushed himself up from the ground. Sat there covered in mud and cow shit as he stared at the latest victim of the choices he'd made.

She lay with her arms splayed out, her eyes and mouth wide open, her hair like a halo of worms risen from the ground.

He would have to live with this. He knew he would keep telling himself that she would have killed him if she'd had the chance. But he also knew that, like her son Ronan, her card was marked anyway.

A noise to his right made him turn.

'Left it a bit late, didn't you?' he asked.

'I was enjoying the drama. This was better than my Xbox.'

Scott tried to see if the other man was smiling, but it was impossible to tell.

He had put the hood of his parka up again.

*

'I'm giving you a choice,' he'd said in Barrington's flat after he'd put the pistol to his head. 'Option one is I blow your brains out and take your money.'

'I'll take option two.'

'You haven't heard it yet.'

'I don't care, man. That's what I'm taking.'

Scott climbed off him, but kept the gun pointing at his face. 'Option two is you help me out with something.'

Barrington sat up and rubbed his swollen cheek. 'Help you? With what?'

'You know a man named Ronan Cobb?'

'Yeah, I know him. What about him?'

'I plan to kill him.'

Barrington stopped rubbing and started laughing. 'You serious? You want to kill Ronan Cobb?'

'I've never been more serious in my life.'

'Why? What's he done to you?'

'He threatened me. Even worse, he threatened my family.'

'First of all, that's no big surprise. It's what the Cobbs do. You can't make a leper change its fucking spots, man.'

'Leopard.'

'What?'

'It's leopards that have spots, not lepers. Although they possibly have spots too.'

'Okay, whatever. My point is that his go-to solution to any problem is violence, and if that doesn't work he'll use more violence. And my second point is that you don't just walk up to someone like Ronan Cobb with the intention of killing him. The man is streetwise. He can smell danger from a mile away.

Probably better than any fucking spotty leopard. No disrespect, man, but you against him don't sound like no fair match.'

'I know. That's why I need your help.'

'What, to hold your hand while we both get killed?'

Scott didn't answer.

'Why'd he threaten you anyway?'

'You hear about his brother Joey?'

'About him getting sliced and diced? Everyone's heard.'

'Ronan blames me for that.'

Barrington laughed even louder now. 'Sorry, man, but I'm having a hard time picturing that one. Joey Cobb was even more of a psycho than Ronan.'

Again, Scott didn't answer.

'Wait. You're serious? About Joey?'

'I did what I had to do.'

He decided not to tell Barrington that he wasn't personally responsible for Joey's death. He needed Barrington to remain afraid of him.

'Then I can't help you,' Barrington said. 'You're a dead man walking.'

'Yeah, I think that's what's going through Ronan's head too. That's why I need to hit him before he hits me.'

'Then hit him. Don't get me wrong, I'm grateful for the opportunity to keep on living, but why do you need me?'

'Insurance. I've got a meeting with him soon. If it goes the way I hope it will, you won't have to lift a finger. But, like you, I think there's a good chance Ronan will guess what's coming and shoot me first. If that happens, I want you to kill him before he can go after my family.'

Barrington shook his head in disbelief. 'You're asking a lot, man. Especially being a stranger who's just attacked me in my own crib. What are you even doing here? I thought you came to rip off my money.'

'Haven't you figured it out yet?'

'Figured what out? I've been too busy watching that gun of yours to be working shit out.'

'Ronan sent me.'

Confusion settled on Barrington's features. 'What do you mean?'

'You're Ronan's target, not mine. He sent me to kill you and steal the money.'

Barrington's mood darkened. 'Fuck. Knew I couldn't trust that family. Only reason I worked with his brother was because he came up with the goods. Always thought one of them would stab me in the back one day.'

'Well that day has arrived. And it's worse than you think.'

'How so?'

'I knew that a white Adidas bag full of money was being dropped here this afternoon. I know it's supposed to get picked up again at seven. How do I know? Because Ronan told me. How did he know? Because he's got help on the inside. Maybe it's whoever gave you the bag. Maybe it's the guy coming here later to collect it. Point is, you can't trust anyone now, Barrington. For whatever reason, people have decided you're dispensable.'

While Barrington mused, Scott checked his watch. Twenty to seven. Time was running out.

'I need a decision, Barrington. You going to help me or not?'

'Wasting someone isn't a thing I like to make snap decisions about. That's what gets people in jail. Or worse.' He paused. 'What if I don't help you? You really gonna shoot me like you said?'

'Actually, I don't need to. I could just take your money and walk out of here, leaving you to explain it to the pick-up guy. How long do you think they'll let you live after that?'

'They'll come after me anyway. If they don't find me and the money here at seven, I'm still dead. Ronan will be the least of my problems.'

'That's why I'm offering you the money too.'

'What?'

'You can have it. All of it. All you have to do is cover my back for the next hour, and then you can take all the money. You could get a long way from here with money like that.'

Barrington looked at the bag like a dog eyeing a juicy bone.

'How do I know I can trust you?'

'You don't have to. Say no, and I'll walk away now with the bag, meet with Ronan, and take my chances. But you'll be on your own, with no money and a handful of enemies at your door. Your choice, but make it now, because I'm about to leave.'

Scott stood up, hoping to push Barrington into a decision.

'All right,' Barrington said. 'I'll do it. But there's something you need to know.'

Scott glanced at his watch again. 6.45. This was getting too tight.

'What?' he snapped.

'Ronan Cobb isn't your real problem.'

340

'I think I know my problems better than you do.'

'Uh-uh. Ronan is muscle, that's all. He does what he's told.'

Scott didn't like the sound of this.

'Told by who?'

'His mother.'

'His mother?'

'That's right, man. Myra Cobb. She pulls all the strings in that family. Only reason you're not dead already is that Myra will have decided she can squeeze something out of you first. And this scheme to rip me off tonight? That's not Ronan. He doesn't have the brains to come up with something like this, or the connections to make it happen. This is all Myra.'

Thoughts and fears swam through Scott's head. Could this be right? He remembered his first encounter with Ronan at the flat, and how he had gone to the far side of the room to have a quiet telephone conversation before he came back to them with an ultimatum that seemed out of the blue. Had he been talking to his mother? Could all this really have been her doing?

He cursed himself. That call had bothered him since the beginning. Ronan had always talked in the singular, claiming that it was his money and that he was demanding its return. But the phone call left open the possibility that someone else was pulling the strings, or at least knew what was going on. Scott should have explored that further, should have factored it into his thinking, instead of burying his head in the sand and hoping it would go away.

'So what are you saying?' he asked.

'I'm saying that if you're going to kill Ronan, you'll have to

341

waste his mother too. If you don't, she will come after you and she will hurt your family so badly they'll be begging to die.'

Shit, he thought. Not now. After all I've been through, don't tear my plans to shreds now.

Mentally, he felt fully prepared to kill Ronan. The man had pushed him to the edge of a cliff, leaving him with only one way out. He knew that the deal Ronan had offered him was worthless. He couldn't be trusted. It was kill or be killed.

But the man's mother?

He had no idea how to find her. And even if he could obtain that information, he didn't think he had it within him to turn up at her house and murder her in cold blood. In recent days he had cast aside much of his morality out of sheer necessity, but he hadn't yet shucked off all that made him human.

And yet . . .

Ronan would have told her everything. She would know his address, and if all that Barrington said about her was true, she would undoubtedly seek revenge.

Tick-tock.

He had to decide.

'I'll do it.'

This from Barrington.

Scott turned to him. 'What?'

'The mother. I'll do it.'

'Why?'

'Don't get your hopes up. It's not a favour. It's self-preservation. Myra's already got me in her sights. If I help to kill the only son she's got left and then run away with her money, it won't matter where I go. Myra's not the force she used to be, but she can still pull in some favours. After she's finished playing with you and your family, she will hunt me down. Besides, even if she can't cut it no more, she'll be the only one alive who knows the truth about yours truly ending up with a lot of money that ain't mine. Believe it or not, there are people who would kill me to get it back.'

The concern that refused to leave Scott's face must have been obvious.

'No other choice, man. Not if you want to protect your family. And personally, I want to be able to relax when I get to that beach villa.'

'You know where she lives?'

'Yeah. She's got this farmhouse out in the sticks.'

Scott had no more time to debate the matter. He nodded at Barrington. It was something he'd have to come to terms with later.

'You got a gun?'

Not so long ago, this would have felt like the weirdest of questions, but Scott had come to learn that, to the Cobbs and Daleys of this world, strapping on a firearm was as mundane as pulling on underwear.

'Funnily enough, if you'd turned up here a few minutes later, I would have had it on me. I like to be prepared in case a pick-up goes wrong.'

'Where is it now?'

'You're sitting on it.'

Scott stood up from the sofa and lifted the seat cushion. A black pistol stared back at him. He took it and said, 'You've got two minutes to grab some things. Once we leave, it probably won't be a good idea for you to come back here.'

Barrington pushed himself up from the floor. 'Crazy thing is, I'd have signed up straight away if you'd told me all this in the first place. There was no need to get all violent and shit.'

Barrington had followed Scott in his own car, then parked up a good distance behind him to avoid being seen. Scott had left Barrington's gun in his glove compartment for him to collect once he'd started up the path. It had crossed his mind once or twice that Barrington might close the gap, shoot him in the back, and then try to run off with the money before Ronan could get down there, but his fears had proved unfounded.

And now here they were, staring down at their second corpse of the evening.

'Saved me a trip to her house anyway,' Barrington said.

'Guess so,' Scott answered. He hadn't been at all sure about killing this woman, but she'd made things easier in the same way that Ronan had. It was actually a relief to know that she was out of the picture.

'What now?' he asked. He was handing control over to Barrington. He was done with scheming.

'We dump the bodies and the car. Might buy me a few days to get as far as I can.'

'What about the people who were expecting to get that money tonight? You really think they won't come after you?'

'Nice of you to worry. Although I don't recall you raising

that particular concern for my welfare when you were trying to recruit me.'

Scott shrugged. 'I was making a sales pitch.'

Barrington smiled. 'Maybe they will, but I doubt it. I think they'll blame the Cobbs, especially once they find out they've disappeared. If they do enough digging, they'll learn that Myra was asking a lot of questions about that money. And anyone going into my place will find all my stuff still there and signs of a fight. They'll probably think I'm dead or hiding from the Cobbs. They won't believe I've got the balls to wipe out the whole Cobb clan and steal their money.'

They stared silently at Myra Cobb for a few more seconds, then went into action. They loaded both bodies onto the Land Rover and drove it over the hill. On the other side was a bridge across a stream. The Cobbs must have driven in that way. Some distance to the right, the hill dropped sharply down to a patch of tall brambles and weeds bordering the stream. Most people would have no inclination to lower themselves down there or wade to it through the fast-flowing water. Barrington and Scott rolled the bodies unceremoniously down into the hollow and watched them get swallowed up.

Barrington decided that the best place to leave the Land Rover was hidden in plain sight outside Myra's farmhouse, only a few minutes' drive away. Scott followed him in his own car, then transported Barrington back to his Corsa on the lane.

Before they parted, Barrington reached into the Adidas bag and grabbed several bundles of cash. He proffered them to Scott.

'Call me sentimental, but I get the feeling you need this as much as I do.'

Scott lowered his gaze to the money. It would certainly come in useful after all his losses.

But then he shook his head. 'I can't take that. It's drug money.'

Barrington waited for a few seconds longer, then pushed the packets back into the bag.

'You know your problem, don't you?'

'What's that?'

'You're too honest.'

Scott watched him load the bag into the boot of his car, then climb behind the steering wheel.

'One last question,' Scott said.

'Shoot.'

'Why the parka?'

'What kind of stupid question is that? It's cold, bro.'

And then he drove into the night.

Scott went to his own car. As he opened the door, he took one last look up at the hill, remembering all that had taken place there. It looked so unbelievably peaceful now.

He groaned in pain as he lowered himself into the driver's seat.

It was time to go home.

51

After a shit week, this felt good. It felt human. It would seem a small, simple act to most, but to Hannah Washington it was of profound importance.

Screw the force, she thought. Screw Ray Devereux. This is what really matters.

She rang the doorbell and waited.

It was Gemma who came to the door. Alarm rang out from her pale features, but Hannah was used to that reaction from people receiving an unexpected visit from a police officer. Their first thoughts were always that her arrival heralded disaster.

This was one of the few opportunities she would get to do the opposite.

'Hello again,' Hannah began. 'Remember me? I was on your sofa when—'

'Yes. Yes, of course I remember. Oh, God. Is ... is everything all right?'

Clearly, Gemma had it worse than most. The poor woman looked like she was about to have a panic attack.

'Yes. Sorry. I hope it's not too late for me to call. I'm not here on police business. This is personal. My way of showing my gratitude.'

Gemma unveiled a weak smile. 'You don't have to. It's the least we could have done, honestly.'

Hannah raised the plastic carrier bag she was holding. 'I've brought a few gifts for Daniel. I'm sure he told me it's his birthday soon, but my brain was a bit scrambled at the time. I haven't missed it, have I?'

'No, you haven't missed it. It's next week. That's very kind of you, but you shouldn't have, really.'

'No problem. I think he probably saved my life, so this is the absolute least I can do.'

'Well . . . thank you again. I'm sure he'll appreciate it.'

Gemma reached a hand out for the bag, and Hannah felt disappointment wash over her. This was supposed to be a symbolic act. She needed to share in Daniel's emotion.

She tilted her head to insert her gaze into the hallway behind Gemma. 'Is Daniel around? I'd love to give these to him personally. Do you think that would be okay?'

Gemma grew visibly uncomfortable. 'Well, I don't like to get him too excited at this time of night. It takes him ages to calm down again, and he won't sleep.'

Hannah struggled to keep a smile on her face. What an anti-climax this was turning out to be. A shit end to a shit week.

'Oh. Right. That's fine. In that case, I'll just—'

She was interrupted by a loud yell from behind Gemma.

'*Lieutenant Columbo!*'

Daniel's head appeared over his mother's shoulder.

348

'You've come back!' he said. 'How's your head now? Are you better? Did you catch the man who did it? Is he in jail? Did you find your phone? Have you watched any more *Adam-9*?'

'Hi, Daniel. Actually, it's Adam-9 I wanted to talk to you about. I've got a few things here you might like.'

Hannah didn't care if she was overstepping a mark. She was already being pulled into his enthusiasm. She couldn't simply walk away and miss what was to come.

'Oh my gosh,' Daniel said, staring at the bag of goodies. 'Mum, did you hear that? She brought me stuff. Adam-9 stuff.'

Gemma put on a more welcoming smile. 'I think you'd better come in.'

They all went through to the living room. Daniel continued to jabber, almost exclusively about Adam-9. Gemma stepped away, giving them some space but maintaining observation.

'Okay, Daniel,' Hannah began. 'You said you've got tons of Adam-9 stuff, right?'

'Yeah, tons. I collect everything.'

'All right, but have you got one of these?'

She reached into the bag and pulled out an action figure. Daniel's eyes bulged.

'Oh my gosh! I've never seen one like that before. Where did you get it?'

'We brought it all the way from Japan.'

'Japan? You went shopping in Japan for me?'

'Well, actually it was for my daughter. But she said you can have it, because it's your birthday soon and you love Adam-9 so much.'

Daniel took hold of the figure and stared at it in amazement.

The utter delight on his face squeezed Hannah's heart. She was so glad she hadn't missed this.

'Wow. Your daughter is so kind. You said her name's Tilly, didn't you?'

'You remembered.'

'Please, will you thank Tilly for me?'

'I . . . Yes, of course I will.'

She caught Gemma looking at her. Something passed between them. Something only mothers knew.

She distracted herself with another dip into the bag. 'I've got other stuff here. There's this . . . and this . . . and this . . .'

Daniel acted like all his Christmases had come at once. Hannah didn't care if he didn't sleep for the whole weekend, and she didn't care if she never worked for the police again. What she was doing here was starting a new life by letting go of a previous one. If Tilly could see her now, she would be beaming from ear to ear – of that much she was certain.

'I need to put these with my collection,' Daniel said. 'Do you want to see it? Do you want to see my collection? Mum, can Hannah come and see my collection?'

Gemma seemed unsure, but then she looked again into Hannah's eyes, and what she saw there made her relent.

'Just quickly, Daniel. It's your bedtime soon.'

'Oh, Mum, but it's Friday night. I get to stay up later on a Friday.'

'I said you can have a few minutes, Daniel.'

Daniel nodded. 'Come on, Hannah. Follow me.' He was beckoning as he walked out of the living room, but his eyes were already focused on one of his new comics.

Hannah started to follow, but Gemma touched her elbow.

'Please, don't talk to him about police work. It frightens him. It's not like the comics.'

'Don't worry. I'm sick of police work myself at the moment. I'll just take a quick look at his collection, and then I'll get off home.'

Hannah went through to Daniel's room. Almost every inch of wall space was covered in Adam-9 posters. He had an Adam-9 duvet, an Adam-9 lamp, and Adam-9 pyjamas draped over the bottom of his bed. On a cheap desk were Adam-9 toys and precariously balanced stacks of Adam-9 comics, books and DVDs.

'Wow,' she said. 'You really are a fan, aren't you?'

'I'm the biggest fan in the world. I bet Tilly would like to see these. Could she come and see them one day?'

'I hope so, Daniel. I really hope so.'

'We could talk all day long about it, and we could watch all the episodes again and again.'

'She'd love that, I'm sure.'

Hannah wandered around the room, savouring the moment and what it meant. She paused at the desk. Idly, she picked up a scroll of wallpaper onto which Daniel had been drawing with crayons.

'Let me guess,' she said. 'An Adam-9 story, right?'

'Right!' Daniel answered. 'I did it this week. It's the longest one I've ever done. Mrs Collins said it's my best work yet, and she gave me another gold star.'

Hannah started to unroll it. The final frame of the story was revealed first. It showed a figure with a very long arm, its fingers fastened around the neck of another figure.

'Is that Adam-9?' she asked.

'Yes. He can shoot out a long metal arm from his briefcase.'

'I see. And this is the baddy?'

'Yes.'

'And who's this?' She pointed to a third figure.

'That's my dad.'

'Your dad? Do you often put your dad in your stories?'

'No. But he was in this one.'

Hannah noticed how Daniel's mood had suddenly changed. How he had become less garrulous and more guarded.

'And where are you?'

'I . . . I'm not sure.'

She pointed again. 'What's this?'

'That's the lift. Those are the doors.'

'The lift here? In the building?'

'Yes.'

She unrolled the length of wallpaper a little more, travelling back in time through the story. The previous frame showed three figures again, but none of them looked like Adam-9. Two of the characters appeared to be fighting.

'Who's fighting here? Your dad and the bad guy?'

'Yes.'

'And this other person is you?'

'Yes.'

'No sign of Adam-9 yet.'

'No. Not yet.'

'He comes later, right? To rescue your dad?'

'Yes. That's what he does. He stops bad guys.'

Hannah kept unrolling and throwing out questions. There

was a scene at the cinema, and then an earlier scene in which two characters stood next to a car.

'Is this you and your dad again?'

'Yes.'

'Is it your dad's car?'

'No. We fixed it. I helped him.'

'You fixed it? Why?'

'It's my dad's job. He fixes cars.'

'Oh, I see. You mean in a garage?'

'Yes. He doesn't own it, though. It belongs to Gavin.'

Gavin. Where had she heard that name recently?

'Gavin who?'

'Crossland. Gavin Crossland.'

Hannah racked her brain. She definitely knew that name. Crossland.

And then she made the connection. Crossland Garage. She had spoken to Mr Crossland about the Toyota.

What was it the Toyota's owner had said? Something about Gavin Crossland's colleague having a name like the polar explorer.

'Daniel,' she said, 'what's your dad's first name?'

'Scott. And my mum's called Gemma.'

Scott.

As in Scott of the Antarctic.

Shit.

She looked through the story again, in time order now. Daniel with his dad at the garage, then the cinema, then going home and meeting someone in the lift who turned out to be a bad guy. And then . . .

She remembered what Ben had suggested to her. That perhaps the homicide she was investigating wasn't a targeted execution at all. That perhaps it was simply the result of a chance encounter.

Could it be possible?

She pointed to the end panel of the story again.

'This bad guy. Do you know him? Do you know his name?'

Daniel squirmed. 'I'm not supposed to talk about it.'

'It's all right, Daniel. You can tell me. We're friends, aren't we?'

He nodded.

'So what's his name?'

It took him a few seconds, and even though she knew what was coming, it still shocked her.

'Joey Cobb.'

She stared at him.

Oh my God, she thought.

Oh my good God.

52

Scott knew he was a changed man. You couldn't go through something like this and not be altered by it.

He expected he would have nightmares and flashbacks. He would be overwhelmed with guilt. He had seen things he had never wanted to see, done things he had never wanted to do.

He consoled himself with the hope that time would gradually heal him. He would eventually look back at this week of his life in disbelief. Even now it seemed almost surreal. He would never be able to forget, but it would come to feel like something he once dreamt.

That was his hope.

He knew he would be able to live with the pain, because he had won. Daniel and Gemma were out of danger. Life could return to normal.

Normality was all he'd ever wanted from the beginning.

He reached the door of his flat. Found his keys. Opened up. The familiarity of home made him suddenly appreciate how tired he was. He needed his bed. But first he needed his family.

Gemma jumped when he appeared in the living room, and he realised what a mess he must look, his clothes caked in mud.

He started towards her, a reassuring smile on his face. 'It's okay,' he told her. 'It's finally over. I promise you, it's all sorted.'

But she did not smile back. She looked pale and scared, almost as though she didn't want him here.

And then her eyes shifted, looking at something over his shoulder, and so he turned and saw who had come into the room behind him, and his world came crashing down again.

It was not how Hannah had expected to solve this case. But sometimes that's how things went. A stroke of luck. Being in the right place at the right time. Seeing or hearing something that caused all the tumblers to click into place and unlock the secrets.

She had her killer.

This was one in the eye for Devereux and for Devereux's superiors and for anyone else who had doubted her ability. This case had been foisted on her by people who had fully expected – perhaps even *wanted* – her to fail. She had proved them wrong, and it felt amazing.

Or at least it should have felt amazing.

Because look who the killer is, she thought. Look beneath that huge, powerful, manly exterior and see that he is still just a child. Someone who still gets excited by comics and toys and birthday cake and fish fingers. Someone who has pictures of a fantasy hero on every wall and on their duvet and their lamp and their pyjamas.

Someone who saved my life.

Not my problem, she told herself. I'm a police officer. I have a duty to carry out. Let the courts sort out the details.

'Mr Timpson,' she said. 'I know what happened. I've just made a telephone call to my colleagues, and they're on the way. I have to tell the three of you that I'm placing you all under arrest on suspicion of the murder of Joseph Cobb. You do not have to say anything, but it may harm your defence if—'

She didn't get to finish, because Scott Timpson had just pulled out a gun.

Hannah put her hands up.

'Scott, don't be silly. Put the gun away.'

Gemma shrieked his name, but he turned the gun on her and she backed away. Daniel stood where he was, looking bemused but not scared.

Hannah tried again: 'Scott. This isn't helping the situation. Please put the gun down and let's talk about this.'

She could see that something had snapped inside Scott, as though he had already been stretched to breaking point and this latest turn of events had given him that final shove.

'I tried,' he said, his lip quivering. 'I tried so hard. Not for me, but for them.' He waggled his gun from side to side, indicating his wife and son. Gemma flinched as the gun danced in front of her.

'I did everything I could,' he continued. A fat tear escaped down his cheek. 'I was protecting them. You have to understand that.'

'I understand, Scott. I know you were only trying to do what was right. But we can't discuss it properly while you're waving a gun around, can we?'

357

'I had to save Daniel. You've got a kid, right? You should know what that feels like.'

The words stung. She hadn't protected Tilly. She hadn't saved her.

This isn't about me, she told herself.

'Of course,' she said. 'I get what you're saying. And I'm sure once we sit down calmly and look at all the facts of the case—'

'NO!' Scott cried. He suddenly closed the distance between himself and Daniel, then put the gun to the back of his son's head. Gemma yelled his name again. Daniel remained still, apparently oblivious to the extreme danger he was in.

Hannah raised her hands again. 'Scott. Don't do this. I'm begging you. We can work this out.'

'We can't. You know what happened. You know what Daniel did. You're going to hurt him, and I can't allow that.'

'We're not going to hurt him, I promise.'

'Liar!'

'I'm not lying. Daniel told me that Joey Cobb attacked you first. You had to defend yourselves.'

'That's not what you'll say when you get us to the police station. You'll say we overreacted. You'll say we went too far.'

'No. Things just got out of hand. I know that. You didn't mean for any of this to happen. And Daniel certainly didn't. There's a thing in law called diminished responsibility. It's when somebody has special circumstances and can't be held responsible for their actions. All that will be taken into account.'

Scott shook his head. 'I've read up on this. I've seen too many examples of the system failing people like Daniel. People who will never be able to read or write who still get sent to prison or mental hospitals. Even if he isn't convicted, they'll say he's a danger to the public. They'll take him away from us. It will destroy him. I can't put him through that.'

'Scott. Please listen to me. He's your son. Taking his life is not protecting him. He deserves to live like everybody else.'

'EXACTLY! Like everybody else. Tell *them* that. Tell all the people who call him names. Tell the kids who tease him and throw things at him. Tell the people who hounded us out of our last home. We want to be left alone, that's all. We want to be treated like normal people. Like everyone else.'

He was crying freely now. His finger was whitening on the trigger. Hannah had a horrible feeling she was powerless to prevent this death. Images of Suzy Carling running in front of a train flashed into her mind.

Not again. Please don't let that happen again.

'Scott—' she said.

'Look at him,' Scott interrupted. 'What do you see? A big man in his twenties. Strong. Powerful. So powerful that we had to give him a rule to stop him from touching other people. That's what the courts will see, too. What they won't see – what nobody ever sees – is the real Daniel. There isn't a harmful thought in his head. He only ever wants to please people. He loves animals, even though we can't let him have a pet. If everyone was like Daniel, the world would be a better place. Why is it that people always have to destroy what they don't understand?'

Hannah searched for an answer, but none came.

And then it stepped out in front of her.

Tilly.

She appeared from the shadows behind Daniel and she slipped her tiny hand into his immense one. Neither Scott nor Gemma saw her, but Hannah could have sworn that Daniel's gaze lowered to settle on her.

And suddenly Hannah was no longer a police officer, following rule books and procedure.

She was a mother, pure and simple, with all the resourcefulness and intuition that motherhood entailed.

'Maybe there's a way,' she said.

'There's no other way,' Scott answered. 'I tried to protect Daniel, but I failed. I'm tired now.'

He was saying he'd reached the end, that there was no going back.

'Listen to what I'm saying, Scott. Daniel saved my life, so now let me save his.'

The earnestness in her voice made Scott's eyes widen.

She said, 'What you did personally is one thing. You're going to have to face up to that. Daniel doesn't have to.'

'What do you mean?'

'We can change the narrative, Scott.'

'I don't . . . What are you talking about?'

'I'm talking about putting it all on your shoulders, instead of Daniel's. Are you enough of a father to do that?'

Scott laughed when he realised what she was saying. He shook his head. 'You don't know how many times I've thought about that. But here's the problem. Daniel can't lie. He calls things as he sees them. He's as honest as the day is long.'

'I'm not asking him to lie.'

'Forget it. It's too late now.'

Scott flicked off the safety catch on his gun.

'Daniel,' Hannah said. 'I want to ask you a question. Are you ready?'

Daniel nodded.

'Don't put him through this,' Scott warned.

'That day when you met Joey Cobb in the lift. What happened after he attacked your dad?'

'Please,' Scott said. 'Stop.'

'Somebody came and saved him.'

'And who was that?'

'Adam-9. He stops bad guys.'

'Yeah, that's right, he does. And how did Adam-9 stop Joey?'

'He used his robot arm. He's used it before, against the Quark Monster.'

'Good. You're doing well, Daniel. Here's a harder question for you. Who is Adam-9 really?'

'I . . . I don't know. Nobody knows.'

'Well, it couldn't have been Joey, right? That only leaves you and your dad.'

Daniel looked down. Tilly looked back at him.

'I suppose. I think . . . I think it must have been me.'

'You see?' Scott said, wiping tears away with his free hand. 'See how easy that was? They'll tear him apart in a courtroom, and they'll do even worse to him in prison.'

Hannah said, 'I think you need to tell your son the truth now, Scott.'

'What?'

'Your secret. You can't keep it any longer. You have to tell him.'

'I . . . I don't know what . . .'

Hannah turned to Gemma. 'You've got no choice now, Gemma. Go and get the things.'

Gemma looked mystified.

'Please, Gemma. Scott's secret things. The stuff he keeps in the bedroom. You told me about them when we first met. I promised not to tell anyone else.'

It clicked. Gemma took a step towards the doorway, then looked to Scott, checking with him.

'Let her do it,' Hannah said.

Scott nodded apprehensively. Gemma disappeared, but was back in seconds, her hands full.

Hannah saw how Daniel's eyes widened. He said, 'That's . . . that's an Adam-9 briefcase. A real one!'

'Yes it is.'

'And that's one of his masks. He uses that one the most.'

Gemma held up the third item.

'His identity card! How did you . . . ?'

'Only one person could have all these things, couldn't they, Daniel? Only one.'

Daniel turned fully around to face his father. As he did so, the gun muzzle came to rest directly between his eyes.

'Dad?'

In shame, Scott lowered the gun.

'Dad? Is it true? Are you Adam-9?'

Scott looked across at Hannah, then back at his son. He seemed unsure about whether to play along, and then it was as though he'd decided he had nothing to lose. He nodded, blinking more tears away.

'You stop all the bad guys? You stopped Joey Cobb?'

'I . . . I had to, Daniel. He was threatening us. He had a gun. This gun.'

'But . . . but . . . your briefcase. You didn't have it with you that day. You need it for the robot arm.'

Scott looked troubled that the pretence had been demolished so quickly, but then something triggered in his eyes.

'I had my backpack with me. Only it wasn't really a backpack. The camouflage switch, remember? I can disguise the briefcase. I used it that time when I had to hike up that mountain in Tibet.'

'To get to the Ice Lair!'

'Yes, that's right.'

Daniel's mouth dropped open. 'Dad! I can't believe it!'

Scott looked across at Hannah. 'Me neither.'

'Can I see? Can I look at the identity card?'

Scott started to bring his gun up, and for a moment Hannah thought she had lost him again. But then he said, 'Sure. Careful with it, though. I'll be needing it.'

It was as though Daniel's life had never been in danger. His entire focus now centred on his discovery of his father's top-secret identity.

Hannah swallowed hard. It was then that she realised Tilly was no longer in the room. She had disappeared as quickly and silently as she had entered.

She knows she's not needed, Hannah thought. She's done what she came for.

While Daniel was engrossed in the identity card, Hannah took a step towards Scott. She was about to do something she would have thought unthinkable an hour ago.

'You can make a case for self-defence,' she told him. 'Joey Cobb was threatening you and he had a gun. Daniel's story will no longer jeopardise that defence. I will personally supervise the interviews with Daniel and with Gemma.'

She let that sink in. Let him know that she wouldn't be pressing them for any version of events that would endanger him. She wasn't going to tell Scott that, as of tonight, she was no longer the senior investigating officer on the case. She was going to demand that role back from Devereux. He could hardly deny that right of the detective who had cracked the case.

Scott looked across at his wife, who was doing her best to keep Daniel occupied while staring at her husband with frightened eyes.

'Gemma,' he muttered.

'She knew nothing,' Hannah said, her voice loud enough to ensure that Gemma got the message. 'You brought a man into your flat who was injured. Gemma got annoyed at you for getting into a fight, and she left you to sort it out. The next day, he was gone again, and she thought no more about it. Could Daniel contradict any of that?'

Scott scratched his head, as if to dislodge memories and assess their ramifications. 'I don't think so.'

'There's still the disposal of the body,' she said. No point trying to sugar-coat it. 'You'll have to own up to that. You were frightened. You'd seen the drugs and the money and the gun, and you were afraid of retaliation or jail. You didn't know what you were doing, and you acted spontaneously.'

Scott swayed in uncertainty. From his appearance – the mud, the way he was holding himself as though in severe pain, the fact that he'd casually wandered in here with a gun – she suspected there was a lot more to this story. She didn't want to know. But at the same time she prayed it wasn't something that would undermine the edifice she was desperately trying to construct and bring it tumbling down again.

'It's true,' he said. 'I tried to cover it all up. I didn't tell anyone what I was doing. I only wanted to protect them.'

Hannah nodded. She was almost there.

The sound of the doorbell and then the urgent knocking galvanised all of them.

Hannah reached out. 'The gun. Give me the gun.'

More wavering. More knocking.

'The gun, Scott. You can do this. You know you can.'

Scott handed it over. Hannah opened her bag and pushed the gun down to the bottom. Then she looked Scott in the eyes and nodded. A tacit contract between them.

'Gemma,' she said. 'Could you let the officers in, please?'

53

When it was over, when it had been explained to the uniformed officers what was going on and what they had to do, when they had been instructed that nobody was to interview the suspects until she got back to the station, when she had made it clear how special Daniel was and how he needed to be treated with the utmost care and sensitivity, when they had all disappeared again except for a single officer who would remain at the door and cordon the flat off until forensics specialists arrived – when all that palaver was out of the way, Hannah Washington took one final look around the Timpsons' flat.

Everything she had done in the last half hour had gone against her training and pledges to uphold the law of the land. She knew that.

She also knew that there were justices on a much larger scale than those enshrined in her job description. Her conscience was clear.

She didn't know if it would work out. Scott, Gemma and Daniel would all play a part, and it would take only a mere slip from one of them to drag the others down too. There was also the possibility that whatever Scott had been up to would come back to bite him. If that happened, she might be unable to save him. Might even be unable to save her own hide.

She was willing to take that chance.

And afterwards, when she had seen this investigation through to its conclusion, she knew she would hand in her resignation. She wanted to see the look on Devereux's face as she went out on a high note, rather than in the disgrace and humiliation he had tried to engineer for her.

Right now, though, there was plenty of work to be done.

She went to the front door. As she reached for the lock, she thought she heard a noise behind her. She turned.

Tilly was there, in the doorway to Daniel's bedroom.

Hannah raised her hand and gave a slight wave.

'Mummy loves you,' she said.

Tilly smiled the sunniest of smiles. And then she went back into Daniel's room to play with her toys.

Hannah opened the front door and left the building, knowing she would never see her daughter again.

ACKNOWLEDGEMENTS

The Rule is my tenth published novel, which feels like some kind of milestone. Going into double digits should make me an old hand at this, but in fact I'm learning all the time and hopefully getting better at it. One of the most important lessons I've learned is the value of a good editor, and Miranda Jewess is undeniably one of the very best. She's also one of the most modest, but I'm afraid she'll have to suffer some toe-curling while I praise her as Queen of the Editing Spreadsheet. And although Miranda acts as my interface and sounding board, I'm fully aware that surrounding her is a talented and dedicated team that has worked wonders on this book. My heartfelt thanks go out to them all.

In *The Rule*, Daniel is fixated upon the exploits of his fictional secret agent Adam-9. I have my own not-so-secret agent in the form of Oli-1, or Oli Munson, to reveal his true identity. Oli has an endearing habit of surprising me with the outcomes of his covert activity when I least expect it, and long may it continue. Again, my thanks go not only to him but to all the wonderful gang at A.M. Heath.

I cannot overstate my gratitude to all the authors who have

kindly agreed to read early copies of my books and who have provided such amazing quotes. Their support has been incredible, as has that of the many book bloggers who have spent their valuable time in writing reviews and spreading the word.

A major turning point for me in the past year was giving up my day job to become a full-time writer. I have only one regret about that, which is that I will dearly miss all my colleagues at the University of Liverpool. I worked there for a long time, and it was a wrench to leave. My thanks go to every one of them for their friendship, encouragement and many fond memories.

As always, my love and appreciation of Lisa, Bethany and Eden is eternal, not least for putting up with me during a pandemic lockdown. I have seen much less of other family and friends than I would have wished in the past year, but I know that they have been rooting for me too, and I am profoundly grateful.

And, of course, to you, the reader: thank you for sharing this journey with me. It wouldn't be the same without you.